"Doctor! Quick!" The distant voice registered alarm and excitement. Great excitement. "It's a positive, a big one! Jackpot! Hurry!"

Garnet, carnelian, sardonyx. Cameo black-against-white . . . all singing with the colors of an imaginative power he had never felt before, rushing away on the dark tides of his thought into the past. He had no attention to spare now for the ordinary little men and women about him.

Heat—a warmth like that of a fever—was beginning to glow all through him. He felt his thoughts picking up speed under the powerful thrust of the RIV-induced stimulation. A problem lay before him now, and he hurled himself with increasing speed to engage it, like a lover to a tryst, like a warrior to a battle.

THE LAST MASTER

GORDON R. DICKSON

THE LAST MASTER

A TOM DOHERTY ASSOCIATES BOOK

THE LAST MASTER

This is a work of fiction. All the characters and events portrayed in this book are fictional, and any resemblance to real people or incidents is purely coincidental.

A TOR Book

Published by:

Tom Doherty Associates, Inc.
8-10 West 36th Street
New York, New York 10018

First TOR printing, February 1984

ISBN: 812-53-562-6

Can. Ed.: 812-53-563-4

Cover art by David Mattingly

Printed in the United States of America

Distributed by:

Pinnacle Books, Inc.
1430 Broadway
New York, New York 10018

THE LAST MASTER

CHAPTER ONE

Naked under a thin sheet, being floated on an airborne grav table along a white and shining corridor to the injection room, Etter Ho grinned ironically at the gleaming ceiling. The inner pain and fury of the last seven months were set to the side now, under full control; he felt at peace. It came back to him abruptly that there was a quotation that fitted the situation.

Daily, with knees that feign to quake—
Bent head and shaded brow—
Yet once again, for my father's sake,
*In Rimmon's House I bow.**

*"Rimmon" by Rudyard Kipling

Only it was not for his father's sake but for his brother's that he was here, in a situation no different from that of any ambitious deskworker gambling on bettering himself—ignorant of the beauty and freedom of a wanderer's existence on the open seas. His brother, Wally, had bowed down in this particular House of Rimmon long since; now Etter was following him, after twenty-four years of being obligated to no one. Now, at last, even in his own mind, he was no better than any of the billions of other individuals who had ignored the chance of freedom on a Citizen's Basic Allowance, to scurry after the golden manacles of occupation, position, and authority within the machinery that made possible their utopian Earth.

His mind now seemed to be functioning at its best, as if newly sharp, cold, and crystal-clear—as if viewing the world from behind a wall of transparent ice. Like everyone else requesting the RIV treatment, Ett had been offered a tranquilizing agent to soothe his way during the process; but he had refused. In part this was because of his long habit of trusting himself to no drug—not even aspirin. He'd lived forever, it seemed, with the fear that even the mildest drug—anything at all that might affect the nervous system or the psyche— might blur and slow the reflexes of his long-established defenses. His inner, true self, protected by the facade of indifference he had established and maintained flawlessly since he was eight years old, must be kept hidden—well enough that even he could forget it existed, most of the time.

And this was the time, above all others, when those defenses must be alert and ready. He could not know in advance what the effect of the RIV would be—whether it might raise his I.Q. a few points or lower it—but he felt he had to be fully aware of the change as it was taking place, whatever it might be. And even if the freak chance that had struck Wally with a severe loss of his mental acuity, were to hit him too, he wanted no anaesthesia, no blurring of the memory. He must be aware of that, too, as he had insisted on being aware of all things else, as far back as he could remember.

Not, of course, that this worst of possible results was likely. The odds against it were literally millions to one, nearly as impossible as the equally freak chance of the drug stimulating him to supergenius. In any case, he must not think of either extreme possibility now. All possible happenings, everything, must be made secondary to his own purposes—to his plan, and to his own ability to feel and know what would happen to him. Those determinations were his personal imperatives, and he would not let go of them while life was still in him.

The automated floating table on which he was being transported swung abruptly into a right-angle turn, and a new stretch of corridor ceiling unreeled above him. He felt an impulse to raise his head to watch for what was coming to him—although actually he was the one in movement—but he controlled it even as his head was restrained by the padded rest it was cushioned in. At the same time the grav table slowed for another ninety-degree turn, and he passed through a doorway into a room where the ceiling was a soft pink. With that he realized that the corridor outside, too—or at least its ceiling—had been imperceptibly building up its own tinge of pink as he had approached the door to this room.

The room was small; he knew because he could see the tops of the walls surrounding him. And even as he watched them, he could see some of the topmost of the banks of physiological monitors come to life now, as his conveyance stopped and plugged itself in, connecting its sensors to them.

"So this is our patient?"

The voice was a deep bass, and it boomed in the room with a heartiness he immediately suspected as professional.

"Let's take a look at you."

The thin sheet was whisked away, even as the soothing pale pink of the ceiling became a soft-focused, pink-tinted mirror. Still looking up, he found himself gazing at himself and at the possessor of the hearty voice, a bulky shape, foreshortened by the angle of reflection, and green-clad even to face-mask and head-covering.

"Why the gown, doctor?" Ett asked. "This isn't an operation."

The figure moved in the mirror, and a few feet above him a large, green-clad head and shoulders swam into his field of vision. From the small area of brown-skinned face that showed between mask and cap, light-brown eyes looked down at him, and then away at the length of his body.

"Regulations, I'm afraid," he heard. Warm fingers were prodding Ett, palpating his abdomen. "Hmm. You're not overweight, after all, are you?"

"Not that I know of," said Ett. "I've just got big bones."

He lay staring up at the self he saw in the overhead mirror. Oddly, it was like watching someone he had never seen before. Why? Of course. It was because this was the last time he might look at his own image with the understanding of this mind with which he had been born. It was entirely possible that the body he saw would have—well, someone else—in it next time he looked at it in a mirror. He tried to make eye contact with the image above him, but found the focus too soft for that.

So he studied what he could see—a tall stranger with coarse black hair and an oval face. The Polynesian ancestry showed in the smoothness of the flesh that overlaid his muscles and led people at first glance into the mistake of thinking him physically soft. The cragginess of the northern European—those big bones he had mentioned—were hidden under the sleek Pacific flesh. Volcano interior under peaceful ocean island. A trapdoor to hellfire and damnation beneath the blue of calm tropic skies—as it had been for three generations now. Great-grandfather Bruder, he wondered, how easy do your bones lie, back in the cold and stony earth of the Cascades? Do they remember the bright beaches of your Mission?

—Actually, I know the answer, Great-grandfather. They lie uneasy, don't they? I know, because inside me I carry the curse that was yours . . .

The physician's fingers had continued prodding, palpating. Now they stopped.

"You're in very good shape, Etter," said the deep voice.

"Thanks, Jerry," said Ett. "Good of you to say so."

The masked face, which had started to turn away from him, came back.

"Jerry?" it said. "I'm Dr. Morgan Carwell. Were you expecting someone named Jerry?"

"No," said Ett. "Pleased to meet you, Dr. Carwell."

The eyes above the green mask stared down at him.

"You've already met me, Etter," the physician said. "It was brief enough, that's true. But we met just an hour ago, before your final examination. Remember?"

"Yes," said Ett. "I met a Dr. Carwell. Did you meet someone named Mr. Ho?"

Their gazes held each other.

"Sorry, Mr. Ho. They tell us it's a good practice to use a patient's first name. I apologize. Now, please relax. We want you as calm as possible."

"I'm relaxed," said Ett.

"Fine." Carwell turned away. "Now you shouldn't expect to notice physical sensations as a result of being given the medication. Lots of people tell us they feel various kinds of reactions, but the best we can come up with is that these are just the result of their expecting to feel something—something like the placebo effect, in fact. Still, if you think you sense anything at all out of the ordinary, I want you to tell me right away—"

Still talking, he had turned his back to Ett, moving so that, even with the mirror above, his bulk hid his hands from the patient's view. Ett felt the light pressure of something pressed momentarily against his neck, at the nape, and then the table tilted him up and forward, closer to a vertical posture. Immediately the doctor was behind him and a heavier pressure came to his neck, which was exposed in its harness at the back. Almost as quickly it was ended, and the doctor stepped back;

the table put Ett back into a horizontal position. Carwell's voice had continued, quietly and steadily. That was it, then. The RIV was already in him.

"—because, as they've probably told you several times over, that's the whole purpose of administering RIV under the controls we do. There's a countermedication available as a blocking agent, but if it's needed, it has to be used as quickly as possible, to do the most good. And since there's so little physiological effect with RIV, anything you can notice with your own perceptions might be highly useful."

"Doctor—" began Ett, then fell silent again.

"Very good, that's right," said Carwell after a moment. He had checked his own talking immediately when Ett had opened his mouth. "We don't want you to speak unless it's necessary to tell us something important. The reason for that is also, of course, to keep you from distracting the physician, who's trying to observe you, to look for any signs you might show outwardly, of a bad reaction. That's also why you have to lie there without your clothes for some minutes yet, while I watch you. Any physical change at all, even movements, can be important . . ."

Carwell's deep voice went rumbling on in a monotone that was obviously intended to be soothing. Ett had been repeatedly cautioned to relax as much as possible after getting the RIV treatment. He tried to do just that. There was no point in pretending that he had no concern at all about what might happen to him. No normal human being could play roulette with the chance of being turned into either a high-grade moron or a genius, no matter how remote those chances were, without concern about the results. And in Ett's case, there was Wally, to whom the full-scale destruction of intelligence had actually come. Wally, his brother, to whom it had happened just that way, in this same procedure. Wally, who in the dice game of life, had crapped out . . .

CHAPTER TWO

What had happened to Wally, in fact, had been part of the general joke of existence, Ett thought, still watching himself in the mirrored ceiling. If his brother had never decided to try the RIV, Ett himself would have lived out his life happily without ever thinking twice of gambling with a drug that might either expand or cripple his inherent intelligence. But Wally, hoping to get back a woman he had lost—a woman who in Ett's opinion was not worth three months out of his brother's life, let alone the as-yet-unlived two thirds of his lifetime—had chosen the gamble; and now the chain of resulting events had brought Ett in turn to this room.

Wally had always been unlucky in the women to whom he had been attracted. He was three years older than Ett, but they had looked alike enough to be twins, once they had become fully adult. So Wally had not even had the excuse that he was physically unattractive to the opposite sex. Because Ett had been lucky. The women who had liked him had always turned out to be better for him than he had secretly thought he deserved—but it had never seemed to work that way for Wally.

It had been as if there was some sort of reverse magic in Wally that always tripped him up. This last love of his had been someone called Maea Tornoy, whom Ett had met only once, and for no more than a minute or two. At that time Ett had been favorably impressed with her, and thought that maybe Wally had found what he had been looking for all these years. Maea had appeared both clever and beautiful—admit it, Ett told himself now, even in that short moment of meeting it had been clear to him that she was a good deal more clever than Wally. Enough so, that Ett had wondered a little even then at her interest in his brother. Now it seemed clear that the extent of the interest had only been the amusing of herself for a few weeks, before Wally's open-hearted and obvious admiration had begun to bore her. When it had, she had dropped him.

"I'm not intelligent enough to interest her," Wally had written Ett in a last letter, painful to read—"that's the problem." And so Wally had decided on a gamble that might make him into what he assumed Maea wanted. He had taken his physical exams and put in an application for the same RIV treatment Ett was taking now.

Afterward, when the first signs of a negative reaction had appeared, he had been taken quickly and discreetly to a pleasant, large, brick building surrounded by parklike grounds, located outside

Hilo on the Big Island; a place staffed by gentle-voiced people to care for him. The deterioration of his intelligence did not happen all at once, but came on over a period of weeks, by small jumps—and as soon as Wally had realized clearly the end condition toward which he was inexorably bound, he had hanged himself.

Upon Ett, who had masqueraded as a lotus-eater all his life, with his secret inner fires grimly banked and controlled, the word of Wally's action had come like a sledgehammer, utterly smashing his belief of more than twenty years that he could stand apart from the world. For all that time he had kept his mask in place successfully, even before Wally, even in the face of his brother's unceasing attempts to convert him to a realization that he must live in society as it was—adapt himself to it.

But even as a child Ett had already learned that adapting was the one thing that he could not do. So he had slipped aside from the confrontation with the world that his attitude would have demanded. He had left Wally to try to struggle with that world alone; and Wally had so struggled until it had finally destroyed him. His final error had been falling in love with someone who had driven him to face a challenge that he had not survived. It was the crowning touch, Ett thought, in a life that just would not seem to go right for Wally—that Maea should leave him. And so, in the end, he had taken the RIV treatment, and then killed himself.

Moreover, Ett had discovered upon arrival in Hawaii, the world—life—kept right on shafting Wally after his death. For after he had killed himself successfully, he'd been discovered and cut down, gotten into cryogenic stasis within minutes.

"Well, then," Ett's relief had been enormous, "he can be revived, can't he?"

"Theoretically," had answered the physician he had been allowed to talk to at the Cryogenics Center in Hilo.

"What do you mean, 'theoretically'?" Ett stared at the other, a small, hard-looking woman with hair just beginning to gray at the temples. The physician had looked at him, Ett thought, a little wearily.

"Mr. Ho," she said, "you'll have to understand something. In the case of your brother, successful revivification is only the remotest of possibilities. The chances are large that he couldn't be brought back to a functioning existence even if he had the best medical team available."

"Then we'll just have to find out, won't we?" said Ett.

"Please let me finish," said the physician. "Even if he should be successfully revived, the chances appear very strong that, rather than his mental deterioration having been halted by the death experience, it'll have been enhanced; so that once brought back he would show no mental capacity at all—in short, he may be no more than a living body without a mind."

"Sure," said Ett. He heard the tone of his own voice, distant and unyielding. "But Wally would want to try, I think. So how do I go about finding the best medical team available?"

The physician looked down at the desktop which lay between them, then once more up at Ett.

"That's another matter," she said. "I'm sorry if

the way I mentioned the best medical team made it sound as if it was possible for you to get something like that for your brother. Actually, the best team for anything like this is a team gathered together by an outstanding specialist in cryogenic revivification. But a specialist like that will have been booked for years in advance."

"We'll make an appointment," said Ett. "Who's the best?"

"Well . . . a Dr. Garranto,"said the physician. "But—"

Ett touched the minicorder button on his wrist chronometer, and aimed it at the woman before him.

"Let me get that down. What's his full name?"

"Dr. Fernando James Garranto y Vega," said the physician. "But I don't seem to be explaining matters to you at all well. Any chance you might have of getting Dr. Garranto to act in your brother's case is—well, impossible. Dr. Garranto specializes in unusual cases and never has any time—"

"Wally's case isn't unusual enough?"

The physician's face tightened. She sat up straight in her chair.

"I'm sorry," she said, "but it looks like I'm going to have to be very frank with you. Dr. Garranto is simply not available for ordinary cases. There's enough work for him among the more necessary and valuable individuals of the world to keep him occupied full-time. Even if he took your brother's name onto his list, he'd never get to it. And if he did, believe me, you couldn't afford the operation."

"Now wait a minute," said Ett. "I may be on basic allowance, but I own an oceangoing sloop—"

"My dear Mr. Ho," said the physician—there

was a slight turn at the corner of her mouth— "if you owned a forty-meter yacht you might have trouble meeting the costs of such an operation. Do you realize what's involved here? Not merely the mechanical requirements, which amount to the use of a small hospital in themselves—but the fees for a team of six to ten physicians and technicians, each one an expert in some particular area, from anaesthesiology to terminal states—plus subordinate medical personnel."

"How much?"

"There's no way to tell."

"Give me an outside figure."

"There is no outside figure," she answered. "I'll make a guess at a minimum for you, if you like— three hundred thousand Gross World Product units."

Ett looked at her across the empty expanse of the desk. He had worked for six years, more or less steadily, while living at a bare subsistence level, to buy the *Pixie*, as his sloop was named. She was worth at most fifteen thousand GWP units, and his citizen's basic allowance was under a hundred units a month.

"So you see, Mr. Ho," said the physician, after a silence. "You see how it is."

But Ett had not yet seen . . .

The official assumption that nothing could be done for Wally finished the work that the news of his death had begun. Something had penetrated his protective facade and, reaching deep into him, had set loose the buried, unyielding self that had always been there.

Through the break in the shell of his outer being had erupted the flames of those ancient, grim fires of decision inherited from his great-grandfather. From hidden volcanic depths had come the antagonism he had spent twenty-four years denying. He had done his best to leave the world alone; but it had chosen to seek him out, with this destruction of his brother. Now, that world must be made to repair the damage it had done, and in the same unsparing, equal measure in which it had meted out its consequences to Wally.

This full reaction had not come upon Ett in one leap. It had only begun to grow as he had started checking on what the physician had told him, about the practical impossibilities of Wally's revival. His first awareness that, if anything, she had been understating the problems of returning Wally to life had come from a Mr. Lehon Wessel, the local underofficial of the World Bank, in Hilo, to whom Ett had gone to arrange financing for the medical costs of the revivification.

"I'm afraid it's a problem," said Lehon Wessel. He was a thick-bodied, long-legged man in his late thirties, with hair bleached and skin burned red by the sun. His voice was soft and regretful. "Your assets and your income simply don't suggest the means to support the expense of your brother's operation."

"I know that," said Ett impatiently. "I knew that before I came in here. But aren't there compassionate grants or special funds from the World Economic Council that could help me out or that I could borrow from?"

Lehon Wessel smiled sadly.

"Of course there are," he answered. "But it's a complicated matter, getting monetary support from them. And to be frank with you, Mr. Ho, in your case any effort like that would be wasted from the start. Such funds are intended for the exceptional situation and the exceptional individual.

"If it's not an exceptional case to have a man commit suicide because of a bad reaction to RIV, what is?" demanded Ett. "That bad a reaction's an exception all by itself. It's as uncommon as the freak good one that makes an R-Master. And how many R-Masters are there? One in a few tens of millions of the people who try RIV."

"Of course," said Lehon Wessel.

"Well?" said Ett. "Can I apply for the funds, or can't I?"

"You can fill out an application," said Wessel.

He gave Ett a thick sheaf of printout forms to be filled in. Ett took them back with him to the hotel where he was staying and discovered that he was required to be an expert not only on his own personal history, but on Wally's. He called up Wessel to protest.

"What is this?" demanded Ett. "Ninety-nine percent of this information's already available in Wally's files and mine, in the Council's central data bank!"

"Of course," said Wessel. "But regulations require the applicant make out these forms. I'm sorry."

So Ett laboriously filled out the forms and returned them to the appropriate offices. After a wait of nearly two weeks, he was called in by a man who was Wessel's immediate superior.

"Come now, Mr. Ho," said the superior, leaning forward confidentially across his desk. He was a lean, smooth man with neatly trimmed brown hair and a smile that seemed to go and come on cue. "You surely don't want to try to push through these requests for funds? I'm not here to discourage anyone, of course, but in your own interest I've got to tell you that your chances of success with this just aren't there. Assistance from these sources is reserved only for those obviously deserving."

"My brother isn't deserving?" Ett stared at him. "It was in an effort to make himself more useful to the world that he had the bad reaction from the RIV that led to his suicide."

"Oh, of course—your brother!" said the other man. "But it isn't your brother who's the applicant here. It's you. And to be frank, Mr. Ho, nothing in your life record shows any promise that you'd ever be able to repay, or justify a free grant of the amount of EC funds you're after."

"What about Wally's value, once he's revived?"

"But we don't know that he'll be of any value, Mr. Ho." He picked up a paper from the far side of his desk and glanced over it. "The medical opinion I've got here is very doubtful of returning him to any kind of useful state in mind and body. Of course, he'd still be deserving, except that he's presently in an effectively noncitizenship state."

"Then suppose I apply in his name?" said Ett.

The man looked up in something resembling a state of shock.

"Oh, you can't do that!" he said. "Not as long as your relationship's close enough to make you responsible. A sibling or a parent automatically becomes guardian for anyone in a cryogenic state where revival is possible. As guardian, you have to apply for aid on your own values as a citizen, not on those of your ward."

"All right," said Ett. "Then I so apply."

The other sighed.

"If you insist," he said. "I'll put these applications of yours through. But I must warn you not to expect very fruitful results. Why don't you talk to your ombudsman, or ombudswoman?"

"I will," said Ett.

And he did.

For the forecast he had been given turned out to be quite correct. His application was turned down. So he found himself an ombudsman, one of those individuals who were supposed to help the ordinary citizen in his tangles with official red tape. But the ombudsman was, it seemed, as pessimistic as everyone else had been.

"We can appeal, of course," he said. "But I wouldn't be doing my duty to you if I didn't tell you you've got damn-all chance . . ."

So they appealed.

They appealed to the Regional Authority, and were turned down. They appealed again to a review board, and were again turned down. Finally they flew to Kansas City to appeal before the Northwest Quadrant Court. Their appeal was denied. As they left the building, Ett asked the ombudsman about the next step.

"We can go on," said the ombudsman. "We can keep this up for years, if you like—there are plenty of boards and courts and authorities and so on. There are just no end of appeals and requests for review you can make."

He paused as they climbed into an autocab for the ride back to the airport.

"But I have to tell you," he said, leaning back as the cab moved off and loosening a tight cuff of his court dress, "you could grow old at this, still getting nowhere. Ett, the problem's with you, not with the regulations. You've never shown them any potential social worth. You're like a man without a credit rating trying to borrow from a lending institution. Take my advice. Give up. Or—"

The ombudsman hesitated.

"Or what?" prompted Ett.

The man sighed.

"Or go out right now, find yourself an occupation, and start working your way up in the active ranks of society," he said. "Maybe in five years, or ten, you'll have climbed to a position of social usefulness where they'll listen to your request for funds. Meanwhile, since he's in cryogenic suspension, the time won't mean a thing to your brother."

Ett looked at the other man, a bland expression on his face.

"But you don't really think I'll do that?" he said.

The ombudsman shook his head.

"No, of course not," he said. "But I wouldn't be doing my job if I didn't point it out to you as a course that's open to you."

"I'm obliged to you," said Ett. "Because as a matter of fact that's exactly what I'm planning to do." He turned his head away from the startled ombudsman. "And I might even make it in less than five or ten years."

"You mustn't get your hopes up," the other said.

"It's not hope I'm thinking of dealing in," replied Ett.

When their plane landed back in Hawaii, Ett left the man. Actually, in the back of his mind he had been making his plans for some weeks now. It had become clear to him some time ago that if he was going to win over the masters of the red-tape jungle in which he— and Wally—were trapped, he must at least pretend to join their game. The bureaucracy owned the ballgame, and would fight him to the death unless he played their game by their rules. And if he did play the game with them, he was sure that he would win—because they, being what they all were, were absolutely bound to play by the rules—whereas he had certain advantages that he would not hesitate to use against them.

As a very young boy, he had become aware that those who let their abilities show were pressured to use them. In his struggle to control his fiery temper and hide that inner self that wanted to fight every opposing force, it seemed to him that the best thing to do was hide himself from that pressure, too, as he hid from all else. And so even in primary school he had learned to keep his score on tests well below what it might have been if he had wanted to do his best. Wally, on the other hand, had not held back; Wally had consistently made good scores—though not near the genius level, to be sure. Secretly, Ett knew himself to be a good deal more than his brother's mental equal, but he had successfully hidden much of that from the records of the world about them.

Now, that restraint would pay off. It gave him a secret edge to play with in this game with a bureaucracy that seemed to hold all the cards. He had foreseen the ombudsman's suggestion and waited for the other to make it. Now, as if trapped by it, he would proceed to take the same RIV injection that had ruined Wally. It was a gamble, admittedly, but the odds were all on his side. The

chance of two disastrous results from that drug in
the same family must be statistically so tiny as to
approach nonexistence. For the rest, the kind of a
small loss or gain in I.Q. that more commonly
took place would be unimportant. A small loss
would not matter much; a small gain would be all
to the good.

The point was that by taking the drug he would
certify to the red-tape society his determination to
make something of himself in its own terms. In
addition, by showing a good slice of his hitherto
hidden ability after his treatment, he could claim
that he'd undergone a rise in intellectual capacity
from the drug, a claim no one could dispute. That
would allay suspicion about his sudden blossoming;
and with that much to go on, plus bluff when
necessary, simple hard work and a grim determination to take any means to power should move
him swiftly up the work-ladder.

In the end, he would get what he wanted for
Wally, from this system that valued position so
highly . . .

"—Mr. Ho!"

It was Carwell talking. Ett had almost forgotten
he was still in the RIV clinic, waiting for signs of
effect from the drug.

"How do you feel?" Carwell asked. "All right?"
Ett nodded.

"Well, then," said the physician. "The immediate period when reaction might be expected has
passed. Let's get you back to the preparation room."

He reached out and touched the table controls
near Ett's head. The grav table rose slightly into
the air and floated out the way it had come, the
door to the corridor opening automatically before

it. The supports behind and around Ett's head and neck fell back, leaving him free to move his head again.

"I'll come with you, of course," said Dr. Carwell.

He followed the programmed path of the table's motive machinery, back to the preparation room, where Ett's clothes waited for him, neatly on hangers.

"You still feel exactly the same?" Carwell asked.

"That's right," said Ett.

"You can get up and dress, then," said the physician. He watched as Ett did so, asking twice again if Ett felt a reaction of any sort.

"I thought," said Ett, as he pressed shut the closure slit on his shirtfront and prepared to leave the room, "you didn't expect anything like that so soon?"

"No physical reaction, of course," said Carwell. "Probably never. But you might be noticing some mental alterations—anything at all, including mild hallucinations."

Ett walked out. Dr. Carwell went with him, stripping off the gown and dropping it in a laundry cart as they walked, along with his mask and cap. They both headed down a short stretch of white corridor toward the lobby of the clinic.

"Not even those," said Ett. He looked sideways at Carwell, who was fully as tall as he was and must weigh over a hundred and thirty kilos. "It's not taking?"

"Too early to say that," Carwell answered. "It's only a large percentage, not all, of our patients who show a reaction during the first few minutes after treatment. In fact, you must have been told by whoever talked to you before I did that there's no telling. Reaction can come any time, up to several weeks later, gradually or suddenly, any way. It can even come in more than one increment."

"It seems to me," said Ett, "I heard that strong positive reactions usually come suddenly, and soon."

"A majority of them, a majority of them," said Dr. Carwell. They were approaching the admitting desk, and the physician spoke to the receptionist on duty there. "Mr. Ho's chart, please. I'll sign him out."

He turned to the white-clad male attendant standing by the desk.

"Looks like we won't need you, after all, Tom," he said. "Mr. Ho has had a fine, uneventful response to treatment. Wait. On second thought, you'd better just walk with him to his vehicle, to make sure."

He turned back to Ett and offered his hand.

"Well, Mr. Ho," he said, as they shook, "you'd better take it easy physically for the next twenty-four hours, just on general principles. Call us right away, of course, if you feel any unusual sensations, mental or physical. And check back with me three days from now, at this time. Say one p.m., Thursday?"

Ett nodded, and turned.

"You really don't need to come out with me," he said to Tom. "I can find my way to an autocar by myself."

"No trouble," said the attendant. "And it's regulations. When you come back on Thursday, check in with the lobby desk here and ask for me—Tom Janus. I'll come get you then, too."

He led the way to the front of the lobby and the transparent glass doors there parted before them.

"See you Thursday, then," Tom said.

"Yes, thanks," answered Ett, and stepped out to the autocar rank. Settled in one of the vehicles, he told it to take him to the Dancing Waters Hotel, and then sat back against the cushions as it pulled away from the clinic. He would rather have returned to stay on board the *Pixie* as he normally did, for reasons of his own preferences as well as his finances; but the conditions under which RIV was given required he spend the next three days in a nearby hotel where the rooms had been equipped to monitor his physical state at all times, and this was one expense which the public grant that paid for the treatment did not cover.

The cost of the hotel was a relatively large expense in terms of Ett's meager savings; but it could not be helped. In any case, cost was beside the point now that he was committed. He stood leaning on the railing of the little balcony attached to his minisuite, watching the sunlight slanting across the green island landscape.

Pixie would have to be sold. There was no other way to raise a fund of immediately available credit in the amount he might need to help him rise in the world; and it was almost a foregone conclusion that somewhere along the way a situation would crop up in which a chunk of credit, instantly available to him, would make possible a leap up that would not be available to him otherwise. The decision to sell the boat was like a decision to part with a living creature; but the hard determination now let loose inside him overrode the pain of parting with her the same way he could trust it to override all other pains that might stand between him and his goal. The loss of *Pixie*, in fact, now functioned in him as a reinforcement to his committment, a price that, once paid, must guarantee delivery—and would guarantee his determination.

The sun extinguished itself, with tropical swiftness, before he left the balcony. He turned from it and went down to eat in the hotel's busiest dining room.

During the next two days he stayed in his room, mostly studying data received over an open phone connection to the local library computers—data on the larger intercontinental consortiums of expediters. These organizations were the largest in the world not directly under control of the bureaucracy itself; and they existed because they served to provide flexible, human interfacing between individuals and the machinery of the bureaucracy itself. In brief, they trained and supplied specialists, from technicians like the woman who had arranged his taking of the RIV treatment in the clinic he had just left, to the highest-priced consultants and ombudsworkers—individuals who found their function midway between citizens like himself and the direct employees of the bureaucracy, such as Dr. Carwell, or the attendant, Tom Janus. Each such consortium of expediters, of course, had its own organizational machinery, and it was possible, within such structures, to climb to a fairly high executive rank.

That was important, because study of the situation in the past weeks, since Ett had made up his mind to take the path that began with having the RIV treatment, had reinforced an unconscious observation he had found himself to have made earlier. This was that the quickest route to executive rank in the bureaucracy was to make a success of himself outside of it and then be invited into its upper levels—rather than starting as one of its lowest employees and working his way up. Also, the chances for unorthodox and opportunistic improvements in job position were greater outside the rigid structure of the bureaucracy's hierarchy—at least, within the lower levels of the bureaucracy.

In the higher levels at which a successful outsider might be invited in, much was allowed to go on behind the scenes that was not tolerated at lower levels; and there were always executives there, one rank up from that at which Ett might be invited in, who were continually on the lookout for unusually capable assistants whose efforts could be used to advance the career of the superior.

On the morning of the day on which he was due to return to the clinic, Ett put his research aside, however, and got up before daylight to take *Pixie* out at dawn for a final time under canvas, alone. Al was already awake when he got there; and, as always when *Pixie* had been left in his care, he had her immaculate and ready. And in his quiet way Al seemed to understand and be sad, when Ett asked him to go ashore and leave him to sail alone— although Ett never mentioned his plans to dispose of her.

The thought of abandoning his plan touched Ett for a moment as he glanced back to see the slim young man watching him quietly from a point near the head of the dock. But then within him there was a crystallizing, the growth of a hardness that caused him to turn away to watch the waves into which he headed *Pixie*'s bow. For several hours he put the boat through a demanding series of maneuvers, before straightening out to rush before the wind, back to the harbor. And it was only then he realized that he'd actually been seeking out the pain each carefully-learned motion of the sloop had brought him, as if clenching a fist-full of broken glass to seal his determination— or perhaps to help him learn to live with it in the future. He shook his head slightly.

When he tied up to his buoy outside the marina, Al was not in sight. Ett inflated the dinghy and rowed ashore, leaving the little boat tied up at the dock. He headed inland toward the clinic and his appointment, walking.

"Etter Ho," he said to the receptionist behind the lobby desk—a tall old man with jet-black hair, this day—"to see Dr. Carwell."

"Thanks," said the old man in a scratchy voice, studying the screen in front of him. "Yes. On recall. If you'll sit down, Tom Janus will be out in a moment."

Ett took one of the overstuffed chairs in the lobby; but almost before he had fitted himself comfortably in it, Tom was standing in front of him.

"This way, Mr. Ho. The consultation offices are over on the left side, here."

Ett followed him into a corridor unlike those he'd seen before, with walls panelled in oak strips. As they went down it, the varying wood colors of the grain caught his eye. It was unusual to find oak used so lavishly these days, particularly in the Hawaiian Islands.

"Just a minute," he said, halting.

He stepped closer to look at a widespread multiple arch of the darker-grained lines on one light brown strip. He could hear Tom Janus' footsteps check and come back toward him. The lines he had stopped to look at held his attention with a strange insistence. Suddenly, as he watched, they seemed to become three-dimensional, like terracing on a hillside, leading his eye away and back into some imaginary land. It was a land where the oak belonged, before the metal of man had begun to scarify the world. On one such naturally terraced hillside, the oak from which this strip came had once flourished, spreading its thick limbs parallel to the earth, as one of its kind might have done back before the first tick of civilized time. Child of the four seasons and no other, it would have stood, in that prehistoric time, safe and enduring, a citizen of the ages under the clean skies of a day out of eternity . . .

Aquamarine morning, the oak would have seen, above the turquoise slopes . . . sapphire noon . . . amethyst and citrine evening . . . topaz twilight . . . tourmaline-into-onyx night: diamond, moonstone, pearl. . . . Colors whirled in his mind.

"Doctor!"

Far, far off, a corner of his busy mind registered the unimportant voice of Tom Janus calling, the hands of the attendant catching him, holding him upright.

"Doctor! Quick!" The distant voice registered alarm and excitement. Great excitement. "It's a positive, a big one! Jackpot! Hurry!"

Garnet, carnelian, sardonyx. Cameo black-against-white . . . all singing with the colors of an imaginative power he had never felt before, rushing away on the dark tides of his thought into the past. He had no attention to spare now for the ordinary little men and women about him.

. . . Amber, serpentine, malachite, cat's-eye . . .

CHAPTER THREE

He woke in a wide nonhospital bed, a dark antique
four-poster—no grav float—in a rose-carpeted, panelled bedroom that looked out through two wide,
heavily-draped floor-to-ceiling windows onto a
broad expanse of green lawn rolling away to walks
of crushed gravel reaching beyond the lawn into a
grove of shade trees. Drowsily he puzzled over
where he was—but the immediate need to find an
answer did not seem urgent. He relaxed once more
into the silence and the peace around him. The
light outside was a clean, clear, dawn light—as if
even the relatively unpolluted air of the tropic
outdoors had been recently washed by a rain
shower.

He felt comfortable and alive. Well, not completely comfortable, on second thought. He had a
small headache, a little queasiness in the stomach,
a little pressure in the bladder; but these were

probably only faint hangover-like symptoms from whatever had hit him, pushing now against the pleasant drowsiness of waking. But what was he doing here?

Memory returned with a rush and he was suddenly fully awake. He remembered the RIV injection, he remembered returning to the clinic. He remembered the colors . . .

He chilled, lying perfectly still, feeling his body about him. As far as he could tell, he felt no change, no sudden increase or decrease of intellect, no new dullness or sharpness of perception, no change in his pattern of thought. Rousing fully, he got up on the edge of the bed, discovering himself naked under the covering. The room remained silent about him.

There were two doors into the room. He tried one and found it locked, tried the other and found it let him into a bathroom whose furnishings were on a par with those of the bedroom. Slowly he shaved and showered, deliberately avoiding coming to any conclusions with the front of his mind, giving the back of his head time to digest what had happened. He came back to the bedroom, found his clothes, newly cleaned, and dressed. No one had yet come in to find out if he was still sleeping. He turned to the bedside phone, hesitated for a moment, and then pressed the operator call.

"Mr. Ho?" said a warm female voice immediately, without an image. "What can I do for you?"

"I don't know," he answered, looking at the coarse brown cloth grill of the antiquated speaker. "Where am I?"

"Dr. Carwell and the clinic Chief of Staff, Dr. Lopayo, will be up to see you in just a short time,

Mr. Ho. They'd like to talk to you as soon as you
feel like seeing them. Would you like some breakfast,
meanwhile?"

"Why not?" said Ett.

"If you'll give me your order then, Mr. Ho."

He ordered the sort of breakfast he usually
ordered—orange juice, eggs over easy, bacon, toast,
and coffee. Waiting, he sat down in one of the
room's padded armchairs, still keeping the front of
his mind carefully blank. After less than ten minutes the food was brought in, not on a grav-float
table, but on a wheeled one, which was pushed by
a dark-haired woman in early middle age, with a
thickened body but a pretty, almost slyly smiling
face, who wore a non-uniform white knit dress and
white calf-length boots. She continued to smile at
him, but silently refused to answer when he once
more asked her where he was. She went out again
quickly and he sat down to eat, alone. But he had
no real appetite and the slight queasiness in his
stomach had increased. He sat back in the chair he
had pulled up to the table, and then pushed the
conveyance away from him. He let his mind open
at last to speculation about what had happened to
him.

A coldness he had held under control in the back
of his mind ever since he had woken came forth
now. Released, it expanded with a rush to take
him over generally. Before signing up for the
treatment, he had considered what he should do if
it should result in his either gaining slightly or
losing slightly in ability. He had even considered
the possibility of ending up with the same sort of
devastating reaction that had been Wally's reward;
so that he was emotionally prepared for even that,

now, if what had happened to him signalled it as a consequence.

On the other hand, he had never seriously considered that he might end up by gaining largely in capability. Like most people who knew themselves to be naturally favored with intelligence, his natural ego had led him unconsciously to doubt that there was much, if any, range of intellect beyond his own. But he forced himself to consider now the possibility that there might be as large a range above him as he knew to be below him—and that he had been lifted considerably in that range—not, of course, to R-Master level, but well beyond what he had considered possible before.

In his mind now he heard again the words of Tom Janus, just before the colors had overwhelmed him—in particular that one word '*jackpot*'. That Tom's shout might have implied the rare type of extreme reaction that could make Ett an R-Master, was of course too outrageous to consider. But it was hard not to imagine that the attendant's excitement implied something very favorable in the way of a response to the RIV.

If, indeed, anything at all like that had really occurred, it was not a cause for unalloyed rejoicing on his part. For one thing, it presented two problems which he hadn't prepared for in his planning, although he now realized that he should have.

One was that as someone known to have gained a large improvement in capability, he might no longer be allowed to work anywhere except within the structure of the bureaucracy—so that his plan to gain status outside that structure before stepping into it might not now be open to him. As a result, his freedom of action to find a short-cut up the professional ladder—and to do what was needed for Wally—might be sharply curtailed by red tape and obligations he did not yet know anything about.

The second problem actually affected his own personal desires more than it did his plan, but that made it no less important. He had assumed that once Wally had been revived and returned to function, he himself would then be free to throw over his position, dropping out of sight to locate *Pixie* and buy her back from whoever then owned her. On her he would resume his old personality, his control and his ways, returning to the socially invisible existence he had carved out for himself before. But now, if his increase in capability were indeed large, he might find himself a marked man, known to such an extent that return to such a retreat from society might no longer be possible.

Whatever had happened to him, it seemed obvious that he was now the recipient of a good deal of unsolicited attention. Already he felt a touch of something akin to claustrophobia, as if the restrictions of the bureaucracy were even now beginning to close about him—for even though as a more valuable member of society he would have access to more resources, he might also be subject to too close a scrutiny for his planning to evade.

Suddenly, all that would come to his mind was the unreasoning image of his great-grandfather, reaching out from the grave, after all Ett's effort to hide himself, to lay an enormous and bony hand upon him. He realized now, after all this time, that always for him the controlling hand of the bureaucracy was one and the same with that other bony hand—in what they had the power to trigger off in him. It seemed he had been aware of both hands, and the danger of their effect on him, ever since he had discovered in himself the nature he had inherited from his grandfather.

The world into which he had been born and grown up was one in which the attractions of conformity were many and the pleasures of nonconformity had been as meager as possible. This was known, but supposed to be the price of progress under the world-wide community and the bureaucracy. It was taken for granted that people would like their work, if they were normal. So it had been something like an act of defiance, on his part, for him to choose to do what he had done, as soon as he had been old enough to break away from the house of Heinrich Bruder. It had been assumed then by his older relatives—and he had fostered the idea—that some weakness in his character had led him to shirk the effort that was every adult's pleasure and duty in this new world. None of them, even Wally, had suspected that he had chosen as he had, literally for the sake of his own survival.

For, unlike his brother, his aunts, uncles and cousins, and everyone else he knew, he had discovered inside himself the same iron intolerance that had made his great-grandfather what he was.

Heinrich Bruder, child of an earlier age, would never have fitted into this new utopia, either, had he been Ett's age. No, he would have fought it instead, with everything that was in him—fought it until it finally destroyed him. Ett had no intention of being destroyed. The situation was as simple as that.

Because destruction for either his great-grand-

father—young again and afire with his convictions—
or himself, would under the present regime be a
matter of course, if either one of them had chosen
to oppose the society of the world as it was now.
The world would have no other choice than to
destroy such as either of them, or else it would be
opening the door to its own destruction.

This was because the cost of what people presently had, in Ett's opinion, was like a stifling blanket wrapped around the spirit of the human race.
Ironically for the ghost of great-grandfather Bruder,
it was the same spirit that Heinrich himself had
ended up by extending over his descendants in the
house where Ett had discovered his spiritual kin-
ship with the old man.

What the race had gained had been only at the
cost of maintaining the massive controlling machinery of the bureaucracy. It took such social
machinery to make sure that all elements of the
new society would work smoothly together to make
that society viable. So much was necessary. So
much, in fact, was not in itself particularly evil;
any more than any tool was evil until it became a
weapon in the hand of someone who wanted to use
it to dominate others. In the beginning, during the
first few decades of the world-wide community,
those who worked in the necessary bureaucracy
that staffed the machinery of a new society, had
done so with high purpose and ideals. It had been
an age of a new pioneering spirit, no doubt.

But, like all bureaucracies since the beginning of
civilization, this one had grown to become an entity in itself, with its own instinct for self-preservation and growth, even at the cost of what it
did to the very society it had been set up to serve.

And its workers—particularly its leaders, the men
and women at its top command posts, had grown
into a new aristocracy of power-holders. The uni-
tary world-wide community had brought about a
rapid development of technology in its early years
of existence, so that all could live well off the
labors of only two people out of every three. But it
had also brought enormous power into the hands
of those top few, and created the need on their
part to ensure that no change occurred in the social pattern which might end up threatening their
positions.

All of this development was seen and understood by the mass of individuals in the world as a
whole, and was tacitly accepted. Life was good,
everyone agreed. Much better than at any time in
history. A few people had to sit in the seats of
power. Rumor and gossip about the abuse of their
authority were swept under the rug, out of sight
and thought. After all, it was to everybody's benefit not to rock the boat, was it not?

The end result was an Earth in which no true
progress, but only maintenance, was the aim. Progress was already beginning to become an evil word.
Which was why, to those few like Ett, the planet
had become a world-wide prison, padded and gilded
but still a prison, in which the one real crime was
to disturb in any way the status quo. There was no
compromise permitted with the official attitudes—
as there had never been in his long lifetime any
compromise permitted by Heinrich Bruder with
his own, personal beliefs.

The fact was, it had only been Heinrich's old age
that had protected him toward the end of his
lifetime. For by then he was out of his time. He

should have been dead, in sober fact, long before Ett was born; let alone alive until Ett and Wally had grown old enough to know him and have their lives warped by him, as had been the lives of all the other descendants who had been trapped into the circle of his personal power.

A literal circle of power it had been, even when Heinrich had become so ancient that he could barely make the daily pilgrimage from the bed where he spent his nights, to the massive armchair in the same bedroom where he spent his days. It had gathered in and enclosed both Ett and Wally, when they had been sent to join his household above Seattle on the death of their mother, when Ett had been nine years old and Wally twelve.

They had left the islands of the sunny Pacific and gone to live in that large house under the cold winter rains; the rambling house filled with four grand-aunts and one grand-uncle, all ancient themselves, plus an assortment of younger aunts, uncles and cousins, who came only when they had to and left again as soon as possible. They left without resentment and without real understanding of why they fled at the first opportunity; but Ett saw them go and came to understand that their flight was the result of an instinct, like his own, to survive.

But the danger his great-grandfather's spirit posed them was not the one with which it threatened him. Where they ran from domination, he had to fly from the instinct in him that drove him to fight back. Controlling and hiding that instinct had been his main occupation for seven long years.

It was all he was able to do; for Wally and he had not been able to leave like the other relatives— at least not until they had graduated from secondary school. They were each trapped there for a number of years by the aura of power that still flowed from the towering, gaunt and ancient figure who hardly acknowledged the presence of either youth, but dominated every moment of their lives as if it had stood over them day and night.

Heinrich Bruder had ceased to be a living individual in the ordinary sense decades before. He had become instead merely the center of his all-powerful and unyielding beliefs; and with those beliefs he had shaped, not only his immediate children, but any of his latter descendants who came within the aura of those beliefs for any appreciable time. He was like an elemental force, forged in the fires of his own convictions and beyond any further shaping that the human race could bring to bear on him.

He had been born during the hard times of the first truly world-wide economic collapse, which had taken nations and potentates down into rubble with it. His parents had originally been blue-collar workers who had struggled to feed themselves and their children during the long recovery from that collapse that had led to the present world community.

Witnessing that process as he grew up, Heinrich had been drawn in and recruited by one of the fanatical fundamentalist sects that had sprung up like weeds in the ruins of the former world society; and in that he had found his way of life. Heinrich was, in fact, a throwback to the fire and brimstone preachers of two hundred or more years before. He saw salvation for himself and everyone else only in terms of the narrow and basically ignorant beliefs of his own personal version of the religion he had adopted.

As such, he had volunteered as a latter-day missionary to the rest of the world; and, meagerly financed by his sect, had set out to travel the islands of the South Pacific, on a crusade to rescue souls from their sure journey to that hell which lay at the end of any way other than the grim and joyless one he himself preached.

The core of his belief was that he, alone of all men and women, had been vouchsafed a clear sight of the way to salvation, and all others must follow and obey him without question if they were to have any hope of being saved themselves.

But his was no shallow or accomodating belief. Physically outsize, utterly fearless, and respecting nothing that did not agree with his own convictions, he drove those he met in the direction he believed in like a hurricane—a looming, black-browed, massive-framed man who shouted the precepts of his personal religion aloud in any place and in the midst of any gathering, unimpressed alike by the forces of public opinion and law. He was not liked— but it had never concerned him that he should be liked. It was salvation, not human approval, he was concerned with. He burned with an inner conflagration and that fire consumed or captured any who lingered in his vicinity. Few did.

But some lingered and were captured, beside the already captive members of his own family. There was a minority among the human race, as there always had been, that found comfort in trading a personal freedom of mind and body for the relief of clinging to a stronger certainty than they were able to produce within themselves. Those so captured, like the aunts and uncles of Ett and Wally in the big house, reradiated outward that force of dominion they found in Heinrich, to shape and control those lesser beings—like the two young boys—who came into their sphere of influence, even when the sun-source of their power was the feeble life-force of an ancient and tottering man.

At no time in the house of Heinrich Bruder was physical force used to make Wally and Ett conform to what Heinrich would have ordained if his strength had still been in him. Only there was always the all-encompassing family attitude that no other way was thinkable; and this attitude maintained a constant, relentless pressure upon their minds, night and day.

Just as the pressure of the bureaucracy was coming to make itself felt upon the world-society in general, and shaping it to the contours and purposes of the World Council members. As Heinrich's pressures had shaped Wally; and, failing to shape Ett, had instead made him a lifetime opponent of all such forces.

Because in Ett, who had never until then known anything more than a passing gust of temper, by way of anger, in his young life, before he arrived at the large house—in Ett awoke the shocking discovery that of all his great-grandfather's descendants, he was the one who had inherited the absolute intolerance of the old man, in the fullest measure. Like Heinrich, he could be broken but never bent, and there was in him a burning desire to challenge what he thought wrong, a desire that, let loose as his great-grandfather had let it loose, could lead him to destruction at the hands of some enemy too great to conquer. An opponent, any recognized opponent, was for either of them impossible to ignore; and like Heinrich, once Ett let himself acknowledge an opponent's existence the battle must continue to the destruction of one of them.

Early, Ett had recognized that if he did not avoid confrontation with his great-grandfather and the spirit of his house, then he would fight the old man himself, and everything Heinrich stood for, until one or the other of them was destroyed; and, as he had gotten older, he had come to recognize that the same compulsion could wake between him and the unspoken tyranny of the bureaucracy. For in the bureaucracy he saw the same, Heinrich-like, absolute conviction that all must conform, or be swept aside.

There was no way he could envisage himself winning a battle with the bureaucracy, any more than he could see himself backing off from it, once he had been trapped into it. So he had chosen instead to hide from society, as he had hidden earlier from his relatives and his great-grandfather, and even Wally—in order to survive.

Now, the possibility of an increase in capability large enough to make such hiding difficult or impossible loomed for the first time as a cold threat to the personal security he had maintained the last years—

There was a soft knock at his door.

"Come in," he said.

The door opened, and three men entered the room—Dr. Carwell followed by two others, who entered almost in tandem through the wideness of the door. Carwell was wearing a white physician's coat, as was one of the other men, a man almost as tall as Carwell although about sixty kilos lighter—

leaner and older than Carwell. The man who entered beside him was virtually obscured from Ett's view by the two larger men until they spread themselves somewhat further apart. The third man was then revealed as a short, plump man, apparently in early middle age, wearing matching dark gray jacket and shorts. He was nearly hairless atop a pink, round baby face, and appeared at first glance rather ordinary and innocuous. But as their eyes met, Ett realized there had been a stir of wariness within him.

"Mr. Ho," said Carwell, and there was no doubt about the politeness in his voice this time, "this is the Chief of Clinic, here at our RIV Center—Dr. Emmera Lopayo. And Mr. Albert Wilson."

Ett got to his feet and shook hands with all of them. Lopayo was the older man, Wilson the plump one.

"Mr. Wilson," said Dr. Lopayo, as they pulled up chairs and Ett sat back down on the edge of the bed, "is Director of the World Accounting Section and a Member of Earth Council. He doesn't, of course, usually come to occasions, even ones like this."

Ett sat, silent and expressionless.

"I was in the islands, though," Wilson's round face beamed easily, "and since my Section's responsible for people like you, Mr. Ho—"

"People like me?" Ett said.

"It's an occasion for us, of course, as well," said Dr. Lopayo. "I take it you haven't guessed, Mr. Ho?"

Ett looked them over, still without expression. In a slow, flat voice, he spoke.

"What are you trying to tell me?"

"Come now," said Lopayo. He smiled, but not as successfully as Wilson. His voice was a little harsh, as if he spoke about something of which he disapproved. "You must have guessed it by now."

"I think I'd like to hear whatever it is from you—any of you—if you don't mind," Ett said.

"We understand, of course," said Wilson, smoothly. "It's simple enough. You're one of the rare successes of RIV, Mr. Ho. You're now an R-Master."

A hidden shock tore Ett internally, but he kept his face expressionless. It was as if a tiger had leaped upon him from the underbrush that had hidden it until this moment.

"I take it ..." he heard his voice as if it was someone else speaking, "you know what you're talking about?"

Wilson looked past Lopayo, who had begun to open his mouth, to Carwell.

"Dr. Carwell?" he said.

"Oh, we do," said Carwell, hastily. "There's no doubt. We're absolutely sure. How do you feel?"

"No different than I ever did," Ett told him.

"Well, that's natural, very natural," said Carwell. "But I meant, how do you feel physically?"

"A little creaky."

"Good." Carwell nodded. "That's natural too. Very natural. You can't do better than that— particularly if it's just a little creaky. I hope you mean that. There's no need to be brave, you know."

"I know," said Ett, dryly. "I said 'a little' and I mean 'a little'."

He looked at them all. None spoke. It was as if they were waiting for him to make some sort of adjustment on the basis of what they had just assured him had happened. But it was too soon for any such adjustment. Ett's survival instincts had already shoved the shock of confirmed discovery to the back of his mind, to be examined in full at some safer, later time. For now, all his attention was given to betraying as little in the way of reaction as possible, so as to let slip nothing that could later be used against him.

"Maybe somebody better tell me more about what's happened to me," he said. "I remember being given a sort of general briefing earlier; but nobody prepared me for what I ought to expect if I turned into an R-Master. How about telling me now?"

"Oh, it's far too soon to start briefing you on that—" Carwell was beginning, when Lopayo cut him short.

"Nonsense, Morgan," said the Clinic Chief. "Mr. Ho is presumably able to understand the whole process better now—" there was something almost malicious in his tone of voice. "Besides, he can ask any questions he likes, and by law we've now got an obligation to answer them. Isn't that correct, Councilman?"

"Not really . . . not just yet," said Wilson, beaming. "Not until he's legally under the Sponsorship of the Council, as all R-Masters are required to be. We should get that little bit of business out of the way, first."

He turned to Ett, as if in appeal.

"May I call you Etter?"

"He prefers Mr. Ho," said Carwell.

"I'm a public figure now, I suppose," Ett said. "Go ahead and call me Etter if you want."

"Etter, you'd prefer getting the paperwork out of the way as soon as possible, wouldn't you?"

"Paperwork?"

"The confirmation of your new status." Wilson's smile widened a little and then returned to its standard width. "You've got two choices, you see."

"Two choices," Ett said. "What choices?"

"Well, you see," Wilson folded his hands on his knees, "you can choose to become simply a Ward of the Earth Council, or you can be a working citizen, with an Earth Council passport and extra-territoriality."

"What's the difference?"

"Just one thing—work," said Wilson. "As one of the unusually successful results of the RIV program, you can simply live as you like, at EC expense, from now on; the Earth Council will shoulder all your life expenses. Or you can live as you like but also work for the EC, either at some problem we'd like you to attack or at something you choose yourself. As a ward of the EC, in the first place, you have equal protection and perquisites, plus you'll be delegated whatever authority you need to do the work in which you're active."

The word "authority" in Wilson's voice seemed to ring with an almost reverent echo. Also, to Ett's ear, there seemed something very like a faint note of condescension in the words he was hearing. Condescension? To an R-Master?—If that was really what he now was. But there had never been anything wrong with his hearing.

"I suppose I could choose a category now and change it later?" he asked.

"Oh, certainly," said Wilson. "Of course, later it might take a little time and trouble to make the changeover. Red tape, you know."

"I think I'd rather be a worker," said Ett.

THE LAST MASTER   53

"Very good," said Wilson. He leaned over toward the phone unit on the table by Ett's bed. "Send in Mr. Erm with the papers." He straightened and addressed Ett. "Rico will be your executive secretary."

A slim, young-looking man—perhaps about thirty—in light gray business shorts and a matching tailored shirt, came in through the still-open door. He carried a thin leather paper-holder under one arm, and as he approached Wilson he peeled back the top surface to expose a sheaf of papers—obviously bureaucratic forms. Ett was put to work signing a series of them. He carefully but quickly scanned each before he signed it, and discovered that in turn he was renouncing his ordinary citizenship, declaring himself a stateless person, petitioning the Earth Council for EC citizenship, and, finally, accepting that citizenship on a class AAA level.

"Very good," said Wilson, when Ett was through. "Let me be the first to welcome you to the ranks of EC personnel, Etter. Now, what would you like to do?"

Ett's answer was as ready to his tongue as if he'd planned this all out in advance. "What I'd like," he said, "would be to find out how to go about getting a medical team and financing for the revivifying of my brother, who's in a cryogenic state at the moment."

"Oh, yes." Wilson turned briefly once more to Rico Erm, then back to Ett. "I noticed that matter in your records, that you'd been trying to arrange compassionate funds for the revivification of—what's his name—Wally. Of course, you could afford to draw on your own credit as an R-Master for that now, if you wished. But there's really no reason why the compassionate funds shouldn't be used."

"There isn't?" Ett asked.

"Of course not. If you'll just sign this D-71439EC form, here—" he produced the paper he had just gotten from Rico Erm, and handed it to Ett. "These local officials! Still, you have to make allowances. There really are a tremendous number of forms and routes for a request like this to take. No, just your single signature is sufficient, Etter, and the whole matter will be funded."

"What is this?" Ett asked, glancing at the form. "Instant certification as a citizen useful enough to be entitled to compassionate funds?"

"Nothing so complicated," said Wilson, good-humoredly. "Just a waiver of responsibility in the case of your brother. Naturally, once you waive responsibility, he becomes a Ward of society and entitled to compassionate funds for rehabilitation on his own. Actually, this form was the only thing you ever needed. What a shame that the people you talked to didn't realize that!"

"Yes," said Ett. He signed and passed the paper back. "A real shame. By the way, there was a temporal sociologist my brother knew. I'd like to talk to her. A Maea Tornoy."

"We'll locate her for you, Mr. Ho," said Rico Erm.

"Yes, well, the rest of us ordinary citizens have to be moving along now," said Wilson briskly. "Duties, Etter. Constant duties. Would you care to walk out to the aircraft with me, Rico? I can brief you on the way."

He led the younger man out of the room. As the

door closed behind both of them, Ett turned to the two physicians.

"Good to have met you, Dr. Lopayo," he said. Both Lopayo and Carwell stood up, Carwell's hand going to the right-hand pocket of his white coat. "I hope we meet again sometime," Ett continued. "Dr. Carwell, I think we were going to have a talk."

CHAPTER FOUR

Dismissed, Lopayo left. Carwell hesitated, still on his feet. As the door closed behind the clinic chief, he finally brought his big hand out of his pocket, holding a small container of white pills about the size of aspirins. He stepped over and handed these to Ett.

"What's this?" Ett asked, not looking at the bottle.

"An analgesic and a tranquilizer of sorts," Carwell said. "To clear up any minor discomforts you may be feeling."

"Thanks, no," Ett said. He tried to hand the pills back. "I don't take drugs. I'll put up with the discomforts."

Carwell avoided his hand.

"Please," he said to Ett. "I'm required to give them to you. Besides, in the long run you'll find—I think you'll find you want them, after all."

"Oh?" said Ett. "We'll see."

Carwell was still standing. Ett waved him back to his chair and reseated himself on the bed, after first putting the container of pills in his pocket.

"Now tell me about my new increase in intelligence."

"Well . . ." Carwell hesitated. "I'm not really the expert you want for that. I mean, I've had the necessary training for the job I do in the RIV Center, but that's a long step from being one of the handful of physicians who've specialized in the health care of R-Masters themselves. You'll have one of those assigned to you, and he or she can do a much better job of answering your questions than I can."

"You'll do for now," Ett said. "Tell me what's happened to me. How much brighter am I?"

Morgan Carwell looked uncomfortable. He sat almost lumpily in the chair facing Ett, a big brown man clearly struggling with himself.

"I don't even know if you should be told this just yet," he said, "but we're told to answer any questions an R-Master asks. The truth of the matter may be you actually aren't any brighter at all. Or at least that's the best theory on the R-Master reaction at the present time."

"Not brighter?" echoed Ett. He did not astonish easily, but he felt astonishment now. "I don't understand. You mean RIV doesn't increase intelligence? If that's so, what's all this excitement where I'm concerned?"

"No, no," said Carwell hurriedly. "From a practical point of view, you might as well consider your intellectual capacity's been raised. It's not that the effect isn't essentially the same; it's that we don't believe the mechanism creating individuals such as you've become actually raises their innate intelligence."

"Then what's the explanation?" Ett asked.

"Well, if you order it, I can get you a number of books and papers on the subject," said Dr. Carwell. "Most of them are on the restricted list—not for you, I suppose. But some of them I haven't had EC clearance to read myself. I assume those just go a little farther into detail than the ones I'm acquainted with. To put the thing in nonmedical language, we think what happened in your case— and a few rare others—is like becoming sensitized to some allergenic substance. For some reason, in the case of a very, very few people injected with RIV, the whole being of the person develops either an unusual sensitization to intellectual demands—so that he immediately puts forth an unusual mental effort—or he becomes desensitized to any and all intellectual demands." He coughed. "What's known as an extreme negative reaction."

"Such as my brother had," said Ett grimly.

Carwell stopped, looking at Ett almost apologetically. His face maintained that expression while his voice, as he began again, seemed to carry an appeal for understanding.

"I don't know if I'm making myself clear," he said. "As I say, I haven't been trained to give this sort of explanation—" He stopped.

"Just keep talking," said Ett. "You haven't said anything yet that I can't follow."

"Well . . . ," said Carwell, and then paused, obviously fumbling for words. "As you probably learned in school," he went on, "late in the twentieth century the medical sciences made a lot of spectacular advances in molecular biology." As Carwell settled into a lecturing mode he seemed to become more comfortable. Ett let him proceed.

"RIV-I was developed in one of those projects. The program was originally instituted to look for a way to compensate for cases of severe brain damage. Of course it was known that in some cases the body and brain somehow managed to compensate without help—but that wasn't generally the case, particularly in cases of senile dementia."

"The idea at first was to try to understand the basic mechanism the body used in those natural compensation cases—such as people who learned to talk again after a stroke destroyed their normal speech centers—and extend the principle to other cases. It was decided pretty early that the most likely procedure would have to involve something that could permanently correct a problem without resort to a lifelong course of drug therapy. And that meant something that could get into the brain cells and stay there, constantly working."

Carwell stopped momentarily, smiling now as he looked across at Ett. He leaned back in his chair and spread his arms wide.

"It was one of those brilliant times, when knowledge seems to come together from a dozen directions, in a kind of chain reaction. All those great advances they were making around the world—in virology, in molecular biology, in cerebral biochemistry and even in genetic engineering—it just all built on itself."

He leaned forward, elbows on knees and voice lower, confidential.

"They decided what they needed was something that would live inside the brain cells, would stay alive there—and would enhance those cells' capacity. So they designed and made a small, single-strand RNA virus that they called RIV-I—"

"And RIV stands for 'renatin-inducing virus,' as I remember," Ett interjected.

"Yes, exactly," Carwell beamed, unstoppable now. "The virus consisted of RNA with associated unenveloped nucleocapsid protein—" as Ett frowned at the technical terms he rushed to explain. "That means, it lacked the lipoprotein coat, and so could penetrate the cell membranes better." He paused momentarily as if to get himself back on his track.

"So, RIV—in our time, RIV-II, an improved version—can become a permanent resident of the body's neurons, reproducing itself and migrating to new cells as the older body cells die."

"Yes, but what is it that the drug does, to change people's intelligence level?" Ett asked.

"Well, as I said, RIV-II is actually a virus, and not really a drug," Carwell answered. "And we're not sure just what it is that it does, or why it seems to affect some people more than others. The theory is that the virus has been genetically engineered—still a bit of a probing-in-the-dark process, after all—to produce the polypeptide known as renatin—"

"And it's really the renatin that causes the changes?" Ett asked.

"Yes, we think so," said Carwell. "The renatin tends to dissociate into a number of smaller polypeptides, which serve as neuro-transmitter mediators. Do you understand what a neuro-transmitter mediator is?"

"I think so," said Ett. "It's a sort of chemical messenger with news that affects the situation at its arrival point."

"Er—yes," said Carwell. "In fact, that's a pretty good description. The point is, the particular polypeptides involved seem to fine-tune the cerebral biochemistry."

"Or un-tune it?" Ett asked.

Carwell looked uncomfortable again, but nodded. "In a way, yes," he said. "To us the subject seems unaltered physically, except for a few rare side-effects. But in the case of a rare individual, he or she seems to show a striking degree of change in *sensitivity* to intellectual stimulation—either more or less sensitivity."

"So," said Ett thoughtfully, "an R-Master just gets a little more excited than anyone else, when it comes to intellectual matters—is that it? I thought it was going to do something more to me than that."

"Oh, it has," said Carwell. "That's the point. We've found that Masters seem able to reach back into personal resources we wouldn't think they'd have. Put it this way, if I can use an analogy. Ordinary subjects who get some benefit from RIV can demonstrate feats of mental strength unusual for them. But R-Masters can demonstrate the mental equivalent of hysteric strength, with more understanding and conclusion than their tested intelligence ought to permit them to show."

"Then how can you be so sure their intelligence actually hasn't been raised?" Ett watched the large earnest face closely as he spoke.

"It depends on what you mean by 'intelligence,' of course," said Carwell. "But so far as I know, none of the tests we've developed for intelligence yet show an increase in the mental capacity of an R-Master. They just show greater speed and certainty in the perceptive and reasoning areas. And—one other thing—we've now had R-Masters as a result of RIV for nearly fifty years. Not one of them has shown any real increase in creativity, let alone developed into anything resembling what's classically referred to as a creative genius. If there's a flaw in a highly complex plan, a Master will spot it in minutes where it might take ordinary men and women days. If the solution to a problem is possible, the Master will find it in days where ordinary people would need months. That's all."

"Then why all the fuss about us?" Ett said. "Why give us the best that the world has to offer just for being what we are?"

"Because you're valuable resources, of course," said Carwell. "And I suppose—" he hesitated for a second—"because you represent a phenomenon that's still being studied."

"Ah," said Ett. "So that's it. Guinea pigs."

"I'd guess that's part of it. As I say, you're asking me questions I'm not equipped to answer. A little knowledge is a dangerous thing. Your brother—"

He broke off.

"What about my brother?"

"Nothing," said Carwell. "I just mean there are drawbacks to any physiological state, even that of being a Master—but your assigned physician can explain those things better than I can."

"I'll take your explanation for now," said Ett. "What drawbacks?"

"I—" Carwell was genuinely unhappy—"I'm really not supposed to be the one who tells you things like this."

"You're to tell me anything you know, that I want or need to know," said Ett. "Or is what I've heard about the privileges of R-Masters a lot of nonsense?"

"No. It's true enough. But—"

"Can we put the buts aside? What drawbacks?"

"Well," said Carwell, "there seem to be variations we don't fully understand, in individual susceptibilities to the action of RIV. In a case like that of the rare R-Master, brain function seems to be considerably enhanced, but at the price of interference with the brain's normal opioid system. Some of the endorphins seem to lose function, resulting in discomforts of various kinds—aches, irritation, restlessness, even insomnia. As well, the immune system is affected, and so the R-Master suffers a higher susceptibility to infection and disease. There's also some effect on the endocrine system."

He stopped.

"None of this is mentioned to those who might take RIV, is it?" Ett said.

"You're also much more in danger from anaphylactic shock," Carwell went on. "That's one of the reasons we watch you so closely right after administering the virus. Anaphylactic shock, now, is—"

"That's all right," said Ett. "I know that one. I had a cousin who had bad allergic reactions and always carried medication to keep from dying if he was ever stung by a bee."

"So, that's why you'll be needing the care of a personal physician, yourself, to make you comfortable and healthy in the face of these side-effects." He gestured towards the pocket into which Ett had put the pill container. "That's the reason for that medication I just gave you, that you don't want."

"I'll admit I'm not at my best," Ett said. "But I'll get along."

"You may have some trouble sleeping."

"I never have trouble sleeping," Ett said.

Carwell said nothing.

"I see," said Ett, after a moment. "All right, I'll take your word for it. I'll have trouble sleeping. It just proves what I always felt about any kind of drug: none of them are any good. But I'll tell you one thing."

He reached into his pocket, took out the pill container, and set it on the table beside him. "Sleep or no sleep, I'm not going to be taking these."

Carwell still said nothing.

A moment later there was a soft chime from the phone grill. Ett leaned over to hit the answering stud, and said "Yes?"

"Pardon me, Mr. Ho," said an attractive female voice, "but I thought I should tell you that your staff is arriving, and your personal physician is already here. He asked if he could speak to you and Dr. Carwell, both, before Dr. Carwell leaves."

"He can do better than that," said Ett. "He can leave, himself. Dr. Carwell is going to be my personal physician." He turned to look at Carwell. "That is, unless Dr. Carwell objects."

Carwell was staring at him.

"You want me?" he said. "Oh, no! No—no, it wouldn't work."

There had been no sound from the voice on the phone while Carwell spoke; but now a male voice came over the line.

"Mr. Ho, this is Dr. Lopayo," it said. "I'm sorry, but what you want is just not possible. Dr. Carwell isn't qualified for that position. Earth Council requires that you have a qualified physician in attendance at all times."

"He can be in attendance if he wants," said Ett, "but I want Dr. Carwell as well. How about it, Morgan—and you can call me Ett."

"I . . . I . . ." Carwell actually stammered. "Well, naturally, Mr.—uh, Ett—I'd be, um, fascinated by the job of personal physician to an R-Master. But . . . I've got my work here. And I do have a few private patients." He looked at Ett, disturbed. "I'd like to think about it."

"Think about it all you want," said Ett. "But the slot's open—at least for the next few days."

"Thanks. I . . . I don't mean to sound ungrateful—"

"You don't." Ett waved him out of the room. "Think about it."

"Yes . . ."

Carwell went out, blundering a little in his emotion, through the door even his big bulk could not fill. That door closed behind him, while Ett punched the cut-off switch of the phone. It was silent in the room again. He moved over to take a seat in front of one of the windows, and touched the control to open it. A cool morning breeze greeted him, bringing with it sounds of distant, unthreatening human presences, although no one was in sight on the big lawn. Ett sat back and looked out.

Eventually there was a soft double rap on the door, and immediately it opened. Rico Erm once more entered the room, carrying what looked like a narrow-banded wrist instrument, in a gold finish, on a tray. Before he could speak Ett rose and addressed him.

"Why did you knock?" Ett said.

Erm stopped suddenly in the midst of his movement towards Ett, but his face remained calm and still.

"Sir?"

"Why did you bother to knock, if you weren't going to wait for my answer before barging in?" demanded Ett. He stopped himself, with an effort, before continuing, although a part of him would dearly have liked to do so.

"I beg your pardon, Mr. Ho," said Rico Erm. "I'm afraid I was following the pattern that was established in the residences of other R-Masters I've been associated with."

More calm, Ett watched Rico Erm now. "Do R-Masters all live to a pattern, then?"

There was a short silence; then: "To some extent, yes, Mr. Ho."

Ett crossed to the table and picked up the pill bottle Dr. Carwell had left with him.

"And is this a part of the pattern?" he said.

"Yes, Mr. Ho."

Ett allowed the silence to linger for a moment, and then lofted the pill bottle gently across the room with an underarm throw, so that it bounced off Rico's chest and onto the tray.

"Get rid of that for me, will you?" Ett said.

"Very good, Mr. Ho." The face and voice of Rico Erm were as bland as ever; but for a short moment Ett thought he had glimpsed a bright gleam in the man's eyes.

Ett started to say something further, but quickly checked himself. "What's that you have on that tray, then? I assume it's meant for me?"

"Yes," said Rico, holding out the wristwatch-seeming device. "This," he said, "is a somewhat more complex instrument than the usual personal communicator. It puts you in touch on a continuous basis with the Earth Council computer center. Will you put it on, please?"

Ett did so. On his arm it looked deceptively ordinary.

"How does it work?" he asked.

"Press the center stud," said Rico.

Ett did so. A small semitransparent figure like the holographic image of a seated Buddha seemed to form above the dial, and a tiny voice spoke to him from what seemed to be a speaker inside his right ear.

"At your service, Mr. Ho. What can Earth Council do for you?"

"Just testing," said Ett.

"Very good, Mr. Ho." The figure disappeared. Ett reached up to touch his right ear as if to locate the source of the voice.

"You hear through a direct beam broadcast from the wrist instrument to the bones of your ear," said Rico. "You're a valuable property, Mr. Ho. The Earth Council wants to serve and protect you."

"I see," said Ett, in a voice he hardly recognized. The cold feeling was back inside him suddenly. He had been watched over by no one since he had left the Bruder household. Suddenly he felt like a dog on a leash.

"So," he said, still in that voice that was strange even in his own ears. "All right, what are my restrictions? Tell me now."

"No restrictions, sir," said Rico. "The wrist instrument's only for contact purposes. You know all men and women are free nowadays, and an R-Master is even freer than anyone else."

Ett watched the other man closely. There had been something unusual in the calm voice just then—something on the one hand just too bland to be real, yet on the other hand—what? The dark eyes in the impassive, delicately-handsome face were impenetrable.

Rico went on. "You can go anywhere and do anything you like."

"Fine," said Ett. The cold feeling still held him. "Let's try that out, then. I think I want to eat at the Milan Tower."

"Yes, sir," said Rico, "eat at the Milan Tower, Milan, Italy. What time, sir? What day?"

"Today," he said harshly, chilling with the cold anger at last let utterly loose within him. "Right now. What'll it be—midnight when we get there? I want to have a late dinner at a window table in the Milan Tower, and I don't give a damn how you arrange it. I think you said I could go have anything I want. Start by getting this for me!"

CHAPTER FIVE

"Yes, sir," said Rico quietly. He turned toward the door of the room, detouring slightly as he went to avoid the table Ett's breakfast had arrived on.

"What do I do, call Earth Council about it?" Ett asked. His voice seemed loud in his ears.

"No, sir," said Rico from the doorway. "I'll take care of everything."

He went out.

Left alone in the room, Ett found himself shivering, shuddering like someone who had just come from a swimming pool into colder air. It was a phenomenon he recognized from his childhood, and it was a sign that his fury was passing from him, now, leaving in its wake the nausea and chills it always had.

Even as a small boy he had always had a violent temper; and even before he went to live with Heinrich Bruder he had begun to train himself out of it. He had always felt sick after letting his temper go, and controlling the latter had seemed the best way to avoid the disagreeable feelings. Of course, he had slipped on occasion; but the feeling of being befouled and depressed that followed his giving way to the furious anger buried in him, always provided its own punishment.

Later he had found—and been perversely glad of it, for it meant that he was not alone struggling with such a devil—that the anger in him was merely a facet of the Bruder heritage within him. And so his fight to hide himself from that thing he might otherwise become, had been built on the foundation of his earlier struggle.

It was a bad sign, therefore, that he had lost his temper with someone such as this Rico Erm, who after all was hardly responsible for his problems. Possibly the emotional upheaval he had been living through had destabilized his carefully-built false front. He also remembered Dr. Carwell's cautioning him that there were drawbacks to the physiological state of being an R-Master—perhaps the general state of unwellness he had been living with, and trying to ignore, since he awakened, had been eroding his controls, too.

Now he realized just how much of a struggle he might have to keep away from those drugs that were being offered him. But he firmly intended to go on being the self he had always been by choice, in spite of them all. If he had to, he would conquer his temper and his inner self, all over again. He would re-learn self-control.

There were two soft knocks from the door. He turned to look at it but nothing further happened.

"Come in," he said.

The door swung open and Rico Erm stepped back into the room.

"Ready to go, Mr. Ho," he said.

Ett looked sharply at the smaller man. He had expected the other to produce something startling in the way of results, from his demands. But this was almost unbelievable.

"Already?" he asked.

"Your own aircar is in readiness wherever you are, of course," Rico explained. "And I chartered a commercial airline's best intercontinental, which we'll meet at Hawaii port. Later, there'll always be an EC intercontinental on permanent standby near any permanent residence you occupy. Your island's got one, but this charter will be faster than sending for it."

"Island?" Ett felt slightly numbed.

"Naturally, an R-Master can choose whatever residence he might prefer," Rico informed him. "But there are several estates which have been set up on individual small, man-made islands in the Caribbean, and placed at the disposal of new R-Masters until they can decide on something else. I had been about to suggest that we move there, but you asked me to set up lunch for you at the Milan Tower. Perhaps after lunch you'd like to go to your island?"

"We'll see," said Ett. He waved for Rico to precede him from the room.

The intercontinental liner fell up into the sky under the negative impetus of her particle engines at three-grav drive. Inside, Ett was alone again, left by himself in the luxurious first-class lounge while Rico attended some unknown business and the stewards vanished discreetly until he should ring for them. Since a compensating internal grav field controlled the interior of the ship, Ett felt no sign of the acceleration of the vessel; he was free to walk about as he wished.

Walk about he did. He found himself in fact prowling the aisles and corridors of the empty suborbital ship, past the rows of easy chairs, through the lounges, all silent. And he never seemed to encounter members of the crew. He knew he was being lifted farther and farther above the surface of the planet, yet it seemed unreal. He would have no trouble with the idea, he speculated, if only there were more people around. If the lounges and rooms of this great ship only hummed with the movements of people and the self-intent communications they made with each other, he would have no difficulty in believing how high and fast they were all going.

For most of his life he had lived behind his wall of controls, giving no one access to the person who really dwelt there. And for almost eight years now he had lived on his boat, with only Alaric for company—virtually alone on the open seas. Yet he had never felt so lonely as this, and he suspected it might very well go on this way for the rest of his life, unless he could find some way to make the world—the bureaucracy—forget that he was an R-Master, forget him altogether.

He dropped into a chair facing a large switched-off vid screen and considered, eyes closed, what this transportation was probably costing the Earth Council. Half loaded, at a fare of twenty Gross World Product dividend units per passenger, this ship in a commercial flight would take in about eighteen thousand GWP units—which was possibly a little over the cost of the flight in materials, salaries, and depreciation of the craft—but not much over.

White-winged as a cloud under the blue-lighted sky of the clean ocean day, the *Pixie* sailed into his mind's eye. Sloop-rigged and clean-hulled, she turned up into the blue mirror of a small bay, straightened for a run at the shore, and then turned on her heel and slid in to tie up at the dock below the large establishment where Wally had lived those last few months of his life. That had been how it was when Ett sailed in, a week after the radio message that had told him of Wally's suicide. He had already been well on his way to Hawaii when the message reached him or he would have docked the sloop, leaving her in Alaric's care while he flew ahead.

Now the *Pixie* was tied at a buoy in a marina on the Big Island, in the company of Alaric—at least, as far as Ett knew they were still together there. It occurred to Ett that he had better get in touch with Alaric and tell him that *Pixie* was all his. Alaric would not want to take her, but—Ett now grinned, a little bitterly, to himself—as long as Ett put it that Alaric was the only one who could be trusted to take care of the vessel, Al could not very well refuse. Not that, in the long run, he had ever refused to do anything Ett had wanted him to do. Al was a born follower.

Suddenly the feelings he had held back while reviewing his memories, broke into his mind; and the sense of loss that his nostalgia inspired twisted below his heart, stabbing strange and fierce as he realized what was gone from his life now. He had

had *Pixie*, the great blue oceans, and freedom; and it was all gone. Here he was now, suddenly—very suddenly—an empty rich man, spending more in this one-hour trip on a whim than his previous subsistence-level allowance could have paid back in decades.

Ninety-four dividend units each month had been his Citizen's Basic Allowance; with that and *Pixie* he had lived as well as he wanted. . . . He had had to work and sweat for six years to get that sloop, but after that there had been nothing more he had needed. His intent was to let the self-busy world spin its own neat wheels and forget him.

His ninety-four units, the minimum adult's basic allowance, kept him in sails and other supplies, and even let him save a small amount. If there was something unusual he needed, or if he simply felt like doing something—he simply put in a day or two of work.

Other aspects of his life had been happy, too—women seemed to like him, but he felt no need to father children who might put him under obligation to society and the population balance. Five more years without progeny, in fact, and he would even be eligible for a bachelor's bonus.

He had felt safe, contented—secure but independent, in a world where all things were good anyway. As little as fifty years ago, he would have had to struggle for a living, perhaps, or even risk his life in a war. Today there were no such problems. For half a century the world had been able to turn its productivity to improving the lot of humankind . . .

Even Bruder had been buried—all the Bruders, around the world; as the world had made the

intelligent decision at last, forsaking conflict, fear
and poverty—as Ett had buried his own inner self,
choosing to live in peace rather than die at the
behest of the raging soul he had inherited.

He found himself shifting irritably in the lounge
chair, and realized that his eyes were still closed.
What was wrong with him? Perhaps this was one
of the side-effects of the RIV treatment about which
Dr. Carwell had started to tell him. He must make
it a point to see that someone came up with more
detail on the subject right away. When he had sat
down and closed his eyes, he'd figured that after
some initial thought he would drop off into a nap—
he'd never had difficulty doing so before. But now
his mind seemed to have been wandering all
over the map, and by now they must be near to
landing . . .

Alaric. He was remembering the first time he
had ever met the little man. The *Pixie* had been . . .
where? Put in at some small Pacific island. There
had been a number of boats tied up at that dock,
not family or pleasure boats but honest tramps
like *Pixie*. He had joined some of the other boat-
men as they got to fooling around with boxing
gloves—yes, that was it.

Ett had been doing well, for all that they were
just horsing around. He had boxed some in secondary school—it was good for self-control—and he
had fast reflexes. He had never done enough to
become really good, not even a good amateur, and
probably he did not have what it took to ever be
so. But for someone who knew very little about the
art, he was not bad, and he'd been successfully
taking on everyone from the other boats, for beers,

and even some of the local people who were down on the, dock.

From somewhere—he was not one of the island people—this kid had shown up, this young man, younger looking even than he actually was because of his shortness and his round, open face. And somehow Alaric had ended up putting on the gloves with Ett.

It was an apparent mismatch from the first, between the giant and the midget—at least until they started. After a bit of sparring, Ett realized that the great length of his arms could pretty much guarantee that Alaric could not get close enough to Ett to land a punch, particularly since the little man obviously knew nothing at all about boxing. But—and at first Ett found this difficult to believe—he himself couldn't touch the smaller man, either.

Without his shirt, the young man showed himself to be more solidly built than he had appeared, not a narrow target. But for all Ett's greater experience and knowledge, as well as his natural advantages of reach and strength, he could neither corner Al nor lay a glove on him—because if Ett's reflexes were good, Alaric's were blinding. It was incredible at first, and then, as happens amid beer and comradeship, it became funny. Before long Ett was laughing so hard at himself that he could hardly move his gloves, and he was soon punctuating bouts of laughter with wild roundhouse swings that never hit the smaller man.

Al had not laughed back. Ducking, hitting out, his mouth remained a tight line. He continued to fight and would not stop until Ett finally managed to grab him in a full-arm tackle and toss him over the side of the dock. And even then Al came swarm-

ing back up the ladder, dripping, still ready to do
battle; and he was only halted by the surrounding
crowd and the fact that Ett had sat down, taken
off his gloves, and begun to drink a beer while
steadfastly refusing to stand up.

What had that been ... five or six years ago?
Anyway, from then on they had been friends. Ett
had no desire to lead anyone, but Al was a natural
follower and in his own way as successful with
women and the casual life as Ett himself. They
had sailed the world together, comfortable, and
nothing had come to bother either of them until
Wally ...

They had both been running away from the
world, Ett thought now.

And with that thought his eyes opened.

It must be the RIV, he told himself. He would
never have come up with such a sour view of their
way of life before.

A chime sounded through the ship.

"Landing in three minutes at Milan port, Mr.
Ho," said the voice of Rico Erm from all the speak-
ers near him. Ett let himself grimace but did not
answer.

The Milan Tower, four hundred and twenty stories above ground, was currently the tallest building in the world, so narrowly tall that its needle
shape could not have existed even thirty years
before, when technology had not yet developed to
the point to permit such structures. Massive grav
plates between the stories counteracted the tremendous vertical load on its base; in addition to
this, at both the two hundredth and four hundredth floors it was horizontally steadied by four

huge particle engines, automatically responding with drive thrusts to counter wind pressures that otherwise would have snapped the high tower like a breadstick.

In this windy Milanese night, the top twenty stories of the tower swelled out into an elongated, transparent bubble without interior floors, like a giant light bulb aglow softly in the sky. Within that tall open space swam and floated grav-balanced platforms that were separate dining pads done in different decors. Their combined capacity for diners was something like five thousand people being seated and served at once; and since the Tower was no more than an hour from any inter-continental pad on the face of the Earth, it had become the most popular dining spot on the globe.

"Who do you recognize?" Ett asked Rico. He had ordered the other man to join him for lunch, and they were at a table on a dining pad momen-tarily floating high in the bubble, so that they could look out and down over its edge on at least half a dozen other dining pads.

"Recognize?" Rico echoed.

"That's what I said."

Rico glanced around the pad they were on.

"I know the two security guards at the table to our left and the three in the dining pit behind you," he said.

"Oh?" said Ett. It had not occurred to him that he might be guarded. "I'm the reason they're all around us?"

"Yes, Mr. Ho," said Rico. "You can choose later whether you want to be protected or not, but with a world population of six billion, there are always many fanatics—"

"All right, never mind that," said Ett. "I'm not interested in guards. I wanted you to tell me who you recognized among the other people on this pad, and on any others near enough to see, who're here for reasons having nothing to do with me."

"Yes, sir." Rico scanned the other pads nearby. "I don't see anyone I know personally."

"Recognize was the word I used."

"Yes, Mr. Ho. As far as just recognizing public figures or people who've been in the public eye, there're a lot of those around. Li Ron Pao, the conductor of the Berlin Symphony, is just five tables over to your left. The Secretary of the Economic Council, George Fish, is the heavy man in the center of that party near the edge of the pad rising up level with us. There are several stage and screen people on the same pad. Marash Haroun of the First Holographists Mentality is on the other pad just beyond and below."

Rico went on. As their own pad changed position, coming into close proximity with other pads, there were more and more newsworthy figures to identify. Ett sat listening, studying each new person Rico named through half-closed eyes. Finally, Rico began to run down. He hesitated and interrupted himself.

"I can go on like this as long as we're here, Mr. Ho," he said. "Do you want me to?"

"No," said Ett. "That's enough for the moment."

"I don't understand," said Rico. "Why do you want me to point out people you probably know as well as I do?"

"Because I don't," said Ett.

"Don't?" Rico stared at him.

"That's right," said Ett. "It appears I've been

living a particularly quiet and sheltered life. I don't know most of the people who make this world turn."

"All men and women make the world turn," Rico said. "These are just the fortunate few whose work puts them into the public view."

"Mere toilers in the vineyard," said Ett.

"Yes, sir," said Rico.

"Who just happen to be able to get reservations for dinner, like me, at the Milan Tower on a moment's notice."

Rico flushed. It was a curious display of emotion. Ett would have sworn the other man was too self-possessed to show any expression.

"Tell me, Rico," he said. "Who's the most important person in the world?"

"There's no one important person, Mr. Ho, you know that," Rico said. "Every man and woman is equally important to society, and that's the way it's been since the Earth Council was formed in 2002 to eliminate national rivalries and criminal activities. Everybody does what he wants—and doesn't have to do anything if he doesn't want to. The result has to be a world of sane people doing the work they do only because it's the work they most want to do. In a society where every man and woman works only for the sake of working, how can any one person be more important than another?"

"Unless he's an R-Master," said Ett.

"An R-Master," said Rico, "has an unusual value. But until someone like you, Mr. Ho, or the Earth Council itself, finds a use for that value, it's like a fine piece of art stored in a closet and forgotten. On the other hand, I fill one busy day after another with my own work. You are certainly more valuable than I am. But if I had to choose between one human unit and another, I'd have to say that at least for the moment I'm no less important than you and maybe more."

"Interesting," said Ett, looking at the other with new curiosity and some respect. "Sometime you and I ought to talk about this at length—"

He broke off, turning his head sharply to look across to another pad which had just floated up level with their own. The corner of his eye seemed to recognize a familiar face, and now that he looked directly toward it he saw that the familiarity was no mistake.

"I was wrong, Rico," he said. "I thought I wouldn't find anyone here I recognized myself. That's Maea Tornoy over there."

"Maea Tornoy?" echoed Rico. "That's the person you asked me to find for you, I believe?" He turned in the direction Ett indicated with a nod of the head.

Abruptly he stiffened in his chair, and it was a moment before he spoke again; when he did, there was a catch in his voice, almost a note of astonishment, that was again very out of character for Rico as Ett had seen him so far.

"Ah . . . I don't know the person. Do you mean the redhead in her twenties or thirties, with—"

He broke off. Ett looked sharply back at him.

"That's right," Ett said. "With the tall dark man and that particularly beautiful black-haired woman. Do you know them?"

"The man's Patrick St. Onge," said Rico. His face and voice now betrayed no emotion of any sort.

"And the black-haired lady?"

"I don't believe I know who she is."

"Who's St. Onge?" Ett asked. "I suppose I should say, what's St. Onge?" He watched Rico closely.

"An auditor, Mr. Ho. For the Earth Council. Auditors are responsible only to the Accounting Section Chief."

"You mean Wilson?"

"Mr. Wilson, yes," said Rico. He looked at Ett a little strangely. "You certainly know that the EC Auditor Corps has the responsibility of uncovering and arresting offenders against the guidelines of the GWP forecasts. For that matter, the black-haired young lady could also be a member of the Auditor Corps—open, or undercover. But as I say, you must know all this."

"No. How would I? I've lived on minimum subsistence almost all my life."

"The work of the EC auditors is necessarily classified under Security," said Rico. "It's good manners not to refer to the fact that a person is an auditor."

"Oh?" said Ett. "As an R-Master, how do I rank compared to an auditor?"

Rico laughed a little. "Of course there's no such thing as rank," he said. "But naturally, there are always people capable of being trained as EC auditors, and the few R-Masters in the world are the result of accident."

"Fine," said Ett. "Do me a favor. Step over to those three people and ask them if they'd do me the kindness of joining me at my table. Explain that I'm a brand-new R-Master and that the occupation of EC auditor fascinates me."

Rico got half to his feet, then hesitated.

"Mr. Ho," he said. "If I might suggest—"

"Don't suggest," said Ett gently. "Just do it."

Rico nodded, straightened up all the way, and went off to a corner where small floating aircars nuzzled the edge of the dining pad, waiting to convey diners from the pad to the elevator at the base of the bubble, or from pad to pad. A second later, Ett saw him in one of the cars, sliding across through the open air to the pad on which Maea Tornoy sat with Patrick St. Onge and the unknown girl with the black hair and the face of a cameo beauty.

Rico landed on the outer edge of the pad and walked across toward the three. Before he had quite reached the table, though, Maea stood up abruptly and left the other two, hurrying off in the opposite direction from that in which Rico was approaching, and vanishing among the leaves of a jungle garden in the middle of the pad. Thus, when Ett's secretary reached the table, only the two were left there. Ett watched as Rico stood and spoke to them, and their heads turned in his direction. He smiled and beckoned. Their heads nodded—at least St. Onge's did—and turned back to Rico. There was a little more conversation, and then, somewhat slowly, they both got up and followed Rico back to his aircar.

A few seconds later, Rico had them at Ett's table and was introducing them.

"Mr. St. Onge, this is Mr. Etter Ho," said Rico. "Miss Cele Partner, Mr. Ho."

"Good of both of you to come over and talk to me," said Ett, when they were seated around the table. "I wouldn't have imposed on you, but I saw you were friends of Maea Tornoy—"

"Tornoy? Oh, yes, that was her name, wasn't it?" St. Onge said, looking at Cele Partner. He glanced back at Ett. "I'm afraid I hadn't met her before today, myself."

"Maea," said Cele Partner, in a soft voice as attractive as the rest of her, "was working on the societal impact of deep-level gold mining in the Philippines at a time when I was there, and we got to know each other. I ran into her today in Lucerne and brought her along to lunch with Patrick."

"But she's an old friend of yours?" St. Onge asked Ett.

"Of my brother's. He's dead," said Ett. He smiled at both of them.

St. Onge smiled back. He was a lean, handsome knife of a man with a level mouth and level dark eyebrows over shadowed eyes that seemed as devoid of depths as the eyes of a hawk or an eagle.

"It seems something almost like a misunderstanding has brought us together," the auditor said.

Cele Partner, who was sitting between St. Onge and Ett, reached out and laid a hand gently on Ett's arm.

"I wouldn't have missed the chance to meet an R-Master on any terms," she said. "There's only a handful to begin with, and they seem mostly to be recluses. I've never met one—well, except for Malone, and he doesn't count."

"Malone?" Ett said.

"Lee Malone," put in St. Onge, smoothly. "He was one of the first of the R-Masters. Actually, he's more of a recluse than any of them—of you, I ought to say, Mr. Ho—but he shows up at World Council Center every so often to agitate for some

wild idea or other that couldn't possibly be put
into effect."

"He's not right in the head, then?" Ett asked.

"Well . . . you can't really say that," St. Onge
smiled. "His ideas aren't impossible—just imprac-
tical. He's eccentric, rather than . . . something
else. And he *is* an R-Master, so the Council always
listens to him."

The tall man's note was light and amused, but
Ett's alert perceptions—for some reason they
seemed keyed up for this encounter— caught what
he felt was a shade too much casualness about the
explanation. He also found himself wondering why
this other R-Master's name should come up in
conversation between strangers so quickly. Was he
being probed to see if he was also likely to be—
what St. Onge termed "eccentric"?

"Never mind Malone, though," said Cele. "As I
say, he doesn't really count. They mustn't have
had the RIV properly developed back in his time. I
want to know about you. Tell me, what's it like
being an R-Master? What does it feel like?"

"Truthfully," said Ett, "I haven't been able to
notice any difference in feeling so far."

He smiled back at her. It was not the first time
someone of the opposite sex had seemed to take an
immediate interest in him—but something inside
him stood on instinctive guard in the case of Cele
Partner. He felt—for what reason he could not
say—that the interest she showed was not to be
counted upon. At the same time, the touch of her
hand, the scent of her perfume, and her startling
beauty stirred him, made him breathe a little faster
and more deeply, in spite of the instinct for caution inside him. It all served to push the low-level

physical discomforts he was still feeling out of his consciousness.

"Tell me about yourself—about yourself before you took RIV," she was saying.

And he was complying . . .

CHAPTER SIX

It was probably an hour or more, but it seemed only a few minutes before St. Onge reminded Cele that it was time for both of them to leave. Her black hair shook in rich, thick waves as she protested the need to depart—she was enjoying Ett's company thoroughly, she said—but she allowed Ett and St. Onge jointly to pull back her chair, and stood up.

Parting ceremonies took a few minutes more, but then the dining pad was the sole province of Ett and the ever-silent Rico Erm. And that made the whole vast cavern of a room seem rather dull, Ett thought, though in fact the highest of beautiful society glittered on the pads all across the Tower.

No sound from those tables could penetrate the pressure walls that separated them one from another. Ett picked at his meal, which he'd hardly touched while Cele and St. Onge were with him, but realized he had less than no appetite—in fact, the food seemed rather distasteful. Another RIV side-effect? he wondered.

The clink of his silverware on the china seemed offensively loud in the silence, and he threw down his napkin atop his plate, shoving his chair back from the table a bit. Across the table from him, Rico Erm looked ready to depart at any moment, but not eager—of course, never eager, thought Ett. That would hardly be competent.

Ett looked across the table at the secretary, wondering how much the man had read of Ett's reactions—to Cele, to St. Onge, to being an R-Master—and what he made of it all. Or perhaps he hadn't seen it, or didn't care, for there was no sign on the other man's features to show he understood that anything more than a polite and pleasant lunch-table meeting had taken place.

Ett watched Rico Erm a few minutes longer, but gained no information from the bland face, not-quite-smiling before him. And it occurred to him to wonder just who Rico Erm was here to serve.

Pushing his chair back and sideways, Ett punched at the service button. Then he addressed Rico.

"Now," he said, "I'd like to go to Hong Kong for a little gambling."

"Yes, Mr. Ho," said Rico.

When the secretary returned Ett was lounging back in an easy chair, several meters from the table, with a wide-mouthed bell glass of cognac in his hand and his feet on an overstuffed hassock. Ett looked relaxed and comfortable. He had barely touched his drink, though, and his eyes were focused out the window.

"By the time we reach the intercontinental they'll be ready to go, Mr. Ho," Rico said.

Ett nodded and pulled his gaze from the lights of Italy which dotted the night—except for parts of the ocean—as far as he could see. He arose and they went.

In less than an hour they were back in the intercontinental liner—at least Ett presumed it was the same vessel they had come in, although it could certainly have been switched for an identical one— and rising into the night on a Hong Kong trajectory. Once more Rico had vanished and Ett was left alone. He closed his eyes and leaned back.

The image of Cele Partner as she had laughed and watched him came before him, her cameo face white against the frame of black hair. He frowned and shook his head slightly, without opening his eyes, wondering how she could do this to him. Perhaps this was another thing that RIV had done to him—certainly he had never been swept off his feet by any woman before the treatment . . .

Of course, he had never encountered anyone like Cele before RIV, either. In fact, he had never imagined that a woman like that could exist in real life.

Well, he told himself, it had been part of his reason for going to the Tower, that he see what the uppermost part of the social body was like, that upper part he had always ignored but now was going to have to live with, since he had become a part of it.

And the other reason for his travels was to test the extent of the demands he could make on the funds and services of the World Economic Council— the Earth Council. So far, evidently, he had not stretched things to the limit. Well, Hong Kong might bring some reaction . . .

A small sound nearby made him open his eyes, and he saw Rico in the act of putting down on the service table beside him a glass filled with some yellowish liquid that effervesced slightly.

"Try this, Mr. Ho," Rico said. "It should make you feel better."

"What makes you think I'm not feeling all right?" demanded Ett. In truth, he was slightly dizzy, and there was a small headache behind his eyes, which would not go away. Altogether he had a general physical feeling of cranky uncomfortableness. But he could not believe any of this had shown.

"Merely a guess," said Rico. "You had a bit to drink at lunch."

"To drink?" Ett stared at him. He had had two cocktails and part of a bottle of some sparkling German wine, which he had divided with Cele and St. Onge—Rico himself evidently did not drink. "What are you talking about? I've handled half a liter of rum between six p.m. and midnight and still gotten up at dawn to take my sloop across open ocean, without trouble."

"Yes, Mr. Ho. I'm sure. But that was before you had the RIV treatment."

Ett found himself glaring at the secretary. Even as he glared he had to admit what he felt now was at least very like the few rare hangovers he had experienced.

"All right," he said at last. "Is this part of being an R-Master, too?"

"It seems to be common among R-Masters to react like that, Mr. Ho."

"Even if there's something to what you say," Ett said, "I don't like medicines. I've told you that."

"It's only an analgesic."

"No," said Ett. He closed his eyes again.

There was more faint movement. When he lifted his eyelids once more, a few minutes later, the glass had been taken away.

He tried to sleep. But again, as on the flight from Hawaii, the easy slumber he had been used to all his life would not come to him. He barely dozed, fitfully running from memory to memory again. It was almost a relief when Rico spoke to him again.

"We'll be landing in two minutes, Mr. Ho."

The most elaborate, and therefore glamorous, gambling colony of the mid-twenty-first century was maintained in and about what had been for a long time the British crown colony of Hong Kong, and for a brief time an autonomous member of the short-lived Chinese Federation. Naturally, their presence meant that the area also had the best-supplied stores, the most expensive health clubs and spas, and—on the island of New Macao—the most fashionable beaches in the world. It was a place to get rid of dividend units, pure and simple.

Biggest, and most famous, of the gambling establishments was the Sunset Mountain, a multi-level complex that climbed the sides of the 280-meter-high feature for which it was named, on Lan Tao Island. The complex included stores, health clubs and pools, and a great deal of hotel, restaurant, and theatre space, but they were merely sidelines to the main business of the Mountain.

Ett swept through the lobby of The Dragon, the

most exclusive of the hotel sections of Sunset Mountain, without stopping to check in. Rico had already arranged that, and they went directly to the best suite of rooms in the building, high up on the Mountain with a striking view of the new archipelago, aglow in the warm noon sun on the turquoise sea.

Still feeling out of sorts, Ett proceeded to the health club for a short workout and a few laps of the pool. The exercise seemed to refresh him, but when he returned to his room to try to nap, he found himself in the same sort of mental treadmill he'd begun to grow all too familiar with. Finally he gave up and dressed once more.

"Have you arranged credit for me?" he asked Rico in the suite's main lounge.

"Yes, Mr. Ho."

"And how much credit have I got?"

"As much as you need," said Rico.

"Unlimited?" Ett looked more closely at his secretary.

"For all practical purposes."

"Well," said Ett, "let's go see." He'd decided that he might as well proceed with his experiment, regardless of the fact that the most popular hours for gambling activity had not yet arrived.

The St. George Room was the specialty of Sunset Mountain, renowned throughout the world. The size of a very large ballroom, it contained only one piece of gambling apparatus—which was a single vertical shaft, upon which were mounted, one above the other, a dozen transparent, crystalline roulette wheels, ten meters in diameter. The wheels rotated independently, two meters apart, and players could bet on the play of one wheel, in the ordinary

fashion of roulette, or on more than one. Sociable
players could bet and watch the play on vid sets,
from booths and tables around the hall; but the
more serious players rode in grav chairs directly
above the wheels, looking down at and through
them while a tote board on each chair kept track
of wins and losses. The ultimate bet was on a
series of numbers to come up in sequence on all
twelve wheels.

Ett went immediately to a grav chair and rode it
up to the top level, while Rico came behind him in
another chair. Floating above the wheels, looking
down through the layers of crystalline plastic, Ett
began to play. He went right to complex sequen-
tial plays, and bet heavily; and even though he
was riding above the wheels, his attention was
soon totally engaged by the displays of the tote
board on his chair.

The perversity of luck ran true to form. Ett, who
had come just to see how much money Earth Council would let him throw away, began by winning.
Ignorant of the various alternative bets he could
make, he'd bet a series of numbers and hit the
button for "Show." And on his fourth wager, the
numbers he punched in all showed up on one or
another of the wheels—he had won; and because
the odds in this room were so very large, he won
an incredible amount.

He stopped his play for a moment while he consulted the Directory as to the rules of the play
here, and determined that for his purposes he
should be playing for a strict sequence of appearance of the numbers he chose. He returned to play.

For practical purposes this roulette room had no
house limit on the size of the bet, but that turned

out to be only because the house limit was so large. Ett quickly found out that his tote board would not let him wager more than 50,000 dividend units at a time, although he could see the manager for an override. But he decided he preferred not to make his purpose as obvious as that; and continued, playing 50,000 units each time.

By the end of a couple of hours word of his playing had spread through the casino, and a large crowd was on hand. Most of the other gamblers on the wheels had withdrawn from play, although a few began to try to ride with his bets. In those next hours he bet and lost an incredible sum of money—but twice in six hours he won an immense amount by hitting a partial sequence on the wheels.

After the second of those wins the room was full of onlookers, although no one was betting now except the few who were still trying to ride his luck. At the moment he had won more than he had lost, by a small margin— but that was enough to strike up the rumor that he might in fact break the bank in the roulette room.

The local gaming laws forbade the breaking of Sunset Mountain as a total entity. Other gamblers in other rooms had to be protected in their own right to win. But he would be allowed to break the bank in this room, if he could do so—and the bank in this room was estimated to be worth more than the combined total of the banks in all the other gambling rooms combined.

Each time Ett had won on a partial sequence wager, it had taken him over two hours to get rid of those winnings again. Those two partials alone, and the size of his wagers, were enough to set the crowd buzzing; for a while they bothered him, but eventually he had shut them completely from his mind.

And shortly after midnight, when he was almost two million dividend units into his credit balance, the buzz turned to a dead silence, quickly followed by a full-throated roar. Ett had hit the jackpot— won a full-sequence wager.

Pandemonium swept the great hall while all the lights flashed and great klaxons roared. Ett sagged back in his seat and watched in disbelief as his tote board ran up an incredible balance in his favor. Down below in the hall two little Japanese men, at one table, and a young woman from Toronto, across the room, were also celebrating wildly—for they had bet on Ett's sequence, and so had won, at tremendous odds though for much smaller amounts.

It was some time before play could resume, and Ett had to refuse an invitation to receive his winnings in a ceremony to be broadcast around the world. When play was allowed to resume, Ett proceeded grimly on his course. He began by buying a magnum of champagne for everyone in the building, which used up a considerable sum; then he dived back into his play again. He also hit on the strategy of playing from the tote board on Rico's chair, which he slaved to his own controls; and so he began to double his losses. The tide of his luck had at last turned. As he continued to play at the house limit, his winnings melted away before him.

Ett paused, some time later, to lean back in his grav chair. Beyond the transparent wall which gave him a view down the mountainside, he could look into the sunrise. Possibly it was a glorious one, but his eyes were grainy and the headache behind them nearly a living, malignant force in itself, although he had drunk nothing more than coffee since Milan. He felt more deeply exhausted than he could ever remember feeling before. He turned to look at Rico Erm, feeling the protest of his back muscles as he did so. Rico was leaning back in another grav unit behind him and to his left. He looked as if they had begun their travels together only an hour or so before.

Somehow Rico contrived to look even more attentive, as if physically indicating his eagerness to serve Ett in any way possible. Abruptly Ett felt an upwelling of raw, fiery anger again, and he threw himself back into the game, hunching over his console and punching savagely at the ivory surfaces that registered his wagers. In another two hours he had lost all he had earlier won. Two hours after that he was more than ten million units in debt.

At last he paused again, and sat looking at his board for some moments. Then he turned back to Rico, who still looked chipper although by this time Ett had become too fogged to notice.

"Have I reached my limit yet?" he asked Rico. "Or can I keep going and try to recoup my losses?"

"That's entirely up to you, Mr. Ho," Rico said. "I can order as much more credit as you'd like."

And so Ett gave up. If there was any end to the funds the EC was willing to supply him, finding out where it might be wasn't worth this.

"Let's quit," he said, and fell back on the cushions of his chair, while Rico slaved its controls and began to lower them both to the floor of the hall. Down there, though, waited the swarms of gam-

blers and other watchers who had been attracted
to the saga of his effort. They had no notion of why
he had played as he had, but he had captured their
imaginations in some way—apparently even a loser
could have some magic, provided he lost on a
grand scale.

Seeing them, Rico overrode the chairs' controls
and, surrounded by other men in grav chairs, until
now themselves quite inconspicuous, they passed
over the heads of the great crowd and down a long
hallway, until they had lost the crowd and were
quite alone. They took Ett to his room, where he
stumbled to his bed, and left him.

It was early evening when Ett awoke. He could
remember being helped to his room, but after that
he could recall nothing. He was still in his clothes,
although his shoes were gone somewhere, and he
was lying atop the rumpled surface of the large
foam bed, with a single old-fashioned cloth blanket draped over him. Rico must have done that, he
thought.

He rolled over so that he was no longer lying on
his side, but flat on his back—although the movement made a throbbing start through the back of
his head. When that had died away he pulled a
pillow down and doubled it up behind his neck,
enduring another session of protest from the back
of his skull. Then he simply lay there, looking out
the window at the sky which slowly deepened in
hue, from a milky blue to a pale lavender, to a
cloud-grained purple with orange highlights, as
the sun went down, somewhere beyond his line of
sight.

The sky was a deep, rich blue, almost black,

when he threw back the blanket and rose, slowly
and cautiously, from the bed. His head seemed all
right, though something suggested it might be un-
duly fragile. There was a dull ache in the small of
his back, and he stretched gingerly while undress-
ing and moving towards the large bathroom. That
room's muted lighting and warm gold tones seemed
to comfort him a bit; and he ran a warm bath, in
which he simply lay, eyes closed, for an unknown
period of time.

The bath water never did get cold—this was,
after all, one of the most expensive bathrooms in
the world—but eventually he opened his eyes and
sat up in the tub, reaching for a towel.

Ett and Rico had dinner in the suite, seated on a
balcony that overlooked the boat-filled harbor that
was called the Living Sea. Ett found that he had
an appetite again, although certain dishes now
tasted different and seemed unfamiliar. By the time
he reached the caramel custard, however, his queasiness had returned.

"If you don't mind, Rico," he said, "I'd like to
return to that conversation we were having in
Milan—you might remember, you were saying you
felt you were at least as important as I am, and
perhaps more so."

"I recall, Mr. Ho," said Rico. "I believe what I
said was to the effect that because I function as
well as I can, I am as important as anyone, and
perhaps more important than even an R-Master, if
he's non-functional."

"Yes, that was it," said Ett. "I take it you're
implying you deplore waste and inefficiency, and

that therefore you're aghast at my performance there the last couple of days."

"By no means, Mr. Ho—that is, as far as what you say applies to yourself. I don't pretend to understand what you've been doing—but I do know you've been moving to a plan, and so you must be at work to fulfill a function of some sort. And as far as I can tell after today, you've been working very hard at it, indeed."

"It doesn't matter to you if I define my function myself?" Ett asked.

"Who could be better qualified to define your function than you?" said Rico. "You are, after all, an R-Master—and quite obviously an intelligent and active one."

Ett sat silent for a few minutes, looking at the young man before him. Rico accepted the scrutiny calmly, with no change of expression.

For some time after that, the two of them walked about the great complex, always accompanied at a discreet distance by at least four of the unobtrusive security men. The crowds seemed to have forgotten Ett already, although perhaps it was simply that a whole new clientele had replaced those present during Ett's gambling binge.

The two of them took a table at a glittering floor show, but Ett was still in the grip of the restlessness that had brought him out of the suite in the first place. He left the theatre soon, pulling his entourage, unbidden, behind him. And as he went, a young redheaded woman rose from a table at the back of the room, and followed. Ett's security noticed her movements at once, however, and when Ett noticed her, she was already hemmed in.

He raised a hand to halt the men who were already about to hustle her away, and walked toward her.

"Why, it's Maea Tornoy, isn't it?" he said. "No, it's all right," he told the security men, "she's a friend of my brother's." The men moved slowly away, reluctant, and Ett led Maea along a hanging balcony. Rico fell back from them, and they moved slowly, renewing the brief acquaintance they'd had once.

"Yes, I remembered you when I saw you walk out of the lounge," she said. "I thought I should tell you how sorry I was to learn about Wally. I'm afraid I was in Africa on a temporary assignment when it happened, and I never heard until just a few weeks ago. I was so sorry!"

She paced slowly beside him, generally watching the floor or the vista ahead, except when touching his arm to emphasize an expression of sympathy. Ett's eyes were generally on her, and for the first few minutes he said very little.

"Was there a funeral?" she asked.

"No," said Ett. "They got to him very quickly and put him in cryogenic as a matter of course. I've been told there's no point in trying revival. But we're going to try anyway."

"I see." She looked down.

"Yes." For some reason Ett did not want to discuss Wally directly with her. To some extent his preoccupation with being an R-Master had driven the matter of her relationship with Wally into the back of his mind, it was true. But now that she had appeared to remind him of it, it did not seem so important . . .

. . . He realized suddenly that he had stopped

walking, and been lost in his thoughts for a moment or two. Maea had also stopped, a step ahead of him, stopped and twisted about in place, looking back at him. He put himself in movement, again, smiling jovially for public consumption. Rico was still about ten feet behind them, he noted, and no one else was closer.

"You're not here by accident, are you?" he said quietly to her, as he moved off beside her.

She looked sideways and up at him as they moved— they were walking much closer to each other now—and appraised him for a moment.

"Well, you *are* an R-Master now, aren't you," she said. It did not seem to be a question, but more a confirmation directed at herself. "Still, you can be misled as easily as anyone else. Don't forget that."

"Oh, I won't," he said. "In fact, I'm still not sure I really believe this has happened to me. But don't *you* try to mislead me, too, Miss Tornoy—"

"Call me Maea," she said.

"Maea, then. Why are you here?"

She was silent for a few moments, looking down in front of her feet as they moved along at a leisurely pace. He didn't press her.

"It's going to sound horrible," she said softly, looking at him, "but Wally is only incidental to the reason I'm here."

She stopped. "That was even worse than I thought it would be."

"Go on," he said. His voice seemed noticeably cooler even to him, and she noticed it.

"I belong to an organization which thinks you need to learn a lot more about the world," she said. "Think about it. Ask questions. Any man of good will will be glad to help you."

"What has—had—Wally to do with this?" he asked. But she refused to meet his eyes, and they strolled on in silence. At the next cross-corridor she turned back to him as she stopped, and looked up.

"Maybe you should talk to Lee Malone," she said.

"He's another R-Master, isn't he?" Ett asked.

"Yes," she said, looking at him now with curiosity frank in her eyes. He said nothing, and after a moment she turned and strode rapidly off down the cross-corridor.

When Ett looked away from her, Rico had joined him. Neither of them said anything for some moments, and they both just stood in place, while couples and occasional small groups detoured around them. Eventually Ett decided to return to his suite. His head hurt again.

An empty elevator opened its doors as they reached the bank nearest them, so they stepped into it alone, and Rico punched the code that would direct the conveyance up, across, and around to their suite. But as soon as they began to move, Ett, reflexively, stepped forward and hit the manual override switch. Rico stared at him.

"Sir?"

"I don't know, Rico—call it restlessness," Ett said. "Maybe I'm just feeling perverse." He punched out another code at random on the elevator's control pad. The car began to move again, and through the single transparent wall it began to be plain that they had left the public portions of Sunset Mountain, and entered service routes.

Rico fingered his wrist communicator but said nothing.

Shortly, the elevator doors opened before them and Ett stepped out into a plain, metal-walled corridor. Rico was at his heels.

"Mr. Ho, I don't mean to object," he said, "but while Earth Council has a tremendous amount of authority and even more power of good will, no one can guarantee you absolute protection. It would be safest—"

He broke off. Down the corridor ahead of them a door had opened, and a man, dressed in a tight-fitting black garment, with a hand-laser clipped to his belt, had just stepped through it. He stood in the center of the hallway, looking at them and frowning.

"What are you doing here?" he said. "I don't see any passes."

"Forgive me, sir," Rico said, "but Mr. Ho is a new R-Master—" but the man in the black suit cut him off.

"I don't care who he is. This is a private section. Get back to the elevator and get out of here."

Ett was grinning. He had been feeling miserable for hours, but this situation, which sounded as if it might lead to a fight, had him feeling better. Adrenalin was suddenly pouring into his bloodstream, washing the weariness and the headache out of his awareness. He didn't notice it was gone, but he was feeling better.

"What's in that room you just came from?" he asked the man in black.

"Mr. Ho—"

"Never mind, Rico," said Ett. "The man can answer me. Let him."

"I'll answer you," said the other. He reached back and touched a point on the wall beside the door. A high-pitched humming filled the corridor. The door opened and the two other armed men in black came out. Farther down the hall another door opened to let out three men, and Ett heard yet another door opening behind himself and Rico, beyond the elevator door.

The elevator opened and four of Ett's security men stepped out. They moved forward quickly; all at once Ett found himself surrounded by their bodies.

Rico released the dial of his own wrist communicator, and stepped forward, reaching between Ett's bodyguards.

"Mr. Ho—if I may?" Without waiting for an answer, Rico took Ett's wrist and lifted it, with the arm, before his face, pressing against the stem of the communicator. The small Buddha image appeared above the dial, before his eyes.

"This is Rico Erm, speaking for Etter Ho. Security problem. Please record and locate."

"Affirmative, Mr. Erm—" the voice from the communicator was set on area broadcast, and so could be heard by everyone there—"Do you require assistance?"

The men in black, who had been moving in, had stopped. Rico let Ett's wrist fall and stepped back out from among the security men. He moved forward in front of the man they had first encountered.

"Not at the moment," Ett said. He, too, stepped forward from the circle of his own security men. Then, as he looked at the door behind the man in black, his grin widened.

At a jaunty, relaxed pace Ett walked up to and

past Rico, past the man in black—and opened the door through which the other had come.

He stepped into what seemed to be a balcony with seats overlooking a gym. Those seats were sparsely filled with spectators who were hunched over viewscreens apparently meant to give them a closeup of action on the gym floor. At one end of the gym some kind of tally board burned with lights. Down on the floor of the gym itself, two men in black suits like those worn by the men in the corridor, were engaged in a fencing match.

It was all so commonplace and harmless that Ett halted, ready to feel foolish at forcing his way in.

Then he noticed that neither of the fencers wore masks. Nor were they fitted with mesh shirts for electrical scoring of touches. Instead, they were naked to the waist; and the one on the right had a long red line slantwise across the upper left of his chest.

Ett stepped forward to an empty seat and looked into the viewer before it.

The viewer gave him an excellent closeup. It was as if he looked at the fencers from less than six feet away. He saw then that the weapons had no protective buttons. Their points were sharp. As he looked, the arm of the man on the left straightened and his right leg kicked forward, as he lunged, and the point of his weapon disappeared into the already scratched chest of his adversary.

As the man on the right crumpled, Ett turned and pushed his way back out the door, brushing by Rico and the security men, who'd been waiting for him just inside it.

"Are you all right, sir?" Rico said. He looked

somehow disheveled, for the first time since Ett had known him.

"All right," said Ett thickly. "We'll go."

Silently, they went, the black-clad men moving out of their way as they approached. Still in silence, Ett rode the elevator to his own corridor and his own suite. He fell on his back on the bed, staring at the ceiling. The exhausted feeling was back. The headache was like a tourniquet about his temples. But more than that was churning inside him. He had seen fights, plenty of them. He had even seen knives and bottles and clubs used, and he was aware that waivers could be signed allowing two contestants to fence with naked weapons.

But the presence of the casino's security men and the tote board confirmed that this had been something more, a duel to the death taking place only so that spectators could bet on it.

With that ugly image still floating in his mind, he slid into a light and uneasy sleep.

CHAPTER SEVEN

He dreamed that he was busy building something beautiful and intricate. In a very large room, he was constructing all sorts of different shapes out of small crystalline shapes. Pillars, arches, and fragile enclosures—they covered the available floor surface and stretched from floor to ceiling. The facets and angles of their innumerable tiny crystals reflected points of fire in all colors around him: diamond-white, red, green, purple, yellow. . . .

A hand blundered into the room, a massive chunk of flesh and bone cut off at the wrist, bigger than a man, bigger than Ett. Blindly and brainlessly, it began to draw straight lines along the floor, arbitrarily dividing the room into sections. It followed the line it was drawing without regard for what was in the way, smashing through and destroying the crystalline creations in its path.

The room was being plowed into a shambles.

Desperately, Ett grappled with the hand, trying to stop it. But it was too massive for him to halt or push aside. With stupid but inexorable concentration it continued, leaving ruin and havoc behind it, all the bright firepoints of light extinguished forever, while Ett struggled helplessly with it, in a vain effort to stop the destruction. . . .

He woke to find himself on the hotel bed in a darkened room, with a darker shape that resolved itself into Rico standing over him.

"What time is it?" said Ett thickly.

"Nearly seven a.m.," said Rico, "local Hong Kong time."

"How long was I sleeping?"

"About four hours."

"Only four hours?" Ett felt like a man in hell, exhausted and tense at the same time. His mouth and throat were dry as powder, his head beat with pain to the pulse of his heart, and all the muscles of his body felt as if he had just climbed a mountain.

"Only four hours, Mr. Ho," said Rico, "I suggest we go to your island now. Your doctor will be waiting for you there, a physician who specializes in the problems of R-Masters. You need his help."

"What help?" said Ett, forcing himself up on his elbow. He peered up through the gloom at Rico. "No medicines. No drugs."

"You're not being realistic," Rico said. "The RIV has changed your whole physical system permanently. There are prescriptions to help you live with these changes—only they're necessarily different for each R-Master. Your physician will have to examine you and determine what you need."

"Nothing," said Ett. With a sudden effort he got himself up in sitting position on the side of the bed. "There's nothing I need. Yes—I need food. And coffee. Now! As quick as you can."

"Yes, Mr. Ho."

Rico went off. Ett fumbled his way to a shower; the hot water helped to revive him. He shaved, found some clean clothes laid out on a chair, and put them on. By the time he was dressed, Rico had returned, with another man pushing a wheeled cart on which were covered plates. The good odor of coffee rose into Ett's nostrils.

He drank and ate. Nothing tasted quite right. In spite of its enticing odor, the coffee was harsh and acid, while the omelet and toast that went with it were almost tasteless. But with food inside him he began to feel once more in control of his life.

He made himself drink more coffee.

"Rico," he said. "I want to talk to another R-Master. Will you set that up?"

For the first time since Ett had met him, the secretary hesitated.

"I'll try, of course, Mr. Ho," he said. "But you understand—with other Masters we can only ask."

Ett frowned.

"You mean out of sixty or whatever number there are of them, there wouldn't be one who could spare me an hour or two of talk?"

"They all have their own individual ways," said Rico. He turned to go, then looked back. "I assume you'd rather talk to a Master who was a man?"

Ett blinked and grinned. He had not thought that far into the matter.

"You're right," he said. "In this one case, you're right. I'd rather talk to another R-Master who's a man."

Rico went out. Forty minutes later, he was back.

"Master Lee Malone will be glad to talk to you, his secretary says, Mr. Ho. I'm sorry."

"Sorry? Why?"

"Master Lee Malone is . . . a little eccentric, even for a Master," said Rico. "He's always willing to talk to new Masters, though—but I don't know how informative or useful he'll be. But there's no one else who wants to be disturbed among the others—men or women."

Ett nodded. He was feeling better than he had for some time. The taste of the coffee had come back to naturalness with his third cup, and he sipped at the hot liquid now.

"All right," he said quietly. "I'm thankful to anyone who'll give me the time. I'll have my session with this Malone, and then we'll go to that island you want me to get to. But Rico—"

"Yes, sir?"

"No more talk about medicines or drugs for me."

"I won't mention it again," said the secretary.

"Good. Now," said Ett, "where does Master Malone keep himself?"

"North America, in San Diego, California," said Rico. "The intercontinental liner that brought us here is standing by. We can use it until you reach the island and your own assigned craft."

"All right," said Ett, getting up from his chair and his coffee cup. "We'll go right now."

R-Master Lee Malone did not merely live in San Diego, he lived in one of the old museum sections of San Diego. There were areas of the town that had been carefully preserved, and dated back to before the time when San Diego's residential streets went underground—twenty years before they were disposed of entirely. To get to Malone's residence, it was necessary to take an aircar—one was waiting for them—from the port to the edge of the museum area, and then switch to one of the hovercars which were the only transportation allowed in the preserve. They had gone into the day side of the planet, and found it now early afternoon; but the day was of a fall coolness untypical of the area.

Their hovercar followed its programming faithfully through the cold, shallow concrete troughs of the streets, under old-fashioned street lamps, past cement block and wooden walls that had been erected during the riots of the last decade of the twentieth century, to hide and protect these one-family homes. At last it stopped before a modern metal vehicle door in a poured ceramic wall. Ett got out, but Rico stayed where he was in the hovercar. Ett looked at him questioningly.

"Master Malone specified he would see you only," said Rico.

Ett nodded. He turned toward the vehicle door and saw that a personnel slot had now opened in it. He walked through, and the slot closed behind him.

He found himself in an area about four times the size of the individual lots he had seen pictured in history books. Under the heatless sun he saw ahead of him a large rambling structure that seemed to be made of wood. Between this building and himself was an extensive grassy area thickly shadowed by large old trees; he recognized oak and what seemed to be cottonwood, among others. But the house was unkempt appearing and badly in need of paint. The grass of the lawn stood high. Cardboard and wooden signs were inexpertly nailed or glued to the tree trunks, bearing strangely-worded exhortations to reform, while various specimens of broken lawn furniture and other bits of household debris lay scattered about. The whole area had the look of the scene of a destructive lawn party that had not been cleaned up for several years.

One of the shallow cement troughs, which had evidently been intended once as a driveway, led up to the house. Ett walked up it, leaving it finally for the front door, a wide and tall surface of dark wood, across which had been clumsily painted in red letters MOGOW.

The word—if it was a word—rang a faint bell of familiarity. Ett turned from the door to look back into the front yard. Several of the signs on the trees had the same combination of letters, either as part of a longer screed or by themselves. He turned back to the door and looked around for an annunciator plate. There was none visible. Remembering the room in which he had awakened on the morning after passing out at the RIV Clinic, he bent the knuckles of his right hand and rapped on the wood surface itself.

The door opened to reveal a short, thin, but broad-shouldered man with a wispy yellow beard and yellowish gray hair.

"Come in! Come on, then!" he snapped in an old man's voice. "I'm Malone; you're Ho. Come in before I change my mind and kick you out, after all."

Ett grinned.

"What's funny?" demanded Malone, as the door closed itself behind them.

"I was just thinking," Ett said. "I haven't felt

like any kind of an R-Master so far. And you certainly don't look or sound like one."

Malone looked at him. Suddenly the old face changed. The lines of irascibility smoothed out, the down-curving line of the old lips became level, and the eyes darkened, hooded under the tangled gray brows.

"Don't be a damn fool," said Malone quietly, in a younger voice. "Keep your mouth shut until you know what you're talking about."

He turned and led the way through a series of dark rooms and hallways and at last through a door that let them into a room miserly of window space but rich in interior decoration and a warmly lighted fireplace. The furniture was heavy, ancient, and comfortably overstuffed; the rugs were thick and dark colored.

"Sit down," said Malone, throwing himself into one of a pair of high-backed chairs flanking the fireplace. "I suppose you found out I was the only one of us who'd talk to you."

"That's right," said Ett.

"Of course it's right," said Malone. His voice was back on its cracking, irascible old-man's tone. "But don't blame them. In fact, make a good start of it. Don't blame anyone—except yourself. No one twisted your arm to make you take the RIV. So forget about blaming and concentrate on what can be done; that's my advice."

He looked into the dancing flames.

"Not that you'll take it—probably," he said.

"Why shouldn't I?" Ett asked. "It makes sense."

Malone looked up from the fire at him and their gazes locked.

"People seem to run on rails, no matter what I

tell them," said the older man softly. "Take you, now. So far you've done everything wrong, every time you had a choice. To begin with, what status did you opt for with the EC, Ward or Citizen? No, don't tell me. I'll tell you. You picked Citizen status, didn't you?"

"I shouldn't have?"

"Hell, no!" snapped Malone. "Couldn't you see that choice was being forced on you?"

"I've got things I want to do," said Ett. "I needed the extra freedom."

"Extra freedom!" Malone snorted. "The only status that gives you anything approaching some freedom is Ward. What do you think I am?"

"Ward, obviously," said Ett.

"That's right. But then I was one of the early ones. Know how long I've been a Master?"

Ett shook his head.

"Forty years."

Ett looked at him closely. It was not that Malone looked hardly more than his late fifties, until he spoke. There were ninety- and even hundred-year-olds around nowadays who could pass for Malone's younger brother. It was the fact that if Malone was telling the truth, he must have been among the first half dozen or so of the Masters to be produced by RIV.

"That's right, forty years," said Malone. "And I'm the only Master left that goes anywhere near that far back. But you won't listen to me, any more than any of the others I've talked to ever did."

"You keep insisting on that," said Ett gently, "and maybe you'll end up talking me into it."

Malone stared at him for a second and then

burst into a shout of laughter, not an aged cackle, but a full-throated roar of humor.

"All right!" he said. "All right! Maybe you're worth the trouble, after all. But let's look at what you've done so far."

"I—" began Ett, but Malone cut him short.

"Don't tell me. I'll tell you," he said. "I have myself briefed on what every new Master does, as soon as he reacts to the RIV. Not that I need briefing any more. I know without being told what you or anyone else is going to do first—and it's always the wrong things. Take you. First you tried to see how much the EC would do for you. Then you tried to see how much they'd spend on you. Then, when you got nowhere with both tries, you finally thought of doing what you should have thought of in the first place—asking somebody who knows. But nobody who knows would talk to you but me. And the way things are set up, I don't look like anyone you can trust, even if I do tell you."

"Look," said Ett. He had liked the other man without reason, from the first moment of seeing him. But he was heavy with tiredness and his head throbbed. "Just answer a few questions. Why don't I feel like I'm an R-Master, if I am one?"

"Why, now," said Malone, "don't tell me you feel just like you always did?"

"Of course I—" Ett broke off. "You mean the way I feel now? I'm out on my feet and uncomfortable right now. But don't tell me . . ."

He paused.

"Or," he went on slowly, "do tell me, come to think of it. Do you mean anyone who has the kind of reaction to RIV that makes him an R-Master is bound to go around feeling this bad? You mean all sixty-three Masters feel like this all the time?"

Malone chuckled.

"I don't," he answered, "but I'm different. The rest—yes, they feel like you do, most of the time. The only time they don't is when they get worked up about something, worked up enough to override their ordinary sensations with excitement, such as when they're figuring something out, or when they're doped up with medicines that damp out their discomforts."

He laughed sarcastically.

"Shakes you up, doesn't it?" he said. "You thought being a lucky ticket holder in the renatin sweepstakes was nothing but peaches and cream. Why should it be? Your whole system's been kicked out of focus to gear up with a mind that's now overgeared. Ever hear of medicines with side effects? Hell, they've all got side effects, even the ones where you don't feel the effects consciously! The history of medicine is lousy with side effects, loaded with drugs that would have been perfect in their main effect if there just hadn't been a few lousy kicker results there, too, that might kill the patient or make him wish he'd never been born. All right, RIV makes men or women into R-Masters, all right, in a few stray cases. But when it does, the heavy effect it has on intelligence is matched by just as heavy effects on the rest of the person it works on."

Ett nodded. "I see," he said.

"Come on, now," said Malone. "Don't just sit there and pretend to shrug it off. Wait until the chemicals in you wear off—whatever drugs your

EC doctor first pumped into you—if you think you feel bad now!"

"What drugs? When?" Ett demanded.

"How do I know what drugs? I wasn't there when you had your first RIV reaction!" Malone snapped. "As for when, you know that better than I do. When did you last see the physician EC assigned to you?"

"I haven't seen him at all yet," said Ett. "And when and if I do, he can keep any medicines he's got on hand. I don't take them."

"You don't mean you haven't had anything but the initial RIV injection?"

"Not unless they pumped something into me while I was asleep or unconscious."

Malone leaned forward in his chair and peered into Ett's eyes with a suddenly sharp gaze.

"You sure you're telling me the truth?" he demanded. "How do you feel?"

"I don't feel good," said Ett grimly. "But I'm alive and moving, and I plan to keep on moving."

"Hmmm," said Malone thoughtfully. "Either you've got some sort of lucky easy reaction to the side effects of RIV, or you're tougher than bull leather. And you never take medicines—any medicines?"

"Not since I could walk."

"How about aspirin?"

"No."

"Tobacco? Alcohol? Cannabis?"

"No tobacco. No cannabis. Alcohol, yes," said Ett. "I used to be able to drink and never have a hangover." He grimaced. "I can't now. You're right about the side effects as far as that goes. I get hangovers."

"Coffee?"

"Coffee's fine. I've even drunk some since the RIV. Tastes a little bad sometimes. But the effect seems good enough."

"Tea? Maté?"

"I didn't use to drink tea much. Haven't tried it since the RIV. Maté I never did drink."

"Cough syrup? Codeine?"

"I wouldn't touch it. Not that I ever had a lot of coughs. Nor did I ever use breath mints, laxatives, antihistamines—"

"You'd better keep some antihistamines around, at any rate," said Malone dryly. "You may find you've become allergy-prone. Something like a bee sting can always happen, and anaphylactic shock can kill you in minutes."

"I'll take my chances," said Ett.

Malone shook his head slowly.

"You're something different," he said, "unless I'm mistaken—and I'm not mistaken about most things. Tell me something. What if you have to give up alcohol and coffee too? Will you suffer?"

"I've just about decided to give up alcohol, and I'd miss coffee," said Ett. "But understand me. Any time I have to, I can give up anything but water, food, and breathing—and under the proper conditions I'd be willing to give those a try."

"Tell me about yourself," said Malone.

Ett did. Starting with his Polynesian childhood, up through his years of education, to the years sailing the *Pixie*—and further, to the death of Wally and his own decision to take the RIV treatment. But while his story was complete, it was not whole, and he left out his long struggle with his inner self, and the campaign of deception he'd used against both himself and the world.

"All right," said Malone at last. He sat back in his chair. The moving firelight left shadows in the lines of his face that made those lines seem deeper and older. "Now I'll tell you a story. The world's going to hell in a handbasket—yes, you heard me right. To hell in a handbasket, in spite of all the peace and prosperity and Citizen's Basic Allowance, and all the services. Can you believe that?"

"I can," said Ett. "Should I, though?"

"Make up your own mind. I'm just telling a story. Here's this world, going to hell, and a man like yourself hits on a long chance that lands him right in the middle of the machinery causing all the trouble."

Ett felt a surge of alertness through him that signalled the same sort of body adrenaline reaction he had had in the hallway of the Sunset Mountain.

"Go on," he said. "What machinery? What trouble?"

"You're an R-Master," said Malone, almost evilly. "Figure it out."

"But am I?" Ett asked. "That was one of the questions I asked you. If I've got all this extra intelligence, why don't I feel it?"

"Who says you've got something you can 'feel'?" said the other man. "Was there ever a time you were able to 'feel' how bright you were? Of course not. The only way you ever knew you had any brains was when you noticed the people around you doing something to show they didn't have as many as you."

Malone snorted. "You offered to work for the

EC," he went on. "Wait six months or so, until their people come to you with a problem and you take a look at it and see there's no real problem there. But you tell them what to do anyway, and they thank you and go away. You'll wonder if they were just pretending to have a problem, because certainly anyone ought to be able to see what you saw. Then maybe—just maybe—you'll begin to understand the gap between you and other people, and see what they mean by 'R-Master.' But then, even then, you won't feel any different from the way you felt since you first opened your eyes on this world."

He stopped.

"On the other hand, in these side effects," he added, "you've got a whole fistful of feelings—if body sensations are what you want."

"If there's something extra there in the intelligence area, I ought to be able to sense it," said Ett stubbornly.

"Who says it has to be something extra?" growled Malone. "Nobody understands fully what RIV does. They think it's only an irritant, a superpep pill that makes your thinking machinery whir twice as fast as it's designed to whir. R-Masters don't live long, generally; they average about ten years or so after they've taken the RIV."

"How about you?"

"I told you I was different."

"Why are you?"

"Who knows?" snarled Malone. "If anyone had the answer to that, I would, being the man concerned and having a Master's mind to figure things out with. I don't know why I'm different. I am, though. For one thing, I've been a Master forty years and I've never needed their medicines. You understand? I didn't just tough it out, the way you're doing; I never felt bad at all."

"All right," said Ett. "What's your advice for me? What should I do?"

"Why should I give you any advice?" snapped Malone.

A surge of adrenalin cleared Ett's head for a moment. "Well, I'll tell you," he said, quietly and slowly. "You struck me as a fairly reasonable sort the moment you opened the door. Now, if you'd asked me for advice, I probably would have given it to you, just for the reason that there doesn't seem any reason not to. It seems to me you've got as little reason not to help me as I'd have not to help you."

Malone snorted. But the snort died and there was a moment of silence.

"All right," he said, after that moment. "I'll tell you what I'll do. See if you can last a year of it—with this business of yours of not letting them help you with medicines. Then, if you haven't figured it all out yourself by that time, come back here and I'll tell you anything I know. And that's that! End of interview!"

"If that's the best you can do," said Ett.

He got to his feet. Malone also stood up and led the way back out the way they had come in. Malone himself opened the front door—Ett had seen no sign to indicate that even one other person shared the house with the other man—and Ett stepped back out onto the front steps.

He turned as the door was about to close behind him.

"What does MOGOW mean?" he asked.

Malone almost glared at him.

"What you were one of once yourself," he said, back again into the high voice of age, "whether you knew it or not. Man of Good Will!"

He slammed the door shut. Ett turned and walked back down the long drive, past the unmowed grass, the litter of the lawn and the signs on the trees. The personnel slot on the door was open, and he went through it to find the hovercar with Rico Erm still waiting for him.

"To the island, Mr. Ho?" Rico said, as the car started up.

Ett nodded. Now that it was all over, he was too exhausted to talk. He closed his eyes. Against the darkness of the inner eye, lids closed, enormous, glowing letters danced crazily: MAN OF GOOD WILL.

CHAPTER EIGHT

The trip back to the intercontinental and the ride across to the Caribbean passed in a daze for Ett. He roused only when he had to move from vehicle to vehicle. Finally, when the island was reached, he was conscious of stumbling along under an indigo night sky, soft with tropical moistness and warmth. From the pad on which the intercontinental had landed, Rico and one of the security guards took him up a ramp to a slidewalk, which happily relieved his heavy legs from the effort of transporting him toward a chain of interconnected buildings.

The slidewalks carried them eventually through the entrance of one of those buildings, into simulated daylight and a small crowd of waiting people. Among them was Carwell, standing—looming—beside a shorter man with jet-black hair and a bushy black brush of a mustache, that gave him an irritable look. But Carwell and the other man, as well as all but one of the others waiting, evaporated almost immediately from Ett's consciousness. The one who remained in focus was Alaric.

"Al!" croaked Ett. "Al, come on with me."

Alaric, who had been standing back in the crowd, pushed past other bodies and joined Ett on the still-moving slideway.

"Stick with me, Al," said Ett. "I'm making you my chief of security."

Al nodded.

The slidewalk carried them on. They transferred to another moving walkway and ended at last before a door that slid aside to let them into a wide bedroom, which at first seemed open to the tropic night, until a glint of reflected light from the wall illumination panels showed Ett that a transparent roof was overhead. He was helped to an enormous, floating grav bed and dropped onto it.

"Al!" he called.

Al loomed up at the side of the bed, pushing his way between Carwell and the man with the black mustache.

"There you are," said Ett, with an effort. "Carwell, no one's to touch me. You know what I told you about drugs. Al, you're in charge. Get everyone but yourself out of here. I need sleep."

"Mr. Ho," broke in the man with the mustache. "I'm Dr. Hoskides, your physician, assigned by the EC. I won't be responsible—"

"Then don't be. I relieve you of responsibility. Out," said Ett. "Carwell, Rico—everybody out."

"Etter—" began Carwell.

"Out. Get them out, Al."

The faces began to move back from the side of his bed, to vanish from the blurred circle of his vision. He looked at the thickly strewn stars above him and then forced his eyelids closed. It was like trying to go to sleep on a hot stove, but he made an image in his mind of a house in the midst of battle, a house with one secret room. And in that secret room he locked himself, lay down, reached out to the light controls, and turned them downward. Gradually the one illumination panel in the secret room dimmed, and dimmed, and went out. . . .

At intervals after that he drifted back to waking again and then forced himself back down under the locks and bolts of sleep.

Finally he came awake beyond all denying, although he lay still for a long time, with his eyes stubbornly closed, trying to hold on to slumber. At last he gave up and opened his eyes. Around him the room was empty, the ceiling overhead was opaqued to a night dimness, and a barely visible Al sat in a tall-backed grav float beside the door.

"Al?" said Ett.

The small man got up from his float, walked to the bed, and stood looking down at him.

"How do you feel?" asked Alaric.

Ett grimaced. He had forgotten how he felt, but now he remembered.

"Not good," he said. "I've got a sour taste in my mouth. A headache, and a backache. I feel starved to death and a little sick to my stomach at the same time. But I got some sleep; my head's clear."

"All right," said Al. "That's all right, then."

"You kept everybody out?"

Al nodded.

"They only tried to come in once or twice. I told them not to push it, and they didn't." Al looked down at Ett. "You slept hard. Most of the time you looked dead. I had to take your pulse a couple of times to be sure you were still alive. Every so often, though, you thrashed around like you were fighting sharks."

"Maybe I was," said Ett. He could not remember specific dreams, but in the back of his mind there was the feeling of nightmares. "But it was worth it. As I say, my mind's clear now. I can think."

Al still stood looking down at him.

"You don't act much different," he said.

"I don't feel different," Ett said. "I don't know—there's more to this whole business than I ever imagined."

"Why did you go take that RIV, anyway?" said Al. "Hell, you hardly saw that brother of yours twice a year before he took it."

"I know," said Ett. "That was one of the reasons."

"Anyway," said Al, "there's a reason I wanted to see you—once more anyway. To see what it'd done to you. Now I do see. It's geared up that old responsibility side of you."

"Old responsibility side?" Ett stared at the smaller man. "What old responsibility side?"

"The one you always had," Al said. "For everything. Women, stray dogs and cats—me, even."

Ett took a deep breath and lay looking at the ceiling.

"I learn something every day," he said.

"You didn't know it showed?" Al said. "You ought to have known."

"I didn't know, period," said Ett. "Never mind. I suppose I'd better eat something. Food and sleep, that's what I have to run on, and I've had the sleep."

"I'll get it for you," Al said. "What do you want?"

"Anything," said Ett, and grimaced again. "I'm hollow, but nothing I think of seems as if it would taste good. Get me a steak and some orange juice. A lot of orange juice."

"Right," said Al. He went toward the door. "Shall I let any of them in? They all want to see you."

"After I've eaten. Then—only Carwell," said Ett.

Al went out. Ett lay back thinking. As he had said to Al, his mind was clear now. It worked. Whether it was working with some sort of super-speed or supercapacity, there was no way of knowing; but it occurred to him that he had de-duced a great deal—a very great deal—in the last day or two, about life and the world. For twenty-four years he had gone on certain assumptions; now, in three days, he had been forced to discover that most of those assumptions either contained errors, or were downright false. If they were false, the world itself could be something he had never guessed. And Wally's part in it could be something he had not understood at all.

He had no definite proof of any of this yet. He had no specifics. But the conviction in him was becoming overwhelming, that he had somehow been dealing with the misleading surface of a world—a surface bearing no relation to the reality under-neath it.

The steak and orange juice were brought in by Al and proved at least partly a disappointment. The steak was as tasteless as the breakfast he had last eaten—in Hong Kong—had been. The orange juice, on the other hand, seemed disagreeably acid.

Nonetheless, the food and drink, once it was down, conquered the slight nausea he had been feeling, and made him feel nourished.

"I'll see Carwell, now," he told Al.

Carwell came in, looking apologetic and stern at the same time. Ett was lying on his bed surface once more, and Carwell seated his bulk on a grav float at the edge of the bed.

"How are you feeling?" Carwell asked.

"Uncomfortable—but awake and fed," said Ett. "I gather you decided to take me up on my offer to take care of me?"

"Yes," Carwell said. "But I don't know how I or anyone else can do much for you medically if you don't take advice. Officially—if I actually am your physician, officially—I have to protest the fact you won't let Dr. Hoskides near you."

"Hoskides is the man with the mustache, my EC doctor?"

"That's right," said Carwell. "And an extremely competent physician, as well as being a specialist in your type of case—which I'm not."

"What is this?" Ett asked. "The EC speaking even through you?"

"My ethics as a doctor speaking," said Carwell. "I'm willing to be your physician; truthfully, it's a job that intrigues me. But I have to tell you honestly that I think Dr. Hoskides is much better able to take care of you than I am."

"All right," said Ett. "You've officially protested, and I've officially listened to your protest and filed it. Now, Dr. Hoskides can do anything he wants. I'll be glad to have him stay around, and you two can talk together, consult or whatever, about me as much as you like. But as far as I'm concerned, I

deal with you and you only. Is that situation going
to work with you, or is it impossible?"

"It's going to have to work," said Carwell.
"There's no way we can bring pressure on you.
Even if you weren't an R-Master, you've got the
right of every competent human being on Earth to
choose his own physician and medical care."

"Good," said Ett. "Now that that's settled, would
you check me over and tell me what you think?"

Carwell did.

"As far as I can tell," he said at the end of about
ten minutes, "you're normally healthy. Your pulse
is a little fast, but your blood pressure is low
normal. You seem to be somewhat more tense
than when I first checked you out before the RIV
injection. What do you feel?"

"Generally hangoverish," said Ett. "Slight headache, backache, heavy-bodied . . ." He ran through
a list of minor symptoms.

Carwell shook his head.

"Are those the standard reactions for an R-
Master?" Ett asked.

"There is no standard, evidently, from what I
can learn," Carwell said. "It's different for each
Master; all each assigned physician does is try to
give his patient as much symptomatic relief as
possible without causing him other discomforts."

"I see," said Ett. "You know, there's an interesting point in connection with that. It occurs to me
that the one thing I haven't got so far has been
information."

"What do you want to know?" asked Carwell.

"In your department," said Ett, "everything that's
known about RIV—its development, its effects on
people: how many people take it, what the true

percentage of idiots and Masters is—everything. How do you like the idea of being a researcher?"

"Everybody who goes into medicine thinks about doing research at one time or another," said Carwell. "I've had my own dreams, too. You want me to look into that?"

"Yes. Tell whoever you have to that you're doing it for me, but don't tell them why."

"I don't know why," said Carwell.

"You don't—" Ett caught himself up short. "Of course you don't. That's right. Well, go ahead; and remember, while you're at it, keep what's-his-name, Hoskides, away from me."

"I'll certainly try," said Carwell. He went out.

Ett lay for a second, watching the closed door through which Carwell had just passed.

"Al," he said.

Al came up to the side of the bed.

"You said something about seeing me once more," Ett told him. "You weren't planning to turn around and leave me here?"

"You won't want somebody like me around now," said Al.

"Why not?"

Al looked down at him strangely.

"All right," Al said, "maybe I wouldn't want to be around someone who knows I'm that much dumber than he is."

"You'll only be dumber than I am if you make yourself out that way," said Ett. "Al, nothing about this R-Master business is the way people—people like us—used to think it was. It may not be a matter of intelligence at all."

"I don't get you," said Al.

"I don't get me, either," said Ett. "I'm all

crocked-up from the side effects of this RIV, and to top it off all of a sudden the world seems to be ninety degrees turned from what I thought it was. All I know is I need help. I need someone to back me I can trust. If you go, who've I got?"

Al frowned.

"You always had an edge," he said. "You don't have to be an R-Master now to talk me into something."

"Will you hang around awhile and then make up your mind about staying?"

"Yes," said Al, after a second. "I can do that, all right."

"Thanks," said Ett. "I mean that. I—oh, hell!"

"What?"

Ett laughed.

"I wanted you to have the *Pixie*," he said. "But if I offer her to you now, it'll sound like I'm trying to pay you for staying."

"That's all right," said Al. "I'll take *Pixie* under any conditions, any time. She's nothing to you, now, but she's still a lot to me."

Ett shook his head.

"I'm glad you'll take her," he said. "But I haven't changed that much. That's one of the things I hope you'll find out. Anyway—who's waiting to see me, if anyone?"

"Mainly that Rico Erm."

"Good. Come to think of it," said Ett, "there's something I want him to check up on for me. Let him in next."

Al opened the door and, putting his head through the opening, said something Ett could not catch. Then the smaller man stood back, and Rico walked in. Ignoring Al, he came directly to Ett.

"Mr. Ho," he said, "there's a large staff involved in running this island. I have to know what you want, so I can give them their orders."

"I want absolute privacy, unless I say otherwise," said Ett. "Especially, I don't want the security men to follow me around. By the way, Alaric Amundssen, here, is to be put on the payroll—I assume there's a payroll?"

Rico nodded.

"I also want him officially named head of my security staff."

"Mr. Ho, I can't promise that. The Security Division comes from the Auditor Corps, and they go to a great deal of trouble to train and educate their workers."

"Ask them if they'd like me to shut them out completely the way I'm shutting out Dr. Hoskides. Come to think of it, I want Carwell appointed my personal physician and put on the payroll, too."

"I'll put the request in, Mr. Ho. Now—"

"I'm not through. I want the most complete library unit made available to me—"

"We already have one here."

"Good. And from time to time I'm going to want to talk to experts in various fields. One more thing. You remember earlier I mentioned wanting to talk to a Miss Maea Tornoy, a temporal sociologist— the woman we ran into in Hong Kong—"

"She's already here."

"Oh, really?" Ett paused.

"Send her in then. No—" Ett made an effort and sat on the edge of the bed; made a further effort and stood up—"wait a minute, I'd better get dressed first."

"I'll send her to you when you're ready, Mr.

Ho," said Rico. "You'll find clothes that fit you in the closet there. May I ask one thing, though? Are you planning on leaving this island again in the next twenty-four hours?"

"I don't think so."

"Thank you. Then I can order the staff accordingly. Good morning." Rico turned toward the door, and this time he crossed gazes with Alaric. "Good morning, Mr. Amundssen."

"Al," said Al.

"Good morning, Al."

"Morning," said Al, as Rico went out of the room, shutting the door behind him. He watched the door close before turning back to Ett. "Actually, it's just about noon."

"Time to move," said Ett, going to the closet and opening it. "I'll get dressed. Have you been around the island? Where's a good place to sit down and talk with someone?"

"There's a terrace looking down a slope to the boat dock," said Al. "I'll show you."

Fifteen minutes later, sitting on a white-painted wrought-iron chair on the flagstone terrace, overlooking a low stone wall and a lawn falling away to what was more like a small marina than a simple dock, Ett glanced up to see Al bringing in Maea Tornoy. He stood up.

"Ett," she said, as they faced each other once more. "It's good to see you again. I've been wanting to apologize for the way it sounded when I mentioned Wally."

After the startling loveliness of Cele Partner, Maea's appearance was not breathtaking—but then, someone like Cele was almost unreal. In her own fashion, Maea had beauty enough. And where Cele had been in her element in the glittering high society of the Milan Tower, Maea was in hers in the sunlight of the terrace. Her hair was long and auburn, shading to red. She was relatively tall, like Cele, but more strongly boned, so that she moved with the odd sort of angular grace seen sometimes in adolescent girls or in very athletic women. In a peculiar way, she was more female and real than Cele, who had a touch of the occult about her, like a figure that had stepped out of a painting.

"Maybe we can talk about Wally a little later," said Ett as they sat down. "Right now, I'm too wound up in adjusting to being an R-Master. If you can help me with that first, I'd appreciate it."

"Of course," she said. "What can I do?"

"Tell me something about what your specialty covers," he said. "I know temporal sociology deals with the development and change in human institutions. But you specialize in making forecasts, don't you, of the changes that'll take place if a community, or a city, puts a particular alteration or development into effect?"

"That's my particular specialty," Maea said. "A temporal sociologist can be involved in any aspect of changing human conditions. It's like being a psychologist—the name covers so many specialties it doesn't mean anything by itself. Like saying someone's an engineer. Unless you specify what kind of engineer, she could be anything."

"All right," said Ett. "What I want from you is a quick survey, or directions from you on how to make a quick survey, of changes since RIV was first invented."

"It wasn't invented, really. They were looking

for something like it, it's true, but it was actually an accidental discovery, like penicillin."

"Whatever," Ett said.

"There's no problem in that," Maea said. "Your secretary says you've got a full-scale library machine here. I can program a course of references for you that will give you a running picture of change from any time to the present. But you'll have to tell me what you're after. General technological development? Development of human emotional patterns? Political developments?"

"I want to know," said Ett, "how much influence RIV, in both its failures and its successes, like me, has had on the general direction society has taken since, say, the year 2000."

"All right. Next question. How extensive a survey do you want to make? I mean, how much studying do you want to do?"

"Give me something I can go through in a day or so, say the equivalent of four or five ordinary-size book-length references."

"All right." She looked at him keenly and a little questioningly. Her face was rounded, and a light dusting of freckles showed across her nose like ghosts of childhood under the golden tan of her skin. "I'll get busy then."

She stood up. He stood up with her.

"As soon as I've had a chance to go through the references, we'll talk some more," he said. "I didn't pull you away from some particularly important job to get you here, did I? I'm sorry if I did."

"No," she said. "As it happened, I was between jobs."

She turned and went off, through the door from

the terrace, back into the house, drawing his gaze after her.

Ett turned back to the lawn and sat down again. During his talk with Maea the adrenaline surge had begun in him, and he felt almost normal. He reached out to the little table beside his chair and pressed the phone stud.

"Rico?" he said.

There was a moment's pause; then Rico's voice answered.

"Yes, Mr. Ho."

"Bring out a terminal to that library machine, will you? I might as well work here as any place else. Oh, and see if you can find Dr. Carwell and have him step out here and speak to me for a moment."

"Yes, Mr. Ho."

A few minutes later Rico showed up, followed by a man pushing a reading screen library terminal along on a table-height grav float. They left, and a few minutes after that Morgan Carwell appeared.

"Just a quick question or two," Ett said to the big physician. "How did I act while I was unconscious—I mean, between the time I collapsed as I was returning to the clinic, and when I woke up in that bedroom with the old-fashioned furniture?"

"I wasn't with you for most of that time," said Carwell. "Our clinic chief—you met Dr. Lopayo, you'll recall—took care of you during those hours. I assumed from what he said that you had the normal reaction."

"The normal reaction?"

"Why, simply a quiet period of unconsciousness

while the shock of the mental change is absorbed—according to the books, that is."

"Check up," said Ett. "Find out if I did go according to the books. And," he said as Carwell turned away, "one other thing. Will you program a short study course for me in RIV, its discovery, its history, and everything else about it?"

"If you like," said Carwell. "But Dr. Hoskides is much more qualified—"

"Dr. Hoskides is to have nothing to do with this—or with me. Now or in the future," said Ett.

"Very well," said Carwell, shrugging. He went off, and Ett turned to the library terminal, typing out his request.

MEN OF GOOD WILL, so-called. Or MOGOW. Any reference or other information under these cues.

Heat—a warmth like that of a fever—was beginning to glow all through him. He felt his thoughts picking up speed under the powerful thrust of the RIV-induced stimulation. A problem lay before him now, and he hurled himself with increasing speed to engage it, like a lover to a tryst, like a warrior to a battle.

CHAPTER NINE

For the next four days Ett immersed himself in the references both Maea and Dr. Carwell led him to—as well as those he pursued for himself through the terminal of his library computer. His days passed quickly as he lost himself in his work, flooded by the adrenaline-like highs that alone gave him relief from the bodily discomforts that plagued him. And when he could do no more, he staggered to his bed, foggy of mind and half-blind with fatigue and aches, to lie still as a log or thrash wildly about, in alternation.

Al was always a quiet, watching presence, somewhere nearby, always the last face Ett saw as his consciousness faded out in the dark and the fatigue, and the first one Ett saw as he awoke, still tired and sick, in the new morning. Rico was there on the perimeter of his world, too—it was Rico who got him what he needed when he asked, and sometimes—as with food—when he did not ask, but forgot.

Several times Ett sent for Maea Tornoy, spending segments of precious time talking with her about her profession and the things she'd learned from it—and, later, about other professions and the world. His talks with her were strange and fragmented, and could not really be described as conversations; they were much more like interrogations, as he sought scraps of information or theory that had escaped him, but which he knew had to be there, somewhere. The puzzlement that was in her face almost constantly now he ignored, although he noted its presence, and that it was often alloyed with some other emotion, very akin to concern. But he had no time to speculate on what he saw, with the drive of his intellectual involvement rushing him on.

Maea always seemed to want to talk with him for a longer period of time; always he dismissed her when he was through, abruptly, politely but firmly.

Dr. Carwell's study program for him on the subject of RIV had been routed to Ett through the library computer, and he avoided the physician until the third day, when he finally sent for him.

"My God, man! You look terrible. Are you all right?" Carwell asked immediately after he'd been ushered into the bedroom Ett was using today. Without waiting for a reply he strode to the wall nearest Ett's bed, where he pulled down a hinged panel to reveal a recessed medical equipment cabinet. As he began to pull out instruments, Ett stopped him and directed him to sit down.

"But you're ill! Didn't you send for me for that?" the physician asked.

"Not at all, doctor. I'm feeling well enough, all things considered. I've just been working hard."

"But haven't you understood even yet," Carwell said after a moment, "that you can't run yourself like this any more? You're not even going to make it to the ten-year average that R-Masters last, these days . . . you're killing yourself! Do you *know* what you look like?"

Ett grinned.

"Morgan, believe me, I have no intention of killing myself, now or at any time in the future. Don't let my appearance fool you."

But the physician insisted on giving Ett a quick examination, and finally Ett let him. After a moment of considering the results he had gotten, Carwell looked up.

"Well, all right," he said. "I guess you're not so bad. You still look terrible, but your blood pressure is just where it was before, and your pulse and temperature are fine. You've got quite a bit of tension building in your neck and shoulders, though—reaction to the aches and pains, I'd say."

Ett nodded.

"I'd like to prescribe something for you," Carwell continued; "and I don't mean drugs," he added hastily, lifting a hand as if to hold Ett off. "You should be getting more physical exercise. I strongly recommend a daily work-out under the supervision of your physical therapist, beginning at a half an hour and working up to a full hour within the next week. And top it off with a steam bath and a good course of massage, every day. Will you do that?"

Ett smiled wearily. "All right, doctor. That makes sense. But I'll be grudging the time."

Carwell frowned.

"What's the hurry? You act as if you have some sort of deadline."

Ett said nothing, and Carwell watched him for a moment; then he began to put his instruments away. When he had finished he nodded and began to walk toward the door.

"Wait, Morgan," Ett said. "We haven't gotten to the reason I sent for you."

The physician turned and stared at Ett questioningly. "You mean there was something else?" he said.

"Yes," Ett said. "You remember I asked you about what happened with me after I passed out in your Clinic? Have you gotten that information yet?"

Carwell frowned, as if to himself, and paused a moment before responding.

"Well, yes," he said. "I hadn't forgotten. But I didn't get back to you because I wasn't sure if I had anything to say or not." He stopped.

"Go on," Ett said.

"Well," Carwell said, hesitating— "I contacted Dr. Lopayo, who if you'll remember handled—"

"I remember," Ett said. "Go on."

"Yes, well . . . Dr. Lopayo agreed with the impression I gave you earlier, that you were simply normally—uh, unconscious." He stopped again, looking at Ett. Ett nodded encouragingly.

"Well, it seems to be standard practice to record continuously such R-Master reactions—all the standard sensory data as well as a running view of the patient. For research purposes, you understand."

Ha paused again, but continued without prodding.

"Dr. Lopayo promised to look up that record and see to it I got a copy. But it hasn't shown up yet."

"I see," Ett said.

After a moment of silence Ett addressed the physician again.

"Morgan, thanks. I appreciate your concern and your help. Please let me know when that record comes in, and what you find on it." He nodded, and Carwell, understanding dismissal, returned the nod and left the room.

Left to himself, Ett stared at the blank wall for a few moments before reactivating the computer terminal and returning to his work.

On the fifth day Alaric came and woke Ett just after dawn, and in the pale lavender light the two of them walked down the hill toward the dock. They went directly over the grass, letting the dew wet their feet through the canvas shoes they wore, rather than along the walkways. Sensitive to the cool breeze, Ett hunched into his windbreaker, thrusting his hands into his pockets and nestling a thermos bottle in the crook of an elbow.

The sun was a red, lopsided ball floating in purple haze just above the horizon as they left the dock in a small sailboat that was part of the island's equipment. Behind them on the shore there were a few loud curses as figures tried—and failed—to start a speedy motorboat. Ett grinned as Alaric looked exceedingly innocent; neither said a word.

Ett really had no intention of going anywhere in particular, though; nor did he want to badly alienate the security men assigned to protect him. So he kept within sight of the shore, and after an hour or so he noticed a small, sleek craft trying to shadow them discreetly. He put it from his mind and concentrated on the sailing.

After a couple more hours they headed back in and tied up at the dock. They had eaten no breakfast yet beyond the coffee Ett had brought along; so they shared one in the sun on the terrace, making no conversation but enjoying it all. Then Ett returned to his room and napped.

When he stepped out again into the early afternoon sun, he did not call for his library terminal, but instead sent for Rico.

"Yes, Mr. Ho?"

"Rico, we've got to do something about these security men who are always hanging around—no, no, listen to me," Ett said, as Rico had been about to speak.

"I understand they've got a job to do; and they do it well," he continued. "But when they're always around it throws my concentration off badly. I believe I've got the right to order them far away from me altogether, but I don't want to go that far—do you think they'd be amenable to a compromise?"

Rico nodded. "I'd have to speak to their leader, of course, sir," he said. "But I think something can be arranged. Might I suggest that we simply ask them to confine themselves to areas away from the immediate compound itself—just the farther grounds, the beaches—ah, and the landing field and staff quarters, too. Would that be acceptable to you, Mr. Ho?"

"That's more like it," Ett nodded. "Do that, would you?"

Rico nodded and walked away.

"Oh, and Rico!"

"Sir?"

"As long as we're about it, how about doing the same for the rest of the staff, too? Let's make it a rule that whenever I'm about, no one at all, except Al and you, of course, comes anywhere near until they're asked for. All right?"

"Yes, sir," said Rico. "I'll arrange it."

"Thank you," said Ett.

As he was finishing dinner that evening, Ett punched the phone stud on his table.

"Rico?" he said. "Will you get in touch with Lee Malone for me? Tell him I'd like to come see him this evening."

"Yes, Mr. Ho."

In a few minutes Rico stepped from the building onto the terrace on which Ett sat. "I'm sorry, Mr. Ho," he said. "Master Malone says to remind you you were told when you could see him next."

"I see," said Ett. He looked up at Rico. "I hate to do this to you, but would you get back to his secretary and—"

"Master Malone has no secretary," Rico interrupted. "I understand he has once more dismissed the man."

"You mean he's answering his phone himself?" Ett asked.

Rico nodded, and Ett thought for a moment.

"Then I'll talk to him myself," he said. "Put me through on this phone, would you? Code the number but I'll hit the activate button myself."

In a moment the blank screen lit up and the testy old face appeared.

"So it's you, is it? I said a year—" The voice was old and raspy, and the face looked tired.

"I know you did," broke in Ett. "I don't want to bother you, and I'm not going to ask those questions I asked before."

Malone snorted.

"But I've been studying some temporal sociology and I need to talk to you—" Ett was interrupted suddenly.

"Temporal sociology?" Malone said. "Have you been talking to Maea Tornoy?"

"Er, yes," Ett said, startled. "How did you know?"

"Oh, I'm able to keep track of things if I want," Malone said. "Is she there?"

"Yes," said Ett, "she's been helping—" Again he was interrupted.

"Good. You can come. Bring her along," Malone said.

He rang off.

Ett stared into the blank screen for several minutes before he began to give the orders that would set up his trip.

"Oh, and Rico," he finished.

"Yes, sir?"

"Notify the security people right away, so they can send their contingent along, would you?"

Rico didn't look startled, but he took a moment before giving his usual quiet acknowledgement of the order. Ett continued.

"You know, you're not going to be able to go inside with us, again; would you rather just stay here?"

"Oh, no, sir," Rico said. "Of course it's my job to be with you, whenever I'm needed."

"Your *job*," said Ett, emphasizing the word, "is

to do what I want. And I'm giving you the choice—you can stay here while we go, or you can wait at the plane in San Diego, or—whatever. I'll manage, either way." He paused for a reply.

"I'd rather stay with you as long as possible, Mr. Ho," Rico said. "I appreciate your consideration, but doing my job makes me happy, and this seems the best way for me."

Ett nodded.

When the door with the red letters opened, Maea stepped forward and put her arms around Malone, who responded with a grin and a hug of his own. Ett simply stood on the top step, watching them in the doorway—and very surprised. After a moment they all stepped inside and Malone led the way through the dim halls to his sitting room.

The evening had been warmer than the last time Ett was here, and now the fireplace was dark and cool, still; but the room retained all its former richness and warmth. Malone again took the old chair he'd used before, and Maea pulled up a large floor cushion and settled comfortably near him. Ett was left to take the other chair, at some distance from the others.

For a few moments Maea and Malone exchanged small talk, explaining to each other why it had been so long since their last contact, and what they had been doing. But in a short time Maea looked up at Ett and then directed Malone's attention back to his other guest. Malone looked across at Ett, and his old face seemed suddenly transformed—younger, and more lively, than Ett had ever seen it. But as it regarded him, it began to change, reverting back to the Malone Ett had met before.

"So, you're here," Malone said. "But why? You know I told you to wait a year."

"I know," Ett replied. "But as I said, I'm not here to bring up that subject again. In fact—" he broke off for a moment, while Malone looked across at him challengingly.

"Actually," Ett continued, "I'm using you. I wanted to set up my own reputation as an eccentric, and it seemed the best way to do that was to visit you more often." Ett was addressing Malone but he was watching Maea for reaction.

She smiled at him; and when he looked up Malone was laughing.

"You're learning, Ho," he said. "But remember that the reputation had some bad aspects, too. Besides, you didn't mention that you're looking me over for good ideas you can use, on how to be eccentric, eh?"

He watched Ett, slyly.

"All right," said Ett, "I'll admit that."

"You won't learn much," Malone said. "There's nobody around but us, so I can't work at it. I fired my secretary and staff yesterday, you know—do that every once in a while and get new ones. Keeps 'em on their toes; don't have time to settle in and spy on me, either." He nodded.

"But then, you probably figured that one out already," he said.

"Yes," said Ett.

Malone nodded again but said nothing. Silence filled the room for some time, until at last Ett stood up.

"Well," he said. "May as well go home."

*   *   *

The following day Al went to Miami and bought a forty-foot yacht, which he had brought back to the island by a temporary crew. Ett gave orders to have him begin training the security contingent as crew for the vessel, even to arranging matching uniforms for them all. One of them was even given a bosun's pipe and put in training to pipe Ett aboard whenever he came down to visit his ship.

Watching from the terrace table as small forms scuttled about the ship, learning the endless tasks that sailors have to know how to do, Ett reflected that his reputation as an eccentric ought to be building by now.

Walking up behind him, Maea said as much. Ett glanced back and up at her.

"Yes," he said, and smiled. "Of course, it keeps them all busy and out of the way, too—not to mention the fact they're very tired when they get back on shore."

She nodded. "And did I see Dr. Hoskides down there?"

"Yes," Ett said. "He's been put in charge of shipboard medicine for me, so he's busy trying to prepare facilities and learn how to be a sea-going doctor."

He leaned forward to hit the phone stud that called Rico. When the secretary appeared, Ett asked him to have Carwell and Al join them all on the terrace.

In a short time Alaric, Dr. Carwell, and Maea were all seated with him at the table. Standing —he had politely declined to sit—was Rico.

"All right," said Ett, with no smile on his face

now, as he looked around at all of them. "It's the witching hour. Time to take off our masks."

They all gazed back at him. It was Maea who spoke first.

"Masks?" she said. "What masks?"

"Everyone here except Al," Ett said, "is wearing some kind of mask. Mine's the mask of an R-Master, for the moment. For the rest of you—Maea, you're a Woman of Good Will. There's an organization called Men of Good Will, and you belong to it."

He turned to Carwell.

"You, too," he said. "You're a Man of Good Will— though I don't know if you knew Maea was a fellow member."

"I didn't," said Carwell, staring across at her.

"Rico," said Ett, looking at the secretary, "you're either a spy deliberately attached to me by the Earth Council, or a Man of Good Will yourself. Being what you are, you ought to be a spy. Doing what you've done since I've known you, you ought to be a member of the same loose organization as Maea and Morgan, here. Which are you?"

Rico looked back at him calmly.

"If I may sit down, after all?" he said.

"Sit, stand, anything you like," said Ett.

"Thank you." Rico stepped forward and seated himself on the extra grav-float seat that Ett had provided for him originally. Seated, he seemed to change. It was a curious change, because there was no single specific sign of it in his face or body. But in some fashion he stopped being obliging and became almost commanding. "As a matter of fact, I'm neither."

"Then you'd better explain what you're doing being my secretary," said Ett.

"I'll be glad to," said Rico. "And maybe you'll tell me how you discovered Maea Tornoy and Morgan Carwell belonged to the Men of Good Will. I wasn't aware of that myself. Which means the EC hadn't identified them as such, or I would have been notified that Security here on the Island was to keep them under watch while they were here."

"In the case of Maea," said Ett, "I found out her type of work had to bring her up against a situation existing on this planet right now, the same situation which has brought the Men of Good Will into existence. She'd have had either to ignore them or to join them, and the way the work she's done the past few years has been directed makes me believe she joined them. Dr. Carwell here, struck me as preferring his work at the RIV Clinic to anything else. But when I asked him to give it up and become my personal doctor, he asked for time to think it over. Then, later, he accepted—still with no reason showing as to why he should leave the job he preferred, to take a position that makes him uncomfortable and offends his sense of order."

Ett broke off and looked hard at Carwell.

"I think he asked for time so that he could check with his own local branch of the Men of Good Will and then took their advice to accept the post because it might put him in a position to do something useful for the organization."

Dr. Carwell did not exactly blush; maturity and solidity had put him beyond blushing. But his embarrassed acknowledgement was marked as plainly on him as if it had been written on a card hung around his neck.

"Now what?" asked Maea.

"Now we consider Rico," said Ett, turning back to the secretary, "who needs to declare himself."

"I've already declared myself," Rico answered. "The word I used was 'neither'—neither spy nor Man of Good Will. I assigned myself to you, Etter Ho."

"Al," said Ett.

Al got up and slipped behind the float on which Rico was sitting.

"Don't be foolish," Rico said, without turning his head. "If I wanted to leave here none of you could stop me."

"Al might surprise you," said Ett.

"I might have a few surprises to offer, myself," murmured Rico. "But that's all beside the point. What I actually am, is a free agent, for all intents and purposes."

"How can that be possible?" Maea asked.

"Why not?" Rico replied. "Etter Ho has been one for a long time; why not someone else?"

She looked at Ett, and then back at Rico. "All right, then," she said, "if you are a free agent—to what end?"

Rico shrugged. "To whatever end pleases me, I suppose."

There was a short silence.

"He's dangerous," said Al, from behind Rico's float. "We should get rid of him."

"That would be foolish," said Rico. "I have no special loyalty to the EC or to anyone or anything but my work. And I can be more useful than any of you dream."

"You think pretty well of yourself," said Maea.

"I should," said Rico. "I may not have quite the intellectual ability of an R-Master, but I'm not far below that level—and that without ever coming close to RIV. I speak twenty-two languages and I have an eidetic memory. I actually hold two degrees in science and one in art, but I could easily hold a couple dozen in either area." He paused for a moment in his catalog, then continued without any hint of self-consciousness.

"I've been working for the Earth Council since I was a very young man, and I've done good work for them. I rose to the position of Special Manager very quickly—that means I would be dropped into any situation or organization which was performing below the optimum level; it was my job to straighten things out within as short a time as possible." He smiled now.

"As you can imagine, that's a challenging field to work in, and one that demands a lot, but rewards the successful. I loved my work, and I loved to think that I was helping the world to run more smoothly. But after some years of this I found myself resenting more and more the fact that the real point of my job was to make my bosses look good—rather than actually worrying about the world. I decided that my resentment would soon affect my efficiency; and so I decided to change jobs." He paused, and looked across at Ett.

"So I decided to transfer to the Auditor Corps." He stopped and smiled as Maea moved on her float, then continued.

"Of course, I investigated the move thoroughly first; and I learned a great deal about the Corps. I'd taken for granted a Security organization had to be efficient in operation; but what I actually learned was that the Corps is just as politically hidebound and wasteful as any other branch of the government."

"And you didn't join them after all?" Ett asked.

"Definitely not," said Rico. "But studying the AC turned out quite useful to me. It led me to a larger study of the entire top structure of the bureaucracy, from which I learned that the entire organization's hardened into one more concerned with itself than with its job. I found myself in the repugnant position of having to work solely for the purpose of enhancing the reputations of people whose sole ability is to rise in the ranks of the bureaucracy."

Rico stopped, seemed about to begin again, then checked himself. He shrugged.

Ett would not let him go easily. "And then what, Rico? What about all this brought you to me?"

Rico shrugged once more. "Well, in my time I had built up my own network of good connections," he said. "It was simple to have myself transferred to work with R-Masters; once there, it didn't take long for me to become what you might call the resident expert in dealing with new Masters. Since then, I've been effectively free to assign myself to each new one who's come along—and been in a position to examine and study each one."

"That's a bit arrogant, don't you think?" said Maea. "Studying R-Masters?"

"Why not?" Rico said. Perhaps, thought Ett, he had been stung a little by the remark, for now he opened up a bit more.

"I know myself well enough to realize that I have no real goals of my own," he said. "I did well at managing organizations, and after that at managing individuals. Now it seems to me that the greatest challenge I can find is to try managing an idea—but I don't have that idea myself. I'm not constructed to strike out efficiently for myself; I do better if I follow the lead of, and work for, a person I can respect, who'll give me that idea I can work for. And what better chance to find such a person and such an idea than among the R-Masters? So far, I have to say, they've been disappointments—all of them lying down and letting themselves be medicated into near insensibility at the bureaucracy's prodding." He shook his head.

Now Carwell looked up sharply, and Ett met his eyes.

"You hear that, doctor," he said. "Drugs."

He looked back at Rico.

"If drugged R-Masters is something you don't want," Ett said, "why did you keep offering the stuff to me?"

"Well, think about it," Rico said; "if what I did was enough to put you on them, then the odds were you'd end up on them anyway."

"A test," said Ett. "All right. I'll go along with that."

"As it stood up to a minute or so ago," Rico said, "I've just been waiting. None of the Masters I worked with before ever got this far into understanding me. But I can't believe you've lined all of us up now, here, and exposed us, out of simple curiosity. So tell us—tell *me*, Etter Ho—what are your intentions? If they're anything like I guess they are, I've found what I've been looking for; and I'll work with you, to the end you're after."

Maea's gaze turned narrowly back on Ett. "The end?" she asked.

Ett sighed heavily.

"You WOGOWs and MOGOWs think in terms of capital letters, don't you?" he answered. "All right. I've got a purpose, but not necessarily with a large P at the front of the word. Until this happened to me I was happy just sailing around the world not worrying about anything. Now I'm involved in what goes on in the world, whether I want to be or not. If it was me, alone, I'd have nothing to do with any of you, or anything else. But I'm going to bring Wally back to life, if it's the last thing I do, and beyond that, my purpose, my end, is just to keep the two of us safe and untouched by the rest of the world from then on."

CHAPTER TEN

Ett turned to look deliberately at Maea.

"Wally was one of you people, wasn't he?" She looked back at him, palely.

"Wasn't he?" Ett repeated.

"Yes," said Maea. Her voice was unnaturally calm. "I suppose he told you about it?"

"No," said Ett. "I didn't even know MOGOWS existed until I got hauled back into society by this RIV reaction. Of course, everything you people say is what I used to hear from Wally himself, back when we were boys. But he seemed to forget it as he got older, so I forgot it. I suppose he was just trying to be more discreet by then. Anyway, he never said a thing to me about it all after he left home."

He leaned back in his chair. "Well, even if he was one of you, once, that's not too bad. I ought to be able to keep him from being one again. But meanwhile, a MOGOW is one thing; a MOGOW with a brother who's an R-Master, that's another. I want some sort of leverage with the Earth Council that'll make them believe me when I say Wally and I just want to be left alone."

"I doubt," said Rico in his precise voice, "that the EC would be seriously concerned by anything short of an R-Master who was himself a MOGOW— an active MOGOW, not just a talking one like Lee Malone. Generally speaking, the EC in my experience considers that particular gathering of idealists to be numerous but harmless, a loose, essentially unorganized movement. Consider the fact that the branch of the organization to which Dr. Carwell belongs clearly doesn't know what's being done by the part of the organization to which Miss Tornoy belongs. This shows just how ineffective they are."

"It's just not practical to build a tight world-wide organization today in opposition to the established order," protested Carwell. "The practical difficulties are too great. Nowadays, no one can move around without leaving all sorts of evidence of where he's been—records of credit payments and the use of public equipment, like automated vehicles, lodging places, and stores."

"It's true," said Maea. "Each of our local cells has had to operate pretty much on its own initiative. We just happen to live at a time when social and technological conditions are against us. It's a fact of life."

"It's a fact of intent," said Ett bluntly. "Do you think it's sheer accident that for nearly forty years the mechanisms of society's control of the individual have developed and proliferated while the mechanisms that would protect the individual have withered?"

Maea and Carwell both stared at him.

"You mean the EC has deliberately . . .? Oh, no," said Maea. "That's impossible. Government today's an open book. It hasn't any secrets for the same reason we individuals can't have many secrets or privacy or freedom."

"God help us," said Ett. "Rico, tell these fuzzy-minded idealists what their real enemy is."

"Certainly," said Rico. "It's the central office or the bureaucracy of the Earth Council. Not all the individuals in that bureaucracy, though they're unconscious accomplices, but the movers and shakers—the top men and women of the bureaucratic system itself."

"But the failings of any bureaucratic system can only merely reflect the lack of good will among its workers . . ." Carwell began, and then trailed off.

"Forget your rhetoric," said Rico. "Look at the simple facts. Just one organization—the bureaucracy that's grown up around the Earth Council and its hundreds of subsidiary organizations and services—is what puts the food before every human on this planet daily, and ensures the roof over his or her head every night. To be able to do that means to have the machinery of control, and the bureaucracy of the EC's got it."

"But you can't do away with that kind of human service," said Carwell. "I mean, somebody's got to do those jobs. All that's necessary is to make those doing it ethically and morally responsible, so that they won't take advantage of their power."

"Nonsense, doctor," said Rico. "You're missing the point. An ethical man survives in a bureaucratic post only if he puts his ethics in second place. A bureaucracy is like a living creature, with instincts of self-preservation and an urge to control all things for its own protection. The bureaucracy of the old Roman Empire didn't die when the Empire died; it transferred its essence into the bureaucracy of the medieval Catholic Christian Church—remember that a bureaucracy lives on even when its members, individually, die. History is full of examples of bureaucratic continuity. So a bureaucrat who doesn't serve the need of the bureaucracy itself, will be sloughed off like a diseased cell."

"Thanks to the amazing advances in the technology of communications and construction over the last fifty years, the bureaucracy of Earth's new form of government has, in that short span, managed to become many times greater than anything dreamed of in the centuries immediately following the decay of the Roman Empire. And this new bureaucracy of ours wants to continue to exist, like any living creature, whether individual humans or human institutions survive its controls or not."

Carwell shook his head, opened his mouth as if to argue, and closed it again in silence. He looked appealingly across at Maea.

"No," said Maea. "They're right. I began to run into it five years ago. It's impossible to work up forecasts for any area or community without having to assume a steadily growing percentage of government workers among the population. The office organization of the EC is gradually taking over all activities on the planet, just as it wound up taking over all controls, even down on the civic level, some twelve years ago. My calculations show that within as little as another thirty years all possible decision-making apparatus will be in the hands of the EC organization, down through its local offices. From then on, we'll be frozen into a pattern with some fourteen percent of the total population as an effective aristocracy, and the rest as—nothing."

"Nothing?" said Carwell. "What do you mean by nothing? People with no rights at all? Slaves?"

"Not even that," said Maea. "The other eighty-six percent will simply be an unnecessary excess, requiring feeding and taking care of, but having no purpose for existing at all. Slaves aren't necessary in these days of modern technology; machinery is much more efficient and reliable."

"And what will happen to this excess, according to your calculations?" Rico asked.

"I can't calculate beyond that point," Maea said. "I can only guess."

"Let me guess for you," Rico said. "The excess of the population—your eighty-six percent—will be an encumbrance. Some means—undoubtedly humane means—will be found to allow it to disappear."

Carwell's face sagged.

"No," he said, shaking his head. "No, no. I can't believe that."

"The idea upsets you, Morgan?" said Rico. "That's because your ethics are at work again. You're trying to read your own moral code into the acts of the bureaucracy. But from where I sit, an end result like that isn't only logical, it's inevitable. I don't find it particularly surprising at all. I wouldn't think a Man of Good Will would be so shocked at this."

Carwell looked back at him without saying anything, and a small silence took over the group.

"Well," said Ett, breaking it. "How about it? Do all of you want to have a hand at trying to change that future?"

Carwell, breathing raggedly, turned to confront Ett.

"What does this have to do with you and us, then?" he demanded. "Why get us together to tell us these things?"

"Because I can use you," Ett said. "I told you what I want—security and safety for Wally and myself. I can only be sure of that if I have something to hold over the head of the bureaucracy. As a system it's got one Achilles heel— its aim is stasis, the maintenance of the status quo. That means its members keep their position in its hierarchy by playing the rules. Only they can't always have played by the rules, or they'd be idealists and angels themselves. And I don't believe any of them are that. So that means that somewhere there's information I can hold over their heads, in case they ever attempt to move against Wally and me. Help me get it, and any fallout—any information we find that I don't need—you can have to put to your own use or MOGOW use, or whatever, and good luck to you."

"Why should we help you?" Maea said levelly. "Why not help ourselves to any information that's available?"

"Because it won't be available to you without me," said Ett. "I'm the R-Master, remember? I've already got an idea of what I'm after—and I'll be keeping that idea to myself unless you work with me. How about it?"

"I'm with you, of course," said Rico.

Al did not say anything, but just matched glances with Ett for a second. He did not need to say anything.

"Yes," said Maea, after a fraction of a moment. "Of course I'll help."

"My God, yes," said Carwell. "You realize," said Ett, "it means that you follow my lead, not that of your local chapter of the MOGOWs?"

Maea and Carwell nodded.

"Fine," said Ett. He turned to the secretary. "Rico, will you get in touch with Lee Malone again? Tell him I'd like to bring some friends to see him tonight."

Rico stood up. In the process of standing, he lost the air of authority that had enfolded him while he sat, and appeared once more merely the obliging secretary.

"Yes, Mr. Ho," he said.

He went inside the building. In a few moments he was back. "I'm sorry, Mr. Ho," he said. "Master Malone said 'Tell him he's got to give me a good reason first' and hung up."

"Call him back," said Ett. "Tell him I already know everything he can tell me, and I've got a few things he doesn't know, to tell him."

Rico went back inside. This time, he did not come out again. But after perhaps three minutes the phone built into the table beside Ett chimed and spoke in the secretary's voice. "Mr. Ho," it said, "Master Malone says he'll expect you and your friends at seven p.m., San Diego time."

"In that case, I think I'll fold up for a bit," Ett

said. "Make the arrangements, please, Rico—but leave out the security people this time."

This time, the southern California evening was milder; the last flush of sunset was still alive in the western sky, if barely so, as the five of them walked up the driveway toward Malone's front door.

"I want him to talk to us alone," Ett said to Rico. "Has he gotten a new secretary or staff yet, do you know?"

"Not yet," said Rico. "I checked on that. He makes do with a maintenance team which comes in during the day, but it leaves before 5 p.m. The whole house is automated, and unless he has house guests Lee Malone should be totally alone evenings."

"He's a real hermit," said Ett.

"No, Mr. Ho. He's known to often have house guests, and he always goes to places where they know him and where EC security has been provided—rather frequently, I think. He's very different from most R-Masters."

A sudden shiver passed through Ett. Borne up on the excitement of the last few days, he had been able to shove his bodily ill feelings into the background. But now a small night breeze out of the warm evening made him shake, and all at once the new discomforts and weaknesses that were always with him made themselves noticed. Suddenly, he was keenly conscious of his own mortality.

"That's right," he said to Rico, "I remember now you saying something about there always being the one crazy individual, the psychotic assassin, to worry about. I didn't pay much attention at the time; is it really a danger?"

"Yes," said Rico. "At least to some extent. Any R-Master can be the peg on which such a mind can hang an irrational hatred or an irrational need for vengeance."

Ett's own secret feelings toward Maea came uncomfortably to the front of his mind. These, like his physical troubles, had been pushed out of the forefront of his thoughts during the last few days. Now he found them back, and himself forced to look at them in close detail.

They were all at the front door now. It opened before they could knock, and Malone looked out at them from the doorway, whiskers bristling.

"Brought a whole crowd, did you?" he said. "All right, all right, bring them in!"

They passed into the interior of the structure, and Malone led them to the room with the fireplace, where he had talked to Ett before.

"Well, then," he said, when they had all been introduced to him and were seated in a rough circle before the now-cold fireplace. "What's this all about, Ho?"

"To begin with," said Ett, "can you tell me how long you were out, after you had your RIV injection?"

"Oh, no!" crowed Malone. "No you don't! You got in here to see me by promising to tell me things, not ask me questions."

"Well, then, I'll answer that question myself," Ett said. "The answer is, you don't know. But it was a long time—a matter of days and perhaps weeks."

Malone glared at him.

"What makes you think so?"

"The same thing that makes me think you're a lousy biochemist."

Malone continued to glare, but this time he said nothing. Ett turned to Dr. Carwell.

"Morgan," he said, "RIV has been under research, constantly, since it was first discovered, hasn't it?"

"Yes, of course," said Carwell. "What I laid out for you to read from the library machine wasn't a fraction of the work that's been done on it."

"Still, even with that, the work of one man with RIV isn't to be found in the library machines at all."

Carwell blinked.

"I don't understand," he said.

"Master Malone, here," said Ett, turning back to face the other R-Master, "has been studying RIV, mainly at night, for nearly forty years. Somewhere in or under this house there's a laboratory that would make your eyes bug out—aren't I right, Malone? The only problem has been that, as I say, he's a lousy biochemist."

Maea, seated on a floor cushion next to Malone, stared up at the old man.

"Etter Ho," said Malone grimly, "you've got the kind of tongue that cuts the throat below it."

"I'm not worried," Ett said. "If there's one thing you'll have made sure of, it's that this place of yours is completely bug-proof as far as the EC's concerned. The only way what I say could get carried beyond these walls is if you or any of these others with me were to repeat it, and they won't. I'm sure of that."

"I'm not," said Malone.

"No. And that's why you've made the mistake of keeping your secret all these years." Ett turned to the others. "Let me tell you a story, one that Master Malone had planned to tell me next year. There was a time when the research being done on RIV was serious investigation."

"Was a time?" said Maea.

"That's right. But for nearly forty years," Ett went on, "the reams of reports turned out by the researchers on RIV have been mainly a reworking of old efforts, old efforts that were already known to lead nowhere. What wasn't a reworking of lost causes was nothing-work, simply a going through the motions of research to justify grants, salaries, and appointments."

"I can't believe that!" exclaimed Carwell. "Are you sure? Have you read all the work that's been done on RIV in the last forty years? And if so, when did you get the time to do it during the last week?"

"No," said Ett, "I haven't read it all. I've read enough to see the pattern. Let me remind you again that we're dealing with a human tyranny and down-to-earth causes and effects. It's not hard to point research into a blind alley and keep it there, if you have authority and control of the funds. For forty years the EC has simply subsidized the incompetent and venal among RIV researchers. Anyone with ability found himself or herself crowded out."

"Why?" It was Maea who made the demand. "What makes you think so?"

"I'll tell you why I think they've done it— and the fact they've done it is a matter of record, if you only look at the record closely—they had to do it because something about that particular research scared the bureaucracy. It must have turned up something they thought was a threat to their system. And so effective research was stopped, even though the appearance of research was allowed to continue."

"You realize," said Maea crisply, "that you're talking about the sort of conspiracy that would be too large to keep under wraps."

"Not necessarily," broke in Rico. "Bureaucrats in a working system don't need to conspire. They're like spiders sitting at points on a community web. If one of them starts doing something for the good of the web, it's because conditions seem to call for it—and those same conditions will also move other bureaucrats, whether they know the whole story or not. It's as if the vibrations travel along the strands of the web, and the rest of them, following their nature, start doing what must be done—all without any direct spider-to-spider communication whatsoever."

Malone jerked his head about to look at Rico.

"Who're you?" the older man demanded. "I thought he said you were his secretary, his EC-assigned secretary."

"That too," said Rico. "But at the moment, the post is only a cover for the more important issues at hand."

"The point is," said Ett, looking at Malone, "you were out of action for several weeks; but when you came completely to yourself, you were different from other R-Masters up until that time. You didn't have any of the uncomfortableness all the others complained about. You got curious about that later on and found out you'd been kept under longer than any other R-Master then alive. Then you began to find out that R-Masters after you were

acting— feeling—just like the earlier ones had.
And they weren't being kept under for days following their injection and reaction. So you guessed
that something new had been tried out on you,
and it had worked."

He paused. Malone said nothing.

"That was a good guess. But then," said Ett,
"you tried to find out on your own what had been
done to you—and that was a bad decision."

"Why?" said Maea.

"Because RIV doesn't change anyone, as far as
his basic character goes," Ett said. He was still
holding his gaze steady on Malone. "That's why
we haven't had any great creative geniuses among
the R-Masters. Whatever RIV does to a human, it
can't make bricks without straw. None of the people who've become R-Masters so far were creative
geniuses to begin with, so they haven't become
such as Masters, either. Malone never had any
flair for biochemical research. He was a hard-
engineering-type tinkerer. But he tried to duplicate a breakthrough in RIV biochemistry all by
himself. It's no wonder he's gotten nowhere in
forty years."

"Do you think one other—even one other person—
could be involved in something like that," demanded Malone, "and the EC wouldn't find out?"

"Of course they'd find out—sooner or later. But
I think we'd have time to find what we're after if
we had the right people doing the searching," said
Ett. He waved his hand at the others he had brought
with him. "That's why I put this team together. Of
course, it's necessary to move fast, if a team is
going to be involved. The trick will be not to duplicate research but rather to find out where the

results of the original research went, and get hold of it."

"But what good will that do anyone?" Carwell asked.

"The EC buried that knowledge," Ett said. "It had to be highly dangerous to them for some reason, and if we find out the knowledge we can find the reason. The one thing that's certain about R-Masters is that we're good problem solvers; and we've got two R-Masters here."

"EC has sixty more," gibed Malone.

"Doped to the eyes or harnessed to other problems," said Ett. "Besides, can you see the EC trusting any of the other Masters with the same knowledge we've got? For some reason they're scared stiff of RIV graduates like you and me having a clear mind in a comfortable body."

He paused, as if waiting, but Malone sat silent.

"Come on," said Ett. "You've tried it forty years your way. What have you got to lose? Try it my way for forty days."

"You expect your results in that short a time?" Carwell asked Ett.

"Yes," he replied. "What I'm planning is a crash program, one that'll put all our efforts into solving this thing. We can't do that without leaving traces the Auditors can follow up, eventually, to find us. But I want to move fast enough that we succeed before they have time to do it."

Carwell looked unhappy as Ett turned back to Malone.

"Well?" he said.

"Or otherwise you'll let them know about my lab? Is that it? Oh, well," snarled Malone, "why not? Might as well be hung for a sheep as a lamb. But what do you need me for?"

"I think you know more about the Men of Good Will than anyone else on the planet," said Ett. "I think you flaunted the fact that you approved of them, as part of your pretended eccentricity—to cover you in your real contacts with them. You planned to use them if you found what you were looking for in the RIV, to use them as troops to get whatever you found to the other R-Masters. All right, I need troops now—I need the benefits of the organization I don't have time to build for myself— to get at the place where the results of the further RIV research have been stored. Because it'll be the same place that holds a lot of information I want."

"What for?" demanded Malone.

"To hold as a club over the EC and force them to leave me alone, and my brother as well—once he's revivified. Outside of that, I've got no interest in what's hidden by the EC. You can use the research information to help other R-Masters, or the MO-GOWs, or anything else you want; that's up to you. We'll just be working together for separate but mutual benefits."

"Well, why didn't you say so to begin with?"

"Malone," said Ett wearily, "will you stop playing word games? I don't have that much physical strength and patience left over, these days."

CHAPTER ELEVEN

The director of the home in which Wallace Gunther Ho had spent his last days led Ett, with Rico and Morgan Carwell, down to a shiny subcellar in which were what looked like eight metal tanks about a meter and a half thick and two and a half meters in length.

"This is essentially a temporary holding room for cryogenic patients," said the director. He was a slim, quick-moving man in his mid-fifties with sparse, straight gray hair. "Anyone who reaches a terminal point in our institution is kept encapsulated in this room until he or she can be moved to more permanent storage quarters or otherwise taken care of. In the case of Wallace, we've delayed beyond the usual time because of Master Ho's new situation, and the fact that he might have special directions for us."

"Glad you did," said Ett. Irrationally, he was

relieved that the metal enclosure had no window, so that he did not have to look at Wally's face. Even though Wally was dead, Ett felt the cold finger of an illogical guilt under his breastbone, at the thought of what had happened to him.

"Mr. Ho," said Rico, "feels his brother would approve the use of his brother's body in a medical experiment which may be of benefit to all the race."

"I'm sure," said the director. "That is, during the short period Wallace was here, he wasn't in a position to discuss such matters with me, but I'm sure Master Ho, knowing his brother, would know what Wallace would want."

He turned to Carwell.

"Doctor?" he said. "I suppose you'd like to check over the unit and the terminal patient?"

"Yes, I'd better," said Carwell.

The director reached for a door which opened in the side of the metal capsule by which they were all standing. Ett turned away, pretending to examine the room at large and the other capsules, as Carwell, and the director, put their heads together over the opening.

Rico followed at Ett's elbow.

"Trouble," he murmured beside Ett's right ear.

"Trouble?" muttered Ett, without turning his head. "What trouble?"

"I don't know any details yet," Rico said. "But I have a few illicit and privately-built warning systems of my own. One just went off, the one that's concerned with EC authority."

"Wilson, maybe?" said Ett.

"No," answered Rico. "Or rather, not necessarily. Wilson is only one man. The warning I get comes whenever there is some EC Central Computer action concerning either yourself or myself. Somewhere in the bureaucracy, in other words, someone has filed a report or asked a permission concerning one or both of us—a report or permission labeled Classified, Secret, Top Secret, or something higher."

"What's above Top Secret?"

"That," said Rico, "I've never been able to learn. But there's at least one higher classification. I've gained access myself to all Classified and Secret data, and a good part of the Top Secret materials; but I found evidence in the Central Computer of other data I could not tap into. Probably the information we're after about RIV would be among that other data."

"Master Ho!"

It was the director, in the far part of the room. Ett turned and saw that Wally's capsule was now on an energized grav table and floating free.

"I'm sorry, Master Ho," called the director, "but you'll have to leave before us. I'm required to be the last one out of this room at all times. Regulations, you know."

"All right," said Ett.

Followed by Rico, he joined Carwell, who was steering the grav table with Wally's capsule. They went out the door together and up the slideway beyond. Behind them, Ett heard the heavy metal door of the cryogenic room boom shut; and a few seconds later the director came trotting up to them, to ride along the slideway on the opposite side of the capsule from Ett.

"Did you ever stop to think," Ett said to him, "what it would be like if we cut down on the number of regulations? Not did away with them entirely, you understand; just cut down on them?"

The director laughed.

"Only criminals break regulations," he said, "so I assume no one but criminals would want there to be less regulations than there are. After all, what else holds civilization together?"

"But what if we did cut down?"

The director stared at him across the coffin for a moment and then laughed again.

"You have to be joking, Master Ho," he said.

"Oh, yes," said Ett. "I'm joking."

They went on up to the director's office, where there were forms to be thumbprinted and signed, by which Wally's frozen entity was formally released to Ett. Then they floated the capsule out of the institution and down the hill to the dock at the foot of the grounds. Ett had planned to use this same trip to Hawaii to arrange trans-shipment of the *Pixie* to his island, and a whim had led him to sail her to the institution to pick up what was left of Wally.

"You shouldn't take regulations too lightly, Mr. Ho," said Rico quietly, as they left the building behind them. "Among other things, they keep you alive."

"I could feed myself if I had to," said Ett.

"I'm not talking about your perquisites as an R-Master," said Rico. "Or even about the Citizen's Basic Allowance you got before you took the RIV. Under the Earth Council the world is like one big piece of working machinery, and regulations are the parts of that machine. The EC won't break regulations because they don't want anyone to tamper with the machinery, even themselves. As long as you don't tamper either, they'll put up with you in the hope that you'll eventually slip and get crushed in the gears on your own. It would be easy enough for the bureaucracy to quietly kill off all the Masters and end the RIV Program—if they were willing to break regulations themselves. But they won't, except as a last resort; the machinery justifies their own existence—it's their god, and its parts are holy."

Ett thought about it. Rico's words seemed to hang in his mind, echoing there with an importance he could not at first pin down; then it came to him. Essentially, what the smaller man was telling him was a typical example of the fact that intelligence—call it intellectual capacity—alone could be helpless in a situation where knowledge or experience was required. Rico knew the EC and the bureaucracy with a knowledge Ett would have to work for years to duplicate. For the first time, Ett considered the unusual value of the other man to his plans and thought about what it would be like if he had to do without Rico—either immediately or later on.

It would not be good if too much depended on any one person, except Ett himself. In this world of regulations, complications, and hidden values, what if Rico was not the ally he seemed? What if the secretary was actually an agent put among them by the very bureaucracy they had come to oppose? Ett was deep in thought by the time they reached the docks, so deep he did not at first notice the two men in the white jackets with the white, pencil-barrelled, laser pistols clipped to their waists, who came forward to meet them as they approached the *Pixie*.

"Master Ho?" said the one on the right. Ett stopped and found himself looking down at a card case the armed man held open before him, an identification plaque within. "We're Field Examiners of the Auditor Corps of the Earth Council. Mr. St. Onge, one of the full auditors of that department, would appreciate it if you could come along with us now for a few words with him."

"Why?" demanded Ett.

"I'm afraid I don't know, sir," said the Field Examiner, putting his identity plaque away in a pocket. "But I assume it's important."

"I can't come right now," Ett said. "I have to take my brother in his cryogenic capsule to safe quarters on my island—"

Rico drew in his breath between his teeth in something like a faint warning hiss.

"I'm sure," said the Field Examiner, "we can ensure the well-keeping of your brother in his capsule while you visit the auditor. We really must insist you come with us now, Master Ho. We have a ship that will take us to Mexico City, where Auditor St. Onge is waiting."

He turned and pointed to an amphibious atmosphere ship rocking on the waves at the end of the dock.

"What do you mean, you must insist?" Ett said. "I've got normal freedom of movement, I suppose? I'm not under arrest—or am I? If so, let's see your warrant."

"I don't know of any warrant for you at the moment, Master Ho," said the Field Examiner in his unvaryingly polite tones. "But I believe that if it should be necessary we might find when we arrived at the auditor's offices that a warrant had indeed been issued."

"Some time since, I suppose?"

"Yes, indeed, sir. Some time since."

Ett looked around.

"My brother in his capsule, Mr. Rico Erm, and Dr. Carwell, here, are all going to have to come with me."

"I'm sure," said the Field Examiner, "that Auditor St. Onge would be the first to insist that you have anyone you wanted with you."

"All right," said Ett.

They moved down the dock and boarded the atmosphere ship. There was a small but adequate lounge inside, which they all shared with Wally's capsule; and the trip to Mexico City took less than an hour. It had been morning when they left the dock. It was just past 1 p.m. when they dropped down into the courtyard landing pad of the EC Western Hemisphere Center, which these days occupied most of the suburb of Gustavo A. Madero.

Here, however, Ett was separated from Rico, Dr. Carwell, and the capsule containing Wally. Politely but inexorably, the Field Examiners explained that the others must wait aboard the atmosphere ship. Ett was conducted alone into the surrounding buildings.

Patrick St. Onge, alone, met Ett in the lounge of an office suite that looked outward and down onto a plaza which held a very large swimming pool, in which some sort of water relay race was being held. Ett found that he was standing behind the weather shield of air flowing upward across a wide window opening, and gazing down at the swimmers fifteen meters below.

"Well, Etter!" said St. Onge, turning to face him as Ett came up, flanked by the Field Examiners. "Good of you to come. I've been looking forward to seeing you again!"

"I got the impression from these two," said Ett, "that there'd be a warrant found existing for my arrest if I didn't."

"You what?" St. Onge turned upon the two field men. "What regulation gave you the authority to hint at anything like that? How the hell dare you approach a Master that way?"

"Sir," began the one who had spoken to Ett on the dock, "procedures—"

"God damn your procedures," snapped St. Onge. "Did you or did you not know Mr. Ho was an R-Master?"

"Yes, sir, we knew."

"Then there's no excuse. Get out of here."

They left. But the whole interchange of words had rung falsely on Ett's ear, like a dialogue in a badly acted play.

St. Onge turned back to Ett. "I don't know what good an apology will do," he said. "But please forgive me. These idiots they're training for field work—give them a plaque and they think they've got all the authority of the Council itself. When I was in the field, we used our heads!"

"And only threatened to arrest people who weren't R-Masters?" said Ett.

St. Onge burst out laughing.

"Well," he said, "at least you can joke about it. But, really, I am sorry something like this had to happen. I did need to talk to you; regulations require it. But there wasn't any need to march you here under guard."

"It's actually business, then, not social—your wanting to see me?"

"I'm afraid so. After we met at the Milan Tower, I asked if I couldn't be assigned to your file. We all have to carry a certain number of files, spread out over the various categories of citizens; it makes for a certain familiarity which makes it much easier to keep audit on someone like you—much easier when something comes up and you have to talk to him."

"Do you talk to most of the citizens whose files you handle?" Ett asked.

"Lord, no," said St. Onge. "Where would I find the time? No, for most citizens, even a full audit is a once-in-a-lifetime thing. But as a citizen's expenditures go up, as his share of the GWP becomes larger—more and more attention has to be paid to the file—it's in the regulations. For perhaps half a million people in the world, a yearly audit is automatic. And for perhaps five hundred or so, there's a running audit being processed in the central computer at all times. We call it a 'keeping' audit. You're in that category, Etter, and what it means is that I get a daily report on any expenditures of yours that exceed the estimates forecast according to your spending profile."

"I see," said Ett. "What have I done now? Or are you thinking about the GWP units I gambled away in Hong Kong?"

"No, no, of course not," said St. Onge. "We expect the new R-Masters to get a bit extravagant as they feel their way into their new life. But—sit down, why don't we?"

They seated themselves opposite each other.

"That's better," said St. Onge. "No, the little

problem that's come up now doesn't actually deal with any current expenses of yours. We'll be wanting to run a special forecast of expenses, if this attempt to revive your brother extends into more extensive work and research than is covered by the grant of compassionate funds—"

"Who told you about that?" demanded Ett. "I only signed the waiver of responsibility a little over two weeks ago."

"But it had to be filed—the waiver form," said St. Onge, with an odd, sudden flashing smile that was like the heatless flicker of lightning. "Any time you deal with forms, the information goes to the central computer, and from the central computer to your file in my office, of course."

"Of course," said Ett. "You'll have to excuse me. I've been used to living without everything I did being recorded and annotated."

"You mean before you became an R-Master?" said St. Onge. "Sorry to disillusion you, but even then you had papers to fill out every time your ship entered or cleared a harbor, or when you drew your allowance or purchased something. Also, the citizens who had anything at all to do with you had their own forms and records to make out. I've no doubt the central computer could give us a day-by-day summary—nearly a diary—of your actions since you were of school age. Would you like me to ask for a printout on that sometime?"

"No, thanks," said Ett. He loosened the neck of his jacket. The room was warmer than he had noticed it being on his arrival.

"Be glad to. No trouble at all, and you might find it amusing."

"No," said Ett. "You were going to tell me why you wanted to talk to me."

"Oh, that. Yes," said St. Onge. "As you know, R-Masters can have pretty much anything they want. But we have a responsibility not to waste funds beyond those necessary for the Master's own needs and desires. Now, you've happened to make some rather peculiar acquaintances since you had the RIV reaction. I don't know if you're aware of it, but Maea Tornoy, the young woman you asked to see, belongs to an organization called the People of Good Will. And we have reason to suspect that the man you chose for your personal physician, over Dr. Hoskides—I mean Morgan Carwell—may be a member of the same group. And of course Master Lee Malone has shown a long-time fascination with that organization, among his other interests."

"Am I supposed to have fallen among dangerous companions?" Ett asked. "Is that it?"

"Dangerous?" St. Onge laughed. "Good god, no! Organizations capable of actual subversion against the EC are a practical impossibility nowadays. Not only does the EC know immediately if anyone becomes a member of any group or organization at all, but of course it controls that individual's wages or allowance and, through ordinary day-to-day records, can tell exactly what he's doing and pick him up the moment he attempts to infringe regulations."

"He'd be smart not to infringe regulations, then," said Ett.

"Of course. And that's why almost none of these odd-group members do so," said St. Onge. "Of course, if they don't infringe on the regulations, they don't do any harm and we don't need to worry about them. So as a matter of fact we don't have to worry about anyone except the actual criminal regulation breaker. But even people like that are no real problem. They may get away with breaking regulations for a little while, but eventually we catch up with them, too."

"In the Sunset Mountain, in Hong Kong," said Ett, "I saw people betting on a fencing match. But the fencers were using sharpened weapons, and one man was killed. I saw him killed myself."

"Oh, you've seen the matches?" said St. Onge. "We know about that sort of thing, of course. Actually, something like that lies in a sort of gray area as far as the regulations go—though of course we keep a quiet but steady eye on it. The duelists are all volunteers, of course. The gambling establishments like to foster the rumor that people are kidnapped, or drugged, or otherwise forced to duel. But drugging, of course, would make a good fight impossible; and kidnapping we'd crack down on right away. And in fact, who could be forced into such a thing? It's impossible to lose more dividend units gambling than you have, these days, due to instantaneous record keeping. So there couldn't be any such thing as paying off losses to the casino by risking your life the way legend has it that some duelists are doing."

"But who'd volunteer for something like that?" Ett asked.

"Why, people bent on suicide, for example," said St. Onge. "As long as they register the intent to do away with themselves, it's all perfectly according to regulations. Or—more common—someone who considers himself a very good fencer and wants to risk' an encounter with real weapons to test his skill. Again, if he's registered his intent, that makes the duel simply a dangerous sport. Someone like that, matched with another such sportsman who's equally skilled—or a would-be suicide, untrained, matched with another like himself—breaks no regulations.''

St Onge gave another of his heatless smiles.

"In fact," he said, "I might tell you that I've tried the sport once or twice myself. I'm really rather good as a fencer. Do you fence?"

"No," said Ett.

"Ah," said St. Onge.

"All right, then," said Ett. "Since these Folk of Good Will are harmless, why bring me here to talk to me about them?"

"Oh, just a word of caution," said St. Onge. "As I say, we want the R-Master to have all the funds he wants. On the other hand—and I'm afraid my department has had to crack down on Master Malone in this respect—we can't have him becoming a funnel by which funds reach other citizens, or groups of citizens, that aren't really entitled to them. You understand I'm sure . . . Is there something the matter? Are you all right?"

"Warm in here, isn't it?" said Ett.

The room about him, Ett thought, had been becoming steadily warmer since his arrival. He had become accustomed, in the weeks since he had first woken from the RIV reaction, to ignoring the minor discomforts to which the drug had rendered him sensitive. But the present heat was raising his feelings of illness above their normal level. He felt feverish and weak. His customary small headache had become a pounding sledgehammer just be-

Gordon R. Dickson

hind his temples, and the air he drew into his lungs now felt thick and unnatural.

"Is it?" said St. Onge, jumping to his feet. "I hadn't noticed. Let me open the window."

He stepped across to the side of the window opening and punched at the control button there. The curtain of upflowing air died, and a cool breeze from the outside atmosphere swept into the room. At first its chill touch was a relief to Ett, but in seconds all heat fled from him and he began to shiver uncontrollably.

"Good Lord, you *are* having trouble," said St. Onge, watching him. "You should remember how frail you are nowadays. Maybe we'd better get you back to your island as soon as possible."

"Don't you," said Ett, between teeth he barely kept from chattering, "—don't you feel that the air from the outside is cold?"

"No." St. Onge shook his head. He stepped across the room again, touched the window control—and immediately the room started to heat up for Ett once more. "To tell you the truth, no," St. Onge continued. "Not really. I'm afraid it's that RIV reaction making you vulnerable to little changes in temperature like this. Damned shame, but you'll have to get used to keeping yourself protected carefully at all times from now on. That's a good reason by itself for your staying clear of political and other matters. You really should start letting Dr. Hoskides take care of you with the proper medicines. A lot of this sort of thing can be shunted off with the correct drugs, they tell me. You'd be much more comfortable under Hoskides' care."

"No, thanks," said Ett, getting unsurely to his feet.

"Here, let me help you to the door . . . Oh, Cele!"

"Ett! What's the matter?" she cried, appearing from somewhere behind Ett and running to him. She put her arms around him. "Here, let me help. What's wrong?"

"The room got a little warm and then a bit too chilly for him," said St. Onge, on the other side of Ett. "You're a godsend, Cele. Could you see he gets back to his ship all right? I can't leave the office. Got an appointment in a few minutes I can't break."

"Of course I'll take care of him," said Cele. "Come on, Ett. Let me get you into one of the inside rooms where there's complete climate control. Then you can lie down while I arrange a way to move you without letting you have any more reactions like this."

She helped Ett out of the office, a short way down the corridor, and into a small room where the temperature seemed to be within comfortable limits and there were no drafts. He was left lying on a couch, alternately shivering and sweating, until she came back with two of the armed Field Examiners—a different two from those who had brought Ett here—and a floating grav surface with what looked like a transparent hood over its full length.

"I'm not going to travel in that thing!" said Ett. "I can walk."

But with Cele's perfume under his nostrils, he allowed himself to be helped in under the hood. He rode back down to the atmosphere ship and, with Carwell and Rico beside him, made the trip back to the island.

He did not, however, improve as he went along. After a while he stopped shivering and simply ran a fever that, by the time they arrived, had made him light-headed, almost drunk. He vaguely remembered being carried to his room on the same hooded grav surface that had brought him out of the EC Western Hemisphere Center.

Later yet, he was vaguely aware of being prodded and examined. But that, too, ended, and he sank into the oblivion and anaesthesia of a sleep for which he was as grateful as a starving man might be for a meal.

CHAPTER TWELVE

He dreamed of Cele. In the beginning, in the Milan Tower, he had found himself both attracted and challenged by her—but not anything beyond that. There was something about her that seemed hidden and out of reach, but the mystery did not attract him; in fact, he did not seem to have the feeling for her that he had had for the other women he had known and wanted. In his way he had liked all of them—and in that same way, a liking for Cele was lacking in him. But this second meeting had increased that earlier measure of attraction and challenge which she presented for him. She was something like the fever that had burned him up on the way back to the island—unnatural, but momentarily intoxicating.

His dreams of her after he got back to the island were confused dreams. He could not remember after he woke just what had been in them. But he knew that Cele had run through them all, like a darkly glittering thread leading him on beyond rational thought. And when, at last, he awoke and found himself again, he found also that his dream concern for her had vanished along with his fever. All at once, he remembered his many other concerns.

He lay now on a grav bed in the room he had slept in since his arrival on the island. He felt weak but newly clean. Rolling on his side with some effort, he reached out to the bedside table and punched the "on" stud of the phone.

"Anyone there?" he called.

"Yes, Mr. Ho," said Rico's voice. "I'll be right in." A moment later, the secretary came in, accompanied by Dr. Carwell.

"How are you feeling?" Carwell asked.

"Limp as an oyster," said Ett. "Otherwise not bad. In fact, better than I've been feeling ever since I first woke up from the RIV reaction. What happened to me?"

"It seems," said Carwell, "you caught a cold."

Ett stared at him unbelievingly.

"A cold?"

"I'm afraid that's all it was," Carwell said. "Evidently because of the RIV you react a lot more violently to small infections than I'd thought. In fact, I had to have Dr. Hoskides examine you."

"That—" Ett started to sit up in bed. Carwell gently held him down.

"Don't worry. All he did was examine. You've got my word he didn't give you any medicines."

Ett relaxed.

"I can't believe it," he said. "Only a cold? I felt as if I was in the last stages of . . . I don't know what."

"Dr. Hoskides said that to you, of course, the sensation of sickness would seem more pronounced. Just as, he said, you thought the room was a good deal hotter than that auditor—St. Onge, was it?—was actually keeping it; and the breeze you felt seemed a lot colder than it actually was."

"I don't believe that," said Ett flatly. "I've been getting used to the way I react since I had the RIV. What I ran into in St. Onge's office was a lot worse than anything I've felt so far. It was hotter and colder than normal. Either St. Onge was pretending not to feel as much of it as I did, or else he's got a pretty powerful lack of sensitivity himself."

Carwell shook his head. He was feeling Ett's forehead and checking his pulse.

"Yes," he said, "you're a good bit improved. But you'd better plan on resting for a day or two."

"Oh, no." Ett tried once more to force himself into a sitting position on the side of the bed, and made it this time, in spite of Dr. Carwell's efforts to push him back down. "We've got to move. I've got to move. There are things to do, with Wally and with the business of finding that RIV information we want."

He checked himself suddenly, looking around at the walls.

"That reminds me," he said to Rico. "Eavesdropping of any kind is against regulations, even for the EC itself—or so I was taught. And I know you said our particular opponents like to play by the regulations. But maybe we'd better check these premises."

"For listening devices?" Rico asked. "I already did, the first day I was here—and everyday since. None."

"All right, then," said Ett. He stood up and was happy to find out he was stronger than he had thought, now that he was fully awake. "I'll get dressed."

He turned to Carwell, who was watching unhappily from the other side of the bed.

"Morgan, how long have I been asleep?" Ett asked.

"About thirteen hours, since we got you home," Carwell answered. "Obviously you feel better, but take my word for it—you don't have the resources to go very far right now. You've still got the cold, even though you're handling it a lot better now; but if you don't take it easy—"

"I understand, Morgan. And I plan to sleep a lot in the next few days. But first I've got to get some things rolling."

The capsule holding Wally had been moved to one wing of the buildings on the island, a wing which was now being expanded and remodeled into completely independent quarters, consisting of a revival theater, a living section, and an area that looked like a combination of a gym and a schoolroom. It would be used for training Wally, however much he might need such help, when and if he should be successfully brought back from the arrested death in which he now lay.

"But you mustn't expect too much," Dr. Carwell said to Ett, as they moved among the workmen making the alterations. "I've been in close contact with Dr. Garranto and his staff, of course, and we've gotten all the equipment and personnel he wants for the procedure. But he asked me to remind you again that the odds are against any revival to any reasonable state at all—I mean, any revival above the basic immediate level of coma. And if something better is achieved, the most we can hope for is that he'll regain a state something below the level of the moderate-to-severe mental deficiency he was showing at the time of his death. It's true the act of his suicide was somewhat beyond what we would have expected from someone with that limited an intellectual capacity—"

"I'm not hoping for any miracle," said Ett harshly. "Just reasonable results!"

He heard his own voice in his ears like the voice of a stranger and enemy. There was something in it he had never heard from himself before, something almost animal-savage.

He was out of words. Carwell walked silently beside him as they crossed the neatly-cropped lawns of the estate, descending gently to the edge of the soft blue-green sea. Ett turned and trudged along the beach, Carwell behind, sinking into the sand on each step and making hard work of it. The effort soon made the muscles inside each thigh feel heavy and flaccid, and grimly Ett admitted to himself that his illness had taken a good deal of his strength, for the moment.

He was panting, as well as perspiring, by the time they reached the concrete section of walkway near the dock, and he saw that Dr. Carwell was eyeing him. Ett suspected the physician was thinking of trying to order him back to bed—and Ett was not sure just what his response would be. Both of them were diverted when they rounded a corner of the rather large boathouse and saw that the atmosphere flyer belonging to Ett was rocking on the waves, apparently ready for flight. Maea was standing on the dock above it, and Rico could be seen inside the vessel, at the controls. He stepped back up to the dock as Ett and Carwell approached.

"What is it?" asked Ett, as they came up to the other two.

"We've gotten a lead to someone who may be able to tell us where the secret EC files are hidden," said Rico. "I had to set up an appointment without waiting to talk to you, and I'll have to leave right away to keep it. But the man doesn't want to talk to any more people than he has to, so I can only take one more—Maea."

"No," said Ett. "I'm going."

Dr. Carwell made a motion as if about to protest, but made no sound.

"We'll see you as soon as we get back," Ett said in the direction of Maea and Carwell, as he was climbing into the flyer.

Maea put a hand on his arm.

"How are you feeling?" she asked.

"How am I? Fine," said Ett. He moved himself away from her and the touch of her hand. The sight of the capsule up on the hill had reminded him of his original feelings against her. He sat beside Rico and let him set up for take-off.

As the vehicle began to move away from the dock, he turned his head and watched the figures of Maea and Carwell, who were watching him in turn. Ett smiled and waved, and saw Maea smile back.

Their destination was one of the underwater, sealed-dome communities in the shallow waters just off the coast of Mexico, in the Gulf of Mexico. It had begun as a retirement community, then been taken over by a new generation of young families that could not afford the units to buy private homes ashore—and had ended up as a sort of third-rate undersea resort area, which catered to people from shore with enough spare credit to buy saltwater fishing licenses.

Among other attractions grown up with the resort character of the community was a sort of amusement park on a high piece of bottom less than thirty meters from the surface. The amusement park offered underwater mazes, tank fishing, and various other entertainments, some of them in their way as seamy as the dueling gym Ett had stumbled into in Sunset Mountain near Hong Kong.

"Don't look in the tank," said the young woman who was guiding them to the man with whom Rico had made the appointment.

She was a local woman—perhaps a housewife—who refused to give her name, but who had been the one to meet them when they had gone to a certain restaurant according to the directions of their contact. She obviously wanted or needed the dividend units she could earn by acting as their guide, because it was clear that she despised not only what she was doing, but the person to whom she was conducting them. But for some unknown reason she had apparently taken a liking to Ett at first sight.

"Why not?" asked Ett. They were travelling on foot through a tubular passageway, surrounded completely by the water of the thirty-meter depth in which the amusement park was located.

Before he could get an answer from her, they reached the pressure door at the end of the tube. It unsealed with a sucking sound to let them through into an area containing what looked like a swimming pool, enclosed by a high wire fence at its very edge and surrounded by bleacher seats. The seats were nearly all filled, mostly by people whose heavily suntanned skins showed them to be land dwellers and probable tourists here in the undersea community. The woman led them to the end of the pool, up to a fat man of unguessable age.

The reason the man's age defied estimate was that he had no teeth in his mouth. Normally, people kept their adult teeth all their lives; even if his lack of them was the result of a birth defect, the man could have been fitted with dentures. It therefore had to be assumed that he preferred to go around toothless. He grinned at Ett with thick, pink lips between a nose and chin that almost touched.

"Which one of you's Rico?" he asked in a high-pitched voice.

"I am," said Rico.

"And your friend here, who wants to be nameless, who's he, I wonder?" The man laughed; then he sobered abruptly and jerked his head at the woman who had brought them. She turned and left.

"Have you got some place where we can talk privately?" Rico asked.

"Sure," lisped the man, "but what's your hurry? The feeding frenzy's due in a second. That's when we lift the barrier. Have a seat and watch, as my guests. I'm the manager here, you know. It won't cost you a thing."

"We don't have time," said Rico.

"You'd better have time," murmured the fat man softly and malevolently. "You'd better have time or I won't talk to you at all. After all, why should I? Sit down or get out!"

He moved over on the bench to give them room. They sat. Looking down into the pool, Ett saw it was divided in the middle by an opaque barrier. In the section farther from him half a dozen white sharks, all about four meters in length, were swimming about. In the right-hand section three bottle-nosed dolphins were darting back and forth underwater; on the bottom of their part of the tank, dead and belly up, were two more white sharks. Ett surmised that the sharks had been introduced, perhaps one at a time, into the section containing the dolphins, and that the dolphins had battered both selachians to death. Now, however, as Ett watched, a chute opened above the shark section and disgorged a couple hundred kilos of bloody meat.

The sharks congregated around the mass. At first they merely fed. Then, abruptly—so abruptly that Ett suspected that some drug or chemical had been introduced to the water around them—the sharks went into a feeding frenzy, a mad swirl of sinuous bodies in which they bit and tore not only at the food but at each other.

And finally the barrier between the two sections split open, drawing aside to left and right into the sides of the pool.

It took a moment or two for the sharks to discover the dolphins. But by this time the original quantity of meat had already been gulped down, and shortly the frenzy became pool-wide. Swifter than the sharks, and many times as intelligent, the dolphins evaded the thrashing appetites for some minutes. But soon one of them was slashed, then another—and the beginning of the end was on hand.

Looking away from the pool at the people in the bleachers around him, Ett saw—or thought he saw— the same faces he had seen staring down at the gym floor where the two fencers dueled with sharpened weapons in the Sunset Mountain. A kind of nausea twisted inside him.

He got up and walked away from the bleachers. After a few moments—as he neared the wall—he felt a touch on his arm. Rico was with him.

"He's still at the—show," Rico said. Only the slight pause showed that he had any reaction at all to the scene they had just witnessed.

"Good," said Ett, turning to face him, in a position from which he could see any approaching person. "Is he your contact?"

"He's the one," Rico said.

"He'll be a problem." Ett paused a moment, then continued.

"If he can tell us what we need to know, he can also tell the Auditor Corps what we're interested in."

"That's true," Rico said. "And we don't have any hold on him."

"No," Ett said. There was silence for a moment. Then the fat man appeared in the mouth of the passageway through the bleachers.

"Follow my lead," Ett said quietly.

"We can talk now," the fat man said from a distance. "Come on." He waved them onto an intersecting course which brought them all together near a door at the end of the pool area. The toothless man opened the door—another of the locks always to be found in an underwater establishment—and led them through it and along another tubular corridor.

At the end of the corridor they passed through another lock and into a single large room, which was evidently the entire inside of a small dome. The room contained a pool, and at poolside was the furniture of a fairly complete office, including desk, office equipment and terminals, and several grav-float seats.

The pool here was partitioned into eight sections by transparent dividing walls that went down to the bottom and rose out of the water a good twenty feet—higher than a bottle-nose dolphin could jump, particularly with no more than three meters of water below them in which to make its preliminary dive. At the far end of each section was a metal gate leading to a water lock and the open sea.

Each section of the pool held a dolphin. Several of these surfaced as the humans came in and swam forward to push their heads onto the near edge of the pool by the desk. The twittering of their voices lifted in the air of the poolside office.

"How do you like that?" said the fat man, waddling forward to drop onto a grav float behind the desk. "Sit down. No, I say, how do you like the way they come up to the edge for me like that? They've got a pretty good idea I'm going to end up shifting them into the other tank and that for some reason they'll never come back. But they still like to be talked to. And if I fell into one of those pool sections, do you think the one in there would hurt me? Never. Probably he'd try to hold me up instead, until I could climb out at the edge."

He broke off, fastening his eyes on Ett.

"What's the matter with you?" he asked, adding, with a blubbery twist of his lips, "Mr. R-Master?"

Ett said nothing.

"Didn't think I'd know, did you?" said the man. "But that's my business, knowing things. That's why you're here, because I know things. Well, let me tell you, Mr. R-Master, you don't impress me. I don't need you or your money or your special position. None of it makes any difference to me. All the same, I'm willing to do business."

"Good," said Rico, calmly and quietly. "Your name is Shu-shu, I'm told? And you're a free-lance ombudsman, as well as being manager of this place?"

"You know what I am," said Shu-shu. He was still watching Ett. "See that brown stud on my desktop, Mr. R-Master? One touch and the gates at the far end of the sections'd be open, and the water lock would let them out. All these little prisoners of mine, they'd go free. Wouldn't you like to push that stud? But of course I can't let you do that—not for any amount of credit."

Rico's voice was still as soft and polite as the voice of an answering service.

"I must ask for your attention, Mr. Shu-shu."

"Just Shu-shu. Never mind any titles." The fat man turned his attention finally to Rico.

"Shu-shu." Rico's voice went on as if he had never been interrupted. "It's unusual for a free-lance ombudsman to have another occupation, if he's any good at free-lancing."

"I'm pretty good." A little bit of spittle moistened Shu-shu's lips with the effort of pronouncing the p. "But this is my hobby, this place with its dolphin-shark fights. Anyway, if you don't want to trust what I can tell you, you can stroll on out of here."

"Of course," said Rico, "of course. But an F.L.O.—a free-lance ombudsman—is someone who hires himself out to help other people, to stand in line for them, to pound on official desks for them. To help them. Naturally, he's paid, but you assume there must be some basic kindness in such an individual. You, on the other hand, seem to enjoy putting on your shark-dolphin fights."

"Mr. Erm," said Shu-shu, leaning far back on his float, "I think you're beginning to bore me. I don't believe I want to tell you what you and your pet R-Master want to know, after all. The door's right behind you. Good-bye."

Rico, however, made no attempt to get up. Instead he turned to Ett.

"Sir," he said in the same polite voice, "this individual is obviously a sadist. I assume he keeps his vices within regulations or the EC would have picked him up long ago. But I think we can safely assume he wants to do business more badly than we do, not for the dividend units involved, but because he receives a certain stimulation from the purveying of information, just as he received stimulations from managing the slaughter of sea creatures that are all but human in their own right. On the other hand, our own schedule is rather tight and he's already wasted some minutes of our time. I suggest we leave."

Ett stood up.

"Wait," said Shu-shu, himself rising behind the desk. "Just a minute."

"Perhaps, sir"—Rico glanced at Ett—"we could give him another two minutes, no more?"

Ett sat down. Shu-shu dropped back onto his own grav float, almost panting.

"All right, all right," he said. "All right! Of course, I don't break regulations. I don't have any information I shouldn't have. But I don't have to. Being an ombudsman I hear things, from my clients and from others—"

Rico glanced at the chronometer on his left wrist.

"All right," said Shu-shu hastily. "Here it is. It seems to me I've heard of certain constructions, originally done very quietly about thirty years ago but added to at intervals since, under the Museum of Natural History buildings in Manhattan, New York City. Of course I've entirely forgotten how that information came to me. It might have been part of something I dreamed one night."

Rico and Ett got to their feet.

"Now, if you'd like to retain me for possible help as a free-lance ombudsman, my retainer is five thousand units."

"A voucher will be sent to you. Not from one of us, of course," murmured Rico.

"Just as long as I get paid," said Shushu. He reached out and touched a white stud on his desk. "Now, just for the record, if I could record the purpose of this consultation—the purpose for which you needed me as ombudsman?"

"Yes," said Ett, leaning forward. "I'd like to promote a regulation to make dolphins a protected species as far as their use in any shows are concerned."

Shu-shu laughed—and broke off laughing suddenly as Ett reached over to press down the brown stud the other man had pointed out earlier. The button went down under Ett's finger. The gates at the far ends of the section began to open.

Shu-shu reached with both hands for Ett's finger. "Don't try it," Ett told him, "unless you want to get your face rebuilt."

Shu-shu looked into Ett's brown eyes and sagged backwards into his seat, lips pressed tightly together. Ett was no longer concerned with what the man might see or think, and he felt his own lips draw back from his teeth as he stood up and leaned over the desk, reaching for the fat man behind it.

Ett was breathing fast now, and his skin felt slightly warm. The fires he had buried so long were coming to the surface, rising in his head like volcanic lava, burying his restraint. He saw what was coming, in a vision flashing at the back of his brain—an anger that might very well consume the man before him—and he found himself welcoming it, eager for the release.

The fat man fell from his grav float chair, onto the concrete surface, and, propping himself up with both arms, stared up at Ett. A large drop of spittle formed on his lower lip and began to run down his chin—Ett saw it clearly as he moved to the side and then around the desk.

Suddenly Rico was there, between them, obstructing Ett's view of Shu-shu—looking up into Ett's eyes, saying nothing. Ett moved sideways as if to get around the smaller man, grasped him by the shoulders, and lofted him lightly over the desk. It seemed to Ett as if everyone were moving in slow motion, and in a preternatural silence; he could feel the play of the muscles under the skin of his shoulders, and it exhilarated him. He laughed.

Shu-shu had already arisen, and when Ett broke his silence the sound seemed to galvanize the fat

man. He turned and ran towards the door by which
they had entered. But when he had gone three
steps he blundered into a small wheeled table that
held a terminal. Before he recovered, Rico had
gotten beyond him and was blocking his access to
the door itself. Shu-shu stopped, looking at Rico.

"I'm afraid we can't allow you to leave us, Shu-
shu," Rico said. His voice was as smooth and pol-
ished as ever, but now his eyes seemed to glint
"We have to make sure you won't go to the Auditors
you see."

Shu-shu turned to face Ett again, and his face
seemed to crumble in on itself, the blubbery lips
twisted in now, in a parody of a large infant about
to bawl. Then the fat man sank to the concrete
floor, closing his eyes and covering his ears with
large, doughy-fingered hands; and lay curled up
there, quivering.

Ett found himself standing over the man, not
really remembering how he had moved there. His
gaze lifted to the pool, and he saw the last of the
dolphins flash out through the gate and into the
water lock that would take it to freedom. He sighed
and looked back down. Rico now faced him on the
other side of the supine Shu-shu.

After a silent moment Ett stepped around Shu-
shu and headed for the door, Rico following—after
a short stop at the fat man's desk and some button-
pushing there. Neither spoke, until they were
through the door and into the tube, heading back
to the main dome.

"That was very impressive," said Rico. "I believe you may have frightened him into something
close to catatonia. And by the time he's likely to

come out of it, we'll be on our way with our plans."
He paused, but Ett remained silent.

"You even had me scared, for a while there,"
Rico said, watching him.

CHAPTER THIRTEEN

The red-and-white intercontinental craft fell to the
pad on the island at precisely 10:13 a.m., local
time, and two minutes later the lean, balding
figure of Dr. Fernando James Garranto y Vega
emerged, glittering in full transparent oversuit and
moving at a good eight-kilometers-an-hour walk.

"Mr. Ho?" he asked briskly as Ett stepped forward to meet him. His voice echoed a little, coming through the breathing filter of the hood. "Come
along, take me to the patient. We can talk as we
go. I'm due back in Sao Paulo early tomorrow."

"I appreciate you coming," Ett said.

"I'm glad you do. I say that not for myself but in
the name of my other patients." They entered the
refurbished wing of the estate's main building,
where Wally's capsule was housed. "I can appreciate—I say appreciate—the fact that you have
good private reasons for asking me to come here

for the revival rather than bringing your brother to me. But the time coming to your island here is spent at the expense of someone else who also needs my services."

"I repeat," said Ett, "it had to be this way, and I thank you."

"Very well. Through here?" said Garranto, stepping into the outer antechamber to the operating room. "Good-bye. I'll talk to you later."

The door closed behind the physician. Ett quickly moved up and around to the panorama window which gave a full view of both the antechambers and the revival arena beyond. He saw Garranto standing in front of the microwave plate which was disintegrating the oversuit that had kept him germ-free during his walk from the intercontinental to this operating theater. Dr. Carwell could be seen off to the side, saying something to the specialist while avoiding contact that might contaminate his clothing. The suit gone, Garranto nodded to Carwell and stepped quickly into the inner antechamber, where six other gowned figures waited for him. Carwell moved to another door, which led to another view window.

"Gentlemen, I know you all, I think?" Garranto's voice could be heard now from the main theater—someone must have turned on the audio system. "Yes, Keyess, Tuumba, Martin . . . there's no one who hasn't worked with me before? Good. You all know your positions, then. There is no change from the situation I outlined for you all earlier. Shall we get to it?"

He led the way into the large, metal-and-plastic revival arena, and his team followed him, moving to their places without a word. They spread them-

selves out at the posts of their equipment, looking
for all the world, Ett thought, like mysteriously-
hooded priests of some arcane ritual. The idea
made him uncomfortable, and he could draw no
relief from the sight of the shiny metal cylinder
that held Wally—which held the place of honor,
the center of attention, like an alloy altar.

Three of the men removed the upper surface of
the cryogenic chamber, while Garranto watched
aloofly. The other team members moved in to help
with the long process of thawing the body, and
removing the special cryogenic solutions from it—
and still Garranto only watched. Only when the
process of locating and repairing physical dam-
ages to the body began, did he step forward—and
then not as obvious director, but rather as merely
one member of the team. At some point in the
process the sound from the arena was cut off once
more, but Ett, watching, did not notice.

For a long while there was little for him to see,
yet still he kept to his post at the window. He
could not be sure when the actual process of reacti-
vation of Wally's bodily processes would begin—
the heart of the effort—but he felt he had to be
there. He was in the grip of an obscure penitential
feeling that somehow demanded that he remain
on watch, sharing the time with Wally—as he had
shared so little before? he wondered.

Finally the now-warm shape of his brother, once
more breathing though in the care of a variety of
mechanical aids, was floated out of the arena. It
would remain in the next room during the initial
recovery period. This was the time when they would
discover how much remained of the Wally that

had been before the RIV, and before death and suspension.

Ett turned away from the window and almost fell over. Abruptly, all the fatigue, the aches and pains that he had forgotten as he stood watching what was being done to Wally, came swooping back to possess him, multiplied by the strain of his unrelieved watch, and by the cold and the strains of his trip to the domed city—a trip he had returned from very nearly unconscious. He tottered like an old man and almost fell, but a hand went around his waist, and an arm steadied him, strong and sure. He looked down, expecting to see Al's hand; but it was Maea.

"Where'd you come from?" he asked thickly.

She looked at him strangely.

"I've been here watching, with you," she said.

She was helping him now, down the hallway and around the corner, as he made his heavy, uncertain way out of the wing and back to his own room and his own bed surface. It was a long trip, and neither of them said anything, until at last he fell on the bed and lay staring at the ceiling.

"You stood there too long," she said.

"Yes." He heard his own voice, talking now from a long way off. "Too long. I'll get a little sleep now—a little sleep."

He heard her footsteps going away. The room dimmed, and there was the sound of a door closing. But he did not go immediately to sleep. Instead he hung there, on the precipice edge of slumber, realizing finally that his determination to bring Wally back to life had been more than a mere desire—it had been a compulsion. If the world had been allowed to get away with killing Wally, it would

have proved itself a real enemy after all, and Ett
would be deeply guilty of letting it conquer his
brother while he stood aside. But now everything
would be all right. He had paid back . . . what? His
exhausted mind could not form the idea of what
he had accomplished. It was something like paying
an old debt. Something like that . . .

He woke abruptly.

For a moment he did not know where he was.
Then memory came back and it seemed to him
that he had closed his eyes just a moment ago. But
the room was now full of morning light, and Rico
was standing over him.

"Wha—?" Ett said.

"I'm sorry to wake you," said Rico. "But Dr.
Garranto is leaving, and he wants to speak to you
before he goes."

"Speak to me." Ett propped himself up on one
elbow, running a hand over his numb and bristled
face. "How long have I been sleeping?"

"Fourteen hours."

"Fourteen!" Ett's mind was jolted into full
awareness. "Wally—how's Wally?"

A little change passed across the polite features
of Rico.

"Dr. Garranto wants to give you a full report."

"Oh." Ett swung his legs over the edge of the
bed and sat up. "Where is he?"

"Just outside the door. If you don't mind, he'd
like to come right in. He's eager to leave."

"Fine," said Ett. "Let him in, then."

He rubbed the last of the sleepiness out of his
eyes as Rico went to the door of the bedroom and
opened it to let Garranto in and himself out. As

the door closed, the narrow-bodied doctor strode briskly over to where Ett waited, pulled up a chair, and sat down so that they faced each other.

"How's Wally?" asked Ett.

Garranto did not answer directly at once. Exhaustion had grayed his skin and deepened the lines on his face. For a second he merely stared directly into Ett's eyes.

"Mr. Ho," he said, "I want you to understand something. I'm a highly trained physician in a medical area where there are never enough highly trained men and women. I don't have enough time to handle all the patients I'd like to handle, let alone involve myself in anything outside my work with patients."

Ett nodded. Garranto's formal and oblique answer to his question had started a small, uneasy feeling inside him, but he repressed it. He felt he had no option but to let the man finish whatever it was he had begun to say in so portentous a manner.

"Fair enough," said Ett, seeing that some sort of reply was indicated. "What about it?"

"We had a very successful revivification in the case of your brother," said the physician. "He responded excellently. Physically, he could hardly be in better shape. Mentally, I'm sorry to say, the case was otherwise."

The uneasy feeling blossomed inside Ett.

"How bad . . ." he began, but the words stuck in his throat.

"I'm afraid"—the voice of Garranto tolled in his ears—"that mentally there was no effective recovery at all. In short, I'm sorry to tell you that your brother is in almost a state of coma—one from which we can't hope to rouse him."

Darkness roared in the back of Ett's mind. He felt the room tilting about him and then felt himself steadied by the strong, bony hand of the surgeon.

"Hold on, there!" Garranto was saying. "Hold on. How do you feel?"

"It didn't work," muttered Ett. He was conscious of himself in the room, with Garranto facing him; but with another part of his mind he was falling, endlessly falling, down into nothingness. Opening out forever before him was the eternity in which Wally would never recover; for the first time he faced the fact that he had never really accepted that possibility. From the start he had ignored all warnings. Inwardly, he had been sure that Wally would be brought back, not merely to warmth and life but to his old abilities and powers.

"No," he said, pushing Garranto's supporting hand from him, "I'm all right. I'd been hoping— but I should have known better, of course."

"No," said Garranto strangely. "No, you shouldn't have known better."

Ett stared at him.

"What do you mean?"

"I mean, damn it, that the odds were there, the odds against your brother being returned to mental normality!" snapped Garranto. "Your own physician must have warned you—Carwell—and I warned you; but in my own mind, Mr. Ho, I actually gave your brother a better than even chance. He was young. The death had been sudden and entirely physical in induction. He had been cryoed immediately. The odds should have been good enough to return him to some form of normal activity both mental and physical."

Ett laughed without humor.

"Why tell me this now?" he said.

"Because." Garranto's tone of voice put a period after the word. Reaching into the side pocket of his jacket, he came out with a small, transparent bottle with a heavy stopper. Within were a few cubic centimeters of what looked like a pale amber liquid.

"I told you I was a busy man," he said. "I've got no time to answer lawyers' questions and sit in courts of justice, no matter how good the cause. When your brother failed to respond mentally to the normal procedure, I did a spinal tap and found traces of a substance which I have never encountered before in the spinal fluid of anyone—following an RIV injection or otherwise—even in the case of someone who, like your brother, had had a bad reaction to the drug. I don't know what this substance is, and I don't want to know. But it appears, among other things, to inhibit the production and liberation of acetylcholine at the postganglionic parasympathetic terminals of the nervous system."

Garranto got to his feet, walked across to a window, and punched the stud that set it sliding open. He opened the container in his hand and poured its contents out into the open air.

Unable to move, Ett watched.

"As I said," the physician went on, coming back across the room to stand before him, "I've got my work to do; I'll deny ever having this conversation with you, if it comes to that. But if I was a betting man, I'd bet your brother had something administered to him other than the normal RIV-II—and that other, whatever it was, was responsible for his mental decay and the fact that now he'll never recover from his present state."

Garranto looked grimly at Ett.

"Forgive me," he said, "but nothing I or anyone else can do can help your brother now. Good-bye."

He turned and went out.

Ett sat still.

There was no darkness roaring at the back of his mind now. There was only a spreading numbness of realization, behind the leaping conclusions of his own RIV-stimulated mind, flogged into extreme activity by the brutal surge of adrenaline called forth by the information that Wally had been deliberately destroyed.

Of course. His mind leaped, as if in magic seven-league boots, taking great and certain strides from evidence to conclusion and on to further conclusions. Wally was known to be a MOGOW. What special knowledge he might have had, or whether he had been only an experimental subject as far as the EC bureaucracy was concerned, did not matter now. What mattered now was only the fact of what they had done to him—and what Ett would guide him, or the shell of him, to do in return.

No longer was it a matter of setting up a situation in which he and Wally would be left alone by bureaucracy and MOGOW alike. Now it was a matter of Wally's living-dead hand which would bring retribution upon the EC—the Council and its agents—itself.

The fatal crack had been made in the shell that Ett had tended so laboriously for so long, around his violent inner self; and now the Heinrich Bruder-like being he knew himself to be was free. A great hatred was filling that being, and it was a good feeling, for it made him feel strong and tall and overpowering.

He had felt that other self in him before, but never like this. Even when he had given way to his fury, so briefly, in the office of Shu-shu, a part of him had watched and, while enjoying the warmth of the great internal fires, known how those fires threatened to consume him whole. But now the fires about his soul were not at all warm; they were cold, so cold, and they took him completely. As they would consume the world about him completely, too.

CHAPTER FOURTEEN

Three days later Rico was waiting for Ett in the workroom that had been set up for the private use of Ett and himself. A large architectural image was three-dimensionally depicted on the viewscreen of a tilted grav-table surface against one wall.

"Mr. Ho—" began Rico as soon as Ett appeared.

"Damn it!" exploded Ett. "Why can't you call me by my first name like everyone else?"

Rico stared at him for perhaps a second.

"I can, of course," he said. "But to be truthful, I feel more comfortable speaking to you formally. You'd rather I called you Ett?"

"No, no," said Ett wearily. "Forgive me. Call me anything you want. Is this the plan of the area under the Museum of Natural History that has the files we're after?"

As he changed the subject, Ett was mentally kicking himself. The strains of his physical discomforts and his recent mental upheaval had given him a hair-trigger temper, and in these last couple of days he had been venting his wrath on those about him more and more often. His resolve to once more regain control of that inner nature of him remained undimmed, but he knew he had already compromised with it, and that that weakened his will. But he could see no way around the fact that he had to, and would, send the world and its society down in ruins—and as he worked to do that, he was aware of the fierce joy in destruction that burned behind the wall in back of his eyes.

His plans would come to nothing, though, he told himself, if he allowed this thing in him to drive off those he needed in the work. Control was once more essential; but this time it would have to be the control of an iron, forceful will, and not that of a mild, bland nothing of a personality.

"Essentially," said Rico, at the table. He picked up a long thin light-pencil and began indicating areas as he mentioned them. "This is the elevator shaft down to it, this is the entrance, and the files are here. Actually, what you're looking at is a composite rendering, built up from a number of sources of information. To begin with, what Shushu told us was no more than a possibility. I've checked it, however, from a number of angles, at several removes—for example, from old records of New York subway tunnels, comparison figures over the years of the number of people going in and out of the museum each day, records of repairs within the museum itself and of the mechanical equipment involved, and so forth—all things which can be safely examined from public sources without alerting EC's Central Computer that anyone is interested in what's underneath the museum."

"Then this is only what you believe it looks like—if it's there?" asked Ett.

"It's a little more than that," said Rico. "Enough things check so that we can be pretty sure it's there, all right. Call its existence certain. Otherwise the amount of coincidence involved in the dovetailing of these pieces of information is beyond belief. It's there, and it's quite a simple layout—which helps protect it. It's simply a secret additional subfloor beneath the museum, with files of records on old-fashioned *emem*—multiplex microfiche. It has one droptube elevator with its upper entrance hidden within an electronically guarded vault entered from the office of one of the museum officials. That official is the only man who knows about the subfloor and the files. All requests for information go directly to him. He goes down, copies the necessary records, and brings the information up again."

"I see," said Ett.

"I should add," said Rico, "that the rock around the sub–basement—and it's sunk in the rock that underlies all Manhattan—is loaded with sensors."

"All right," said Ett. "How do we get to the files?"

"We were expecting the answer to that question from you, Mr. Ho."

"From me?"

"Yes, sir," said Rico. "You're the Master. You have the problem-solving ability. Frankly, I don't see any way into that sub-basement without our being identified and traced back here, eventually—even if we should manage to get away with the

information we want. But if there is a way, someone like you would be the one to find it."

"I see," said Ett.

"Yes, Mr. Ho. Shall I leave you to think about
it?"

"All right. I can try, at least."

Rico went out. Ett was left gazing at the rendering of the sub-basement. He touched the controls
of the screen and brought up an image of the
museum itself, above the sub-basement. To the
right of that image, he punched for a simultaneous
display of data on the museum employee who alone
had access to the file room; following this, he asked
for information on the connection between this
man and the EC itself, and on the route by which
information was channeled through the single individual both to and from the files.

The information was detailed and complete. Rico
had done a good job of setting it up. Ett pulled
over a grav-float seat and sat down, gazing at the
screen and thinking.

When Rico had first left him, he had not felt
confident. Wally's revival had emptied him emotionally. And since then, when not in the grip of his
own personal devil, his optimism and enthusiasm
were drained away; he skirted the edges, he knew,
of a pit of depression in which the various discomforts of his body and mind would become overpowering.

Now, however, as he read the display and studied the rendering of the sub-basement file room,
interest began to kindle in him. Little by little, his
depression and the small complaints of his body
were pushed into the background of his consciousness. His thoughts expanded to encompass

all the information available on the problem and consider it.

The process was self-feeding. As his interest rose, he found himself responding physically, as he had responded during the gambling session at the Sunset Mountain. Self-adrenalized, he began to lift on as strong an emotional push upward as the downward pushes that had sickened him after seeing the fencers and the dolphins. His discomforts began to be crowded off into nonexistence; his body felt light and powerful with energy. His thoughts increased their speed, multiplied, and swelled from something like a slow trickle down a gentle slope, to a cataract pouring down some steep mountainside.

Now he was up on his feet and pacing the room, moving fast and jerkily as excess energy pulled him this way and that. His mind burned in a fire that warmed but did not consume. He rode the furious current of his thoughts as if his attention was a canoe charging among the foam and boulders of a mountain stream, negotiating a course of rapids without a bump. By twos, threes, and dozens, solutions and answers to things he had wondered about all his life came pouring into him—no, they came pouring *from* him, welling up to the surface of his mind and presenting themselves before his watching eyes like a series of birthday presents . . .

Lost among these was the problem that had started it all, the question of how to get into the sub-basement under the museum.

He did not wonder about that now. The problem was still there, he would get to it eventually, and when he did no serious effort would be required to solve it. More important now was the sheer intoxication of cerebration. He thought now, with the sheer joy in pure thinking that could perhaps be likened to that joy a painter feels as color and image leap into life from his brush and onto the canvas, or that the composer feels as notes in an order never before conceived of sing back to him from the piano on which he is developing them.

He was laughing now, he could hear the clear tones of the voice that was his, like bells; and he strode up and down the room, eyes darting from interesting object to fascinating glint of light. His hands rushed about with him, touching and feeling, exploring new things for him to think about and realize within himself. There was no room in all this for that inner fury he'd lived with, and in fear of, for so long; and he didn't notice that it was gone, at least for the moment.

In one great rush he felt that he was reviewing all of Earth and its history up to the present moment. He ran his mind along the times of recorded mankind, as he might have slowly stroked the sleek side of some great cat, feeling the warmth and texture of each hair as his fingers passed. He spread the present before him like a map, then added to it that third dimension built of the characters of those presently alive—the community social pressure, reaching out to create the momentum of an economic and political juggernaut that was now running wild, out of control, headed down the steepening slope of the future to inevitable destruction and ruin against the blank wall of a blind' alley.

There was no way to stop that juggernaut. But it could be diverted. Just a few successive small barriers in its path, at the right points, would jolt the whole massive vehicle aside onto a different vector, one leading it down a different street, where there was no blind wall waiting—

"Ett?"

He broke suddenly from the world of his thoughts to find Maea just inside the door of the room, staring at him.

"Ett?" she said. "I'm sorry. I didn't mean to interrupt. But you acted as if you couldn't even see me, or anything else."

"It's all right," he said automatically.

The torrent of his thoughts had not yet been checked. They were with him still, but they were being diverted around this interruption like the water of the rapids around a boulder in the riverbed.

"What do you want?" he asked her.

"I wanted to tell you about Wally," she answered. "The sensors they've got on him right now show signs he's returning to some sort of consciousness. But, Ett, he can't come back, can he?"

"No," said Ett. And now he was fully back, but he didn't resent her intrusion. "They're right. He can't possibly recover." He looked at her now with different eyes. She, too, had once loved Wally, he remembered, at least in some way; and with that memory he was almost ready to forgive her for whatever influence she had had in Wally's taking the RIV in the first place. Unlike Cele, she was a soft, warm person, human and alive; she had not been the one who had pushed Wally at all. He realized that now.

"Answer some questions for me," he said, in a gentler tone of voice.

"Of course," she said, coming farther into the room. "What about?"

"For one—Lee Malone. He's your grandfather, isn't he?"

She stared at him now.

"Yes," she said. "But how could you know that? It's a secret even the EC doesn't have." She was plainly startled.

"I've seen you two together," Ett said. She frowned. He went on.

"Have you ever seen him acting like I was just now?"

Her frown turned to puzzlement. "No," she said. "Were you all right? It looked—" she stopped, at a loss.

"Never better," he said. "But that confirms something for me. But tell me, how your relationship to Malone is still a secret, and why."

"Well," she began, somewhat reluctantly, "I suppose it's really part of his long campaign of secrecy against the EC. He was very proud, my mother told me, of having evaded their watch so many times." She stopped.

"So he met your grandmother while starting to organize the MOGOWs?" Ett said.

"Yes," she said, and flushed a bit. "They never actually got married. Nor did my mother, who was just a teen-ager, but an idealistic one, when I was born." She paused, looked down, and then continued. Her hands were clasped tightly together now, and she perched herself on the edge of a high worktable, feet dangling free beneath her light-green skirt.

"My parents were both MOGOWs. And they vanished together, somehow, when I was eleven. Lee

Malone saw to it I got another good home—I knew who he was and why he couldn't take me himself. And since I blamed the EC, even then, for what took my parents— well, it kind of pulled us close together."

"And what if you were to find out it actually wasn't the EC who caused your parents to vanish?" Ett asked.

"It wouldn't matter." She looked into his eyes firmly, one hand brushing at a fallen strand of her upswept hair. "It wouldn't change how I feel about my grandfather. I love him."

Ett nodded. "And what about Wally?" he said.

Her gaze had no flinch in it. "I recruited him into the MOGOWs," she said. "But he was in full agreement with our views—he wanted to be one of us."

"Did you love him?"

She hesitated, and looked down at the floor for a moment, before meeting his gaze again. Then she stood up, white canvas shoes hitting the floor with a faint thump.

"No," she said. "Or, in a way, yes. But mostly, I liked him. He was nice, he was serious, and he loved me."

"Yes," Ett said. "That would be Wally." He smiled a little, finally.

"Your field of temporal sociology . . ." Ett went on. She looked up, startled by the change of subject. He went on. "When you make these forecasts of changes that'll be caused in the social patterns and culture of a community because of some planned physical or technological development, how accurate are you?"

"Quite accurate, within limits," she said. "We

can quite accurately identify general trends and project them. Of course, there's no way in the world anyone can imagine what hasn't yet been imagined, invented, or created. An unforeseeable technological improvement, a chemical or medical discovery—anything like that can throw us way off in our picture of how things will be."

"All right," he said. "Give me some examples of how such forecasts have been badly thrown off by discoveries in the last fifteen years."

"Well . . . as a matter of fact," she said, "I can't remember any disruptive discoveries in the last fifteen years. Come to think of it, there hasn't been anything to throw off a modern projection. But of course life's been better for the average person— physically, I mean—and there hasn't been the need to go searching for great new developments in any field."

"Yes. No. Stasis," he said abruptly, his speech unable to keep up with the suddenly accelerating rush of his thoughts. "Development's been ceasing as cultures trended to perfect balance. The whole structure of society's been altered by a constant drive to even up challenge with a response, the response of the EC bureaucracy. It's both a symptom and a result—a result of an attempt to create paradise, right now, in the present."

"People have always tried to create paradise for themselves," she said, staring, fascinated, at him.

"Not in their own time," he said. "In any one individual's time, all he or she can do is lay the groundwork. The next generation comes along and alters the groundwork to suit themselves. So the building never gets finished. But now there's no chipping away at the foundations laid by the previous generation. We're building the fourth and fifth story on our grandparents' foundations."

"The EC," said Maea, "would probably say that at least our four or five stories are an improvement to always reworking the basement. And maybe they've got an argument, but—"

"No. Wrong," he said. "Paradise is perfection. The building going on right now is construction on an imperfect base. See the bad things—duels, dolphin-shark fights, rumors of abuses of authority, hidden files—all signs showing that the building's out of true. Gets worse as it grows. Finally it'll go smash out of its own mistakes." The excitement of R-Master cerebration was kindling in him again.

"The MOGOWs have known that for some time now," she said.

"No. Felt it, thought it, but you didn't *know* it. I know it—now. I could draw you a chart if I had two years to draw it in. But I don't. It doesn't matter anyway . . . You see what I'm driving at?"

"No," she said.

He had gone back once more to pacing up and down the room.

"Imperfection means faults. Faults mean points of weakness. That's what we have to work with. How do you fight a bureaucratic system?"

"Expose it?" said Maea.

"Expose what? You can expose the bureaucrats, if you can show what they did they shouldn't have done. But a system? No. A system—a bureaucracy—is nonphysical. Weapons won't work against it. Even laws won't work. It's a thought, a way of thinking. Even a bloodbath—if you killed off all the bureaucrats—they'd start to appear again the next generation as some people slid back into the same old pattern. The only thing that smashes one pattern is a new pattern."

"What new pattern?"

He shook his head and stopped walking. Suddenly he felt drained to the point of exhaustion. He leaned against a wall with one hand and looked at her.

"You want too much," he said, half to himself. "Too much, too soon. I've got to work it out some more . . ."

He ran down. The headwaters of that furious spate of thought that had been tapped in him were now draining away into the well of an exhaustion deeper than he had ever encountered before.

"I'd better lie down," he said, as much to himself as to her. He started toward the door.

She came close to him.

"Do you need help?" she asked.

"No," he said. "I can make it."

She did not touch him. But she followed along as he made his way to the door of his bedroom and into it. He fell back at last onto the grav float of his bed.

"Lots to do," he said. "I'll have to get back to work soon. But right now, a little nap—"

He was on his way to sleep before he finished the sentence. Still, somehow he had the impression that Maea sat down silently by the bed, to wait and watch . . .

He came to, suddenly. Beyond the windows of his bedroom, it was evening. Maea was gone, but Rico was standing over him.

"Sorry, Mr. Ho," said Rico. "I didn't mean to disturb you."

"That's all right," said Ett. "I shouldn't be asleep anyway."

He felt strangely good, almost abnormally free of his usual small discomforts. It was as if his torrent of thought had washed them clean away. He sat up on the edge of the bed.

"What time is it?"

"A little after eight in the evening," said Rico.

Ett got to his feet.

"I'd better eat something," he said. "If you didn't want me woken up, what brought you here?"

"I was hoping to find you already awake," Rico said. "I've been able to pick up some more information, though I don't know how useful it'll be. For one thing, there's a name for those files, after all. The symbol for them—"

He took a stylus and writing surface from his pocket and marked a couple of glowing swirls upon it, then passed the surface to Ett. What he had drawn was

$$0–0.$$

"In speaking," said Rico, "it's referred to as Zero-zero."

"Cancel out," said Ett, gazing at the symbol.

"Pardon me?" Rico frowned at him.

"Nothing," said Ett. "That symbol just happens to fit something I was thinking about earlier. I got off on a sort of mental binge, did Maea tell you?"

"Yes," said Rico. "Dr. Carwell tells us it was to be expected. Dr. Hoskides says it's a dangerous state to get into without protective drugs."

"I'll bet that's what Hoskides says," muttered Ett. But the memory of what it had been like came back to him. "There may be something in what he's talking about—only not just what he thinks. Never mind that now, though. You wanted to know how we were going to get at these zero-zero files."

"You found a way?"

Ett laughed.

"There's dozens of ways," he said. "But the simplest is to have this museum employee, who also works for the EC, go down and bring them up for us."

Rico looked doubtful.

"I should think a man like that would be electronically and chemically protected against physical coercion or anything psychological or technological."

"He can't be booby-trapped against doing his job, however," said Ett. "The weakest point in the protections set up around those zero-zero files is the pattern of authority to which the one man with access to them responds. We only need to forge an order for him to look up the files we want."

"An order can be forged, of course," said Rico, "although I'd imagine he'd also need voice authority from some superior; we'd have to fake that, too, and find out any codes involved. But getting at the files like that would simply let the EC know what we're after and probably give them enough evidence to trace the whole business back here."

"Not necessarily," said Ett.

"How would you avoid it?" Rico asked.

Ett shook his head.

"That requires a little working out. But it won't be any trouble." He looked at Rico. "Establishing the particular principle behind the action we need was the important part. In this case, we now know

what we want and how we're going to get it. Once
those two things are determined, it's merely a matter of identifying all the inherent liabilities to the
chosen action and taking steps to counter each one
specifically—"

He broke off.

"But you'll have already identified these liabilities,
yourself, haven't you?" he said to Rico.

"No," said Rico. "I'm afraid I haven't."

Ett nodded slowly.

"Malone was right," he said. "The only way I
can tell what the RIV has done to me is when I run
into something which seems plain and simple to
me but not to others. But I give you my word,
Rico, the details I'm talking about are things I can
work out quite easily. You'll just have to trust
me."

CHAPTER FIFTEEN

One week after his revival, Wally's body was clearly as far back along the road to life as it was going to go. In essence, it was not Wally at all, but a flesh-and-blood automaton, something not far removed from catatonic. The body tended to hold any position in which it was put, but only until it became tired. Then it tumbled to the ground. The eyes were open but unfocusing. The jaws chewed automatically when food was put between the lips. Forcing himself, Ett went to see the empty shell—so like his own body—that had once been his brother.

"Try not to let it disturb you," said Carwell, standing beside Ett at the foot of the grav-float bed on which Wally lay. He put his hand gently on Ett's shoulder. "There may be some vestiges of a mind left, but the essential part of the brother you knew isn't here at all. What's here doesn't even have any consciousness of existence. Watch."

He stepped away from Ett, up to the side of the bed, and took a small pencil probe from the pocket of his jacket.

"As a body," Carwell said, "it's got perfect nervous responses. But look."

He brought the point of the pencil probe close to the skin on the back of Wally's left hand, which lay laxly beside the body on the bed. A tiny spark leaped to bridge the last few millimeters of distance between probe point and skin. But Wally remained motionless, and his face showed nothing.

"See?" said Carwell. "Perfect physically, but from a practical point of view there's almost perfect anaesthesia. Skin flinch, which is a reflex, is the only acknowledgement we get. Your brother's body shows an anaesthesia stemming from a lack of mental response, not from any failure of the sensory network. Neither comfort nor discomfort, as we know them, exist for this body. There's no consciousness to record them."

He came back to stand facing Ett.

"Believe me," he said gently, "this is not your brother."

Ett laughed harshly, unable to look away from the figure on the bed.

"According to legend," he said, "they tied the dying Cid on his horse, and he rode out of Valencia to defeat the Almoravids as a dead man. So Wally's body can be used to help destroy the people who cost him his intelligence and then his life."

"Cid?" Carwell stared at him.

"An eleventh-century Spaniard. The most famous of the medieval captains." Ett turned away from the bed. "His real name was Rodrigo Diaz de Vivar. 'Cid' is from the Arabic word '*sid*.' It means '*lord*.'"

They went out. In the room outside were two men in white jumper suits. Around them were various pieces of equipment, looking somewhat like the furnishings of a gym or a weight-training room. Once again Ett was reminded of the gym in the Sunset Mountain, and his lips tightened in a taut line. He knew he was on the verge of giving way to his anger once more, and he didn't want to let that happen here and now. He nodded at the men and strode quickly past, Carwell following, and out a farther door. The resiliency of the gym floor provided a beating reminder of what he was doing, with every step he took.

The second door closed behind them and they stepped onto green lawn. After a few moments Ett turned to Dr. Carwell.

"They're MOGOWs, I suppose?"

"MOGOWs we can trust," the physician said. "And we've managed to get them here without alerting EC alarms. More than that, they're good therapists, good at their profession. You needn't have any doubts that they'll handle—" he hesitated for a moment—"Wally, as gently as you'd handle him yourself."

Ett nodded.

"All right," he said. "I believe you. After looking at Wally just now, though, and remembering all that old business about animal training, it's a little hard for me to warm up to them."

"You're an R-Master," said Carwell. "You shouldn't be affected by old stories."

"I don't know how old they are," Ett said, remembering again the dueling gym and the tank holding the sharks and the dolphins. "What do you want to bet that somewhere in the world some poor damned parrot is reciting the Gettysburg Address or some chimp is playing a whole ensemble of tunes on a flute or a recorder with a special mouthpiece?"

"If there are," said Carwell, "the people who trained them are already under arrest for the regulations they've broken, or about to be made so. Response therapy may have had its inspiration in training animals, small step by small step, to do a whole complicated chain of actions. But it's now become only a medical means to help people, humans suffering from a learning disability because of accidental or genetic mental deficiency or brain disfunction. It's not a toy in the right hands, Ett, it's a tool."

"Morgan," said Ett, looking sideways at him as they walked along. "What does 'therapy' mean?"

Carwell was silent.

"So you see," said Ett, "we aren't retraining Wally so he can live a fuller life. Because there's no life for him to live at all. We're really animal-training him to do a set of tricks that'll fool people into thinking he's me. Remember, doctor? That's the instruction I gave you after Wally was revived. Where's the therapy in that?"

Carwell still said nothing. Only his heavy shoulders hunched a little more. He was like some heavy wounded bear, shambling along, and suddenly Ett's fury melted away again, turned into pain and disgust at himself. Now it was he who reached out, and he put his hand on the other's shoulder. He halted Carwell and turned the man to face him.

"Damn it, Morgan, don't listen to me!" he said. "You know I'm just taking out on you what I

ought to be dealing with myself. It was my idea—
mine alone!—to make a marionette out of Wally,
not yours. I know you're a medical man, with an
oath to relieve suffering, not cause it; and here I
force you into this business with Wally—and then
throw your oath in your face. I didn't use to be like
that. But that's the way I am now. So pay no
attention to me when I talk like that."

"No, no," said Carwell, shaking his head. "It's
all right. I can't wash my hands. Nobody can."

He turned and lumbered away up the slope of
the lawn toward another part of the house. Ett
watched him go and cursed himself. Once again
his inner self, furious and full of hate, had gotten
loose to hurt someone. And this time it was his
own fault, for the things he had had Carwell
do had provided an easy target for the harsh
intolerance, the self-hatred, that waited always beneath his own surface.

It was no longer possible to deceive himself about
this. That self he had buried for so long was rising
nearer and nearer the surface. He was in dreadful
danger of losing out to that other completely. And
he had asked for it all—for he could not deceive
himself on this: it was the course he was on, this
plan of his, that left him so open to all this pain
and fury.

He had determined to destroy the thing that had
brought these degradations to Wally, and he could
not let that go. And because he could not turn
from that course, perhaps he was doomed—perhaps
he had lost already.

Ett turned and walked off down the slope of the
lawn, and as he did so his thoughts wandered off
in another direction. He found himself a distrac-

tion in the chess-like problem of examining all the
possible dangers in his projected scheme to give a
forged order to the custodian of the 0–0 files. He
gave himself up to it, for now.

But in spite of himself, during the next two weeks
while Rico and Maea were arranging for the production of the actual false order, through a variety
of personal connections between MOGOWs and
EC employees, Ett found himself going back to
watch the response-training therapists at work with
Wally. To someone who knew nothing about the
history and scope of this work, the results could
hardly have seemed less than magical. Even to
Ett, what was accomplished was startling.

The principle of response-therapy, or training,
was extremely simple. It was to break down a
complex physical action into a series of very simple movements, and teach these simple acts, one
at a time, to a subject. By this means a sequence of
movements was gradually built up, that became
the complex action. The key to its success was the
practice of rewarding the subject in training for
any movement, even a random one, in the proper
direction, so that an association between the correct movements and pleasure was achieved. As Ett
had said, the principle had first been used by animal trainers, usually in circuses, to produce such
performances as a chicken pecking out a tune on a
small piano, or a dog stealing a wallet from the
pocket of a clown and then hiding it in a series
of different places while the clown frustratedly
searched for it.

The great virtue of the training technique from a
showbusiness viewpoint was that its use could produce acts by animals that appeared to have hu-

man thought and intelligence behind them. Its virtue as a medical therapy—when the principle was adapted to that use, later on—was that it could be used to teach people with crippling mental deficiencies to perform complicated actions necessary to their participation in the society of the normally intelligent. It had been used, for example, to teach the mentally deprived to feed and dress themselves, to operate simple machinery, and, within certain limitations, to acquire the rudiments of normal adult behavior.

Seventy or eighty years of development, however, had brought it almost to the level of a fine art. In Wally's case, starting with a body essentially capable of nothing more than reflex movement, the response therapists began by working to develop what was referred to as "initiating actions." Since the one base on which they had to build in what had been Wally was the feeding reflex, they set to work to build a movement by which a small piece of candy, put in his hand, would be carried by that hand to his mouth. In this case, the reward of the bit of good-tasting food on Wally's palate was reinforced by a momentary mild stimulation beamed directly from a control cap into the pleasure center of Wally's brain.

From getting Wally to carry a morsel of something eatable to his mouth with a single arm movement, the therapists progressed to teaching him first to grasp and then to reach out and pick up the morsel. By the end of the sixth day they had him sitting up in order to reach out and pick up the reward, and from then on progress was rapid.

By the end of the second week, what the therapists called "muscle pleasure" had entered the situation. This was a turn-of-the-century discovery in response therapy, something particularly useful in the case of training humans and the higher anthropoids. It had been discovered that in most warm-blooded mammals there was a distinct, associative pleasure in physical exertion. This had been recognized since time immemorial in the instances of children at play and athletes, both amateur and professional, engaging in physical sports. But it extended beyond that, throughout the animal kingdom as well, exemplified by horses too long confined in a barn who could not be kept from running upon their release, and by trained sled dogs who would continue to try to run along beside a team from which they had been cut loose because they were no longer able to pull properly.

With the awakening of muscle pleasure in the body that had been Wally's, the therapists were able gradually to reduce and finally to abandon the dangerously addictive activity of reward by stimulation of the brain's pleasure center. Meanwhile, Wally was now able to rise from his bed in the morning, to dress himself in a simple one-piece coverall, and even to walk the grounds with one of the therapists in attendance.

For all this, there was still no consciousness behind the eyes of the perambulating figure. Meeting Wally one morning out in the grounds, Ett had made the mistake of looking directly into those eyes; after that he could not bring himself to face Wally directly again.

Ett himself was keeping very busy these days. His new forty-foot yacht was out on the ocean, with Al at the helm and the security men, Dr.

Hoskides, and a number of the estate staff aboard. Ett had gone off with all of them, giving them the impression that he would be on this cruise for some time. But after the second day Rico had picked him off the ship's lifeboat with a helicopter, and all those potential watchers for the EC were stranded on the ship.

Ett kept up a good pretense for them just the same, and returned to the vessel for a few days several times. But he and the MOGOWs now had a goodly amount of privacy on the island, although they had to use some discretion, to be sure.

Meanwhile, he completed the plan for getting at the 0–0 files, and put Rico and Maea to work on it. By the end of the second week after the yacht had sailed, Ett and Rico put themselves in the hands of Cye Morecki, a MOGOW who had been brought to the island in great secrecy a few days earlier with the ultimate purpose of working on Wally. Awaking at 3 a.m. one morning, they sat under Cye's hands for two hours while he, using removable skin parts and other stage tools, changed the two of them so that in the end they looked not only unlike themselves—but enough like each other that the resemblance would disturb the memory of anyone trying to identify them from recollection alone. Then they both went out, took the atmosphere flyer to Miami, and there boarded a commercial ship for New York City.

Two hours later, they were passing the annunciator at the office door of the museum employee who had access to the 0–0 files.

He opened the door himself. He was a man past middle age but vigorous looking in spite of a face folded in deep wrinkles.

"What do you want?" he said. "This isn't part of the public section of the museum—"

"We come from Vienna," said Rico. He pronounced the words very slowly and plainly.

"Ah," said the other, stepping back from the door to let them in and then closing it behind them. "Anyone from Vienna is especially welcome. Who are you?"

"I don't think we need to identify ourselves, Mr. Tolick," Rico said. He was speaking through a throat filter that altered his voice. "We've given the password; you've given the countersign. We've got something to give you here."

He produced a heavy sealed envelope.

"These are to be copied below and the originals returned to us," said Rico.

"Oh?" said Tolick. He spoke into the phone on his wrist. "Code nine thousand—"

His voice broke off. As he had been speaking, he had been ripping open the envelope. As it came unsealed a little puff of almost invisible vapor shot up at his face. He stopped moving and stood with the torn envelope still in his hands, like someone lost in thought.

Hastily, Ett reached out, caught up the old man's wrist, and shut off the phone connection. Taking a small button attached to a short length of what looked like fine wire, he touched the end of the wire to the skin over the bone behind Tolick's ear and spoke. His voice came out through his throat filter, altered and deepened to sound like the voice Tolick was expecting to hear from the phone.

"Tolick. This is Sauvonne. Here are your instructions. Take the entire envelope contents down for copying as you've been told. This is an order."

Ett quickly put the button with its wire back out of sight inside his jacket, even as Rico finished hooking a small vid-transceiver, also button-size, to the shoulder of Tolick's jacket. Rico looked down at his own wrist chronometer and saw, on its tiny screen, a view of them which had been transmitted from the tiny transceiver; Ett could see it over his shoulder.

At forty seconds after the puff of vapor had escaped from the envelope, Tolick stirred, blinked, and turned without a word to the wall behind him. At a touch of his hand, the wall slid aside to reveal an old-fashioned concrete vault entrance large enough to walk into. Tolick put his right thumb into the lock hole and said, "Tolick, entering."

The vault opened. The old man went in, and the door closed behind him. Ett and Rico followed his movements on the screen of Rico's chronometer. For a second or two the vault seemed to tremble around Tolick; then it settled. In another minute its door opened before him of its own accord, and he stepped out—now seventy meters below his office.

The room Tolick entered was small and starkly lighted. Along one wall were a row of filing cabinets with innumerable little drawers ranked in them. Tolick paused and drew from the envelope a thick sheaf of imperishable plastic paper bound with metal clamps into a solid unit and topped with an order form several pages in length. Tolick scanned the form and drew in a hissing breath. On the last page, the signature on the order held his attention for a second.

He turned to a grav-float table surface in the middle of the room, that had what seemed to be a ground-glass screen set in it. He spread out the last sheet of the order holding the signature face down on the ground-glass and waited for a second.

At the end of that time a word suddenly glowed to life on the ground-glass above the sheet: *Forgery*.

Tolick chuckled. He put the order and the clamped bundle of sheets back into the envelope and took the vault elevator back up to his office. There he handed them back to Rico. Brushing against him, Ett retrieved the tiny vid-transceiver.

"You made the copies?" Rico asked.

"Oh, yes," said Tolick, almost chuckling again. "I made them. Good day, gentlemen."

They turned toward the door. As they were going out, Tolick spoke unexpectedly behind them.

"What are you? Auditor Corps men?"

Rico and Ett jerked about.

"Certainly not," said Rico. "What makes you think that?"

"Oh, nothing . . . nothing," said Tolick cheerfully, with a wave of his hand. "Just every so often, one of the other Sections decides they'd like to run a little test on me, that's all."

They went on out. As they closed the door behind them they could hear Tolick laughing.

"We'd better move fast," Ett said, in his altered voice. They went swiftly to the nearest slideramp, up to the street, and took an automated cab to the Harbor Terminal, where they changed cabs. An hour later they were occupying third-class seats on a commercial atmosphere ship back to Miami, using the identification papers of the two MOGOW men; and soon after that they were back at a table in a laboratory room on the island, stripping the envelope from its contents.

Ett let the order flutter to the floor. But with great care he pried off the metal clamps. With these no longer holding the apparent sheaf of papers together, the top half inch of them came off like a box lid. Inside was a space packed with what seemed to be tiny crystals hardly bigger than grains of sand.

"Careful," said Rico. "Don't breathe on them."

He slid the now-exposed mass of crystals into an aperture in a large metal device on the table to their right and sealed the opening behind it.

"Now," he said, with something that was almost a sigh of relief. "The rest of the process is automatic."

Ett nodded. They went off to get Cye to remove their make-up. An hour later they were back in the room, with Maea along; and Rico tended the large machine and took a few readings.

"You didn't explain to me," Maea said, "how this works."

"You're right," said Ett. "But Rico is the one who knew about this, so let him tell you."

Rico nodded. "I will, of course. But you were the one who figured out that something like this ought to be available, and reminded me of it." He turned to face them.

"The crystals are from one of the many research laboratories funded by the EC. So far they haven't been released for commercial use. They're grown completely within a grav field, under no particular stress lines. However, once they're removed from the protection of the grav field enclosing them—as they were when the order paper was detached in the secret file room—they immediately develop stress lines in response not only to gravitational pull but to mass objects within a radius of some twelve meters surrounding them."

Maea frowned. "But how does that help us?"

"These stress lines can be interpreted by computer," Rico went on. "It's much like the process they use when they have a computer enhance— clean up and sharpen—a photograph of Mars or Pluto or any other stellar body. That interpretation of the crystals we have here should give us a complete picture, not only of the files in the basement, but of a good part of the information in them."

Maea nodded. "I see," she said. "You took a three-dimensional picture of the room, and you'll be able to read the files when the picture is developed."

"That's about it," said Ett. "More complicated, of course. And probably objects further from the grains will be too distorted for interpretation. So we have to wait to see just how much we'll get."

Ett and Maea went off to have lunch, and returned some hours later to find Rico poring over a readout on a screen attached to the machine into which he had put the crystals. He looked up, apparently pleased, as they came in.

"We got what we were after," he said. "Everything for five meters in every direction, including the rock structure around the sub-basement and a full set of details on Tolick's insides, came through sharply enough for the computer to give us a copy— beyond that we've got some general information, but small things, in particular, are too fuzzy to be of use. Of course, it's going to be a few days before we can get a good sort on what all we've got, here—it's a good thing there was a system to those files, or we'd have to do the equivalent of paging through a large library to find what we're after."

"But we'll get what we want?" Ett asked.

"Yes," Rico said. "What you're looking for should be here. It'll take a day to pull it out for you."

"Good," said Ett. "Call me if I can be of any help. I think I'm going to have to lie down for a bit."

He went back to his own room. He had been geared up again during the actual visit to the museum and had forgotten all his small discomforts, but now these were back, compounded by the deep weariness that always followed excitement. He dropped off into a dreamless sleep, from which he was roused by the sound of his bedside phone.

He rolled over on one elbow, groggily, in the darkened room, and felt blindly for the *on* stud. The screen surface of the phone lit with the image of Rico, looking once more very secretarial.

"What is it?" asked Ett thickly.

"Cele Partner," said Rico. "Reverberations from our little visit to the museum, perhaps, although the auditors can't have anything much to go on. Patrick St. Onge called just half an hour ago to see how you'd recovered from your cold—but pretty plainly he really wanted to find out if you'd left the island. I told him you were over being sick but were still weak and tired. Now Miss Partner wants to talk to you."

"We still don't know for sure she's connected with the EC," Ett said.

"I'll make you a small wager that we find a dossier on her in the zero-zero files, and proof she's connected with St. Onge and the auditors," answered Rico.

"All right, put her on," said Ett. He knew what he looked like when he was awakened suddenly from one of these deep-fatigue naps; it ought to convince Cele.

Rico's face dissolved on the screen, and in a moment Cele's face formed.

"Ett?" she said. "Ett, are you there? I can't see you."

"Just a minute," he said, trying to make his voice thick even though he was coming thoroughly awake now.

He turned on the bedside light. From the screen he could see her examining his appearance closely.

"You're still sick, then?" she asked.

"Not really," he said. "Just a little wobbly."

"What a shame! I was going to suggest we might get together in New Orleans this evening. I had some business over here, and I'm on your time schedule, more or less."

"Any time I can't make it to New Orleans from here, I'm in bad shape," said Ett.

"How about eight o'clock, this time?"

"Eight will be fine. Eight by your time. Where?"

"I'll be at the Corso. And I'm looking forward to seeing you again. Good evening."

"Evening."

They broke connection. Ett lay where he was for a moment, on one elbow propped up on his bed. Then he called Rico on the phone.

"Did you listen in?" he asked the secretary.

"No, Mr. Ho. Should I, from now on?"

"Yes . . . no. No, on second thought. But you'll

be glad to hear, if you're right about Cele, that they're beginning to take the bait. I'm to have dinner with her in New Orleans at eight. I'll try to bring her back here afterwards to see Wally. Better get Cye to put a mustache on him."

"He'll be ready, Mr. Ho."

CHAPTER SIXTEEN

Flying from the island to New Orleans in his private atmosphere ship, Ett had time to wonder if he was doing the right thing. There was certainly a possibility that Cele, with St. Onge and the Auditor Corps—with the whole EC bureaucracy, for that matter—were laying a trap for him; either to kill him, or kidnap him for questioning under deep drugs. But he had assumed all along that such methods would be avoided by his opponents for as long as possible, until desperation drove them to such extremes—they loved their rules, after all. And Ett, thinking it over, still believed that he'd not given St. Onge reason to feel desperate. His whole strategy was based on that idea, that principle.

No, he was sure he was safe, and that this move by Cele was a probe only. So he would use it for his own purposes.

"My own purposes," he said to himself, out loud in the stillness of the cockpit. It sounded arrogant, when he was alone out here, skimming soundlessly through the night above the barely-visible waves of the Gulf. A few barely-sensed clouds flirted with the stars that dotted the moonless, inky blue-black night; and he realized that for the moment his fiery inner nature seemed well quenched.

Was it the stillness and the dark? he wondered. Did great-grandfather Bruder see nights like this, wandering among those Pacific islands, and did he feel small and insignificant then?

On the day Dr. Garranto had said that whatever had been given to Wally in place of RIV-II, had directly caused his mental disintegration and suicide, Ett had made his decision to smash the system that had brought about those things. In the night he wondered if he could, and if he was right to try. But as he thought about it, he realized once more that he had no alternative to his present course of action. It was a conclusion too simple to be denied.

He was the only one who could be trusted to see the situation in its entirety. No one but an R-Master could hold the complete picture of it in his mind; and the only other R-Master in this matter was Lee Malone, who was unpredictable at best. That meant all the other people involved—Rico, Carwell, Maea—must be brought to act on the basis of a portion of the full facts, as if that portion was the whole story. Cele and St. Onge offered the least problem, because all Ett had to do with those two was sell them a bill of goods. And they wanted to buy. Ett had no doubt that Rico was right; in that

St. Onge had been set, with Cele as his assistant, to keep a special watch over the newest R-Master.

Rico himself would need to know the most and must therefore be the one whom Ett had to trust the most; but Ett felt a strange faith in the smaller man, one that was unusually serene. He had better be right about that, however, because it would be Rico, like Malone, who would have to operate on his own, once Ett had done his part and sent the Section Chiefs of the Earth Council on the way to their own destruction.

Meanwhile, the first step was Cele. She would expect him to be many times her equal, mentally, now that the RIV was in him; but she would also be counting on that part of him that was unchanged, the emotional, instinctive male part, as an arena in which she could win any encounter. At that—a little touch of uneasiness troubled the surface of his mind for a second—she might be right. He was, after all, still only human, only a man.

They went to dinner that evening in the old city of New Orleans, at a historic old restaurant called Brennan's. Just as it had been on the first evening he had called on Malone in San Diego, the weather here was unseasonably cool. They sat at a small round table with spidery ironwork legs, exposed to the stars in a courtyard with old-fashioned radiant heaters set in the high stone walls surrounding them, so that they were half-warmed, half-chilled as they sipped their drinks.

After the drinks, they went inside the weather shield to the terrace of the restaurant proper. There were no live waiters as there had once been, half a century and more ago; but a live maitre d' circu-

lated among the tables in white tie and tails, and
the seafood was memorable.

Cele peered at him in the candlelight as they sat
with coffee and green chartreuse after the meal.

"You do look tired," she said.

"Yes," said Ett.

For indeed he did. The MOGOW make-up expert
who had prepared him and Rico for the visit to the
museum had made some very slight changes in his
appearance in the few minutes available tonight
before he had left the island. Some sort of liquid
injected under his eyes and at their corners had
loosened the skin there, and a faintly dark powder
had been rubbed into the skin below the eyes as
well. Other tiny changes at the corners of his mouth
and nose and along his jawline had faintly aged
him, so that the difference between the image he
presented to the world now, and the one Wally
would present, would be marked by something
more than the mustache he had mentioned to Rico
earlier.

"I'm just worn down a little," Ett said now. "It's
been kind of a tense time. We revivified my
brother."

"Your brother?" said Cele. "Oh, yes, I remember.
Did it go all right?"

"Better than that," said Ett. "He may come out
of it better than he went in. You know, it was RIV
that knocked him down. He had a bad reaction.
But now he seems to be coming back with something like his original intelligence."

"How wonderful!"

"Wonderful and then some," said Ett. "It's a
miracle. Of course the physicians said that a death

shock could conceivably do something like this, but the chances were one in millions. But then, long shots sometimes pay off. I'm an example of that."

"Was he a younger or older brother?"

"Three years older. They say we look like twins, though."

"Oh?"

He thought he caught a new note of interest in her voice.

"Yes," he said. "Come and see me at my island sometime, and you can decide if it's true for yourself."

"Maybe," she said thoughtfully, "I will."

"Of course,"—he leaned a little closer to her—"you could fly back with me tonight, come to think of it. I could take you sailing in the *Pixie*."

"The *Pixie*?"

"My boat," he said. "The one I had before I took RIV. It's not a toy I picked up since; it's an ocean-going sloop. It'll be a good night for sailing tonight, at the island—the moon should have risen by then."

Cele laughed and shook her head.

"I'm not dressed for getting all windblown in a sailboat," she said. "I'm not really in the mood for it, either. But I might take a look at your island anyway."

"Then let's go."

They flew back in Ett's atmosphere flyer. Once they were landed, Ett led her on a general tour of the island, avoiding the route that would take them to Wally's quarters directly. It was necessary to give Rico, Carwell, and the others plenty of time to have Wally ready for Cele to see. Also, he admit-

ted to himself, it was pleasant strolling around in
the night. The moon, low on the horizon, was almost full, as he had said, and the Caribbean night
was soft. For a little while it was almost the way it
had always been with him, in the days before
Wally took the RIV and he himself followed in
Wally's footsteps.

They came at last to the docks, toward which he
had been aiming all along. But when they came
down along the wooden surface, hollow-sounding
under their feet, there was a light in the cabin of
the *Pixie*; and through a side porthole of the cabin,
when they got a little closer, Ett saw the heads of
Al and Maea, laughing together at something.

"Why are you stopping?" Cele asked. "Isn't your
boat here after all?"

"It's here," Ett said flatly. "But I'd forgotten
something. I gave the boat to somebody else."

He turned and led the way back up the dock to
the soft turf and on up to the house, directly now
to Wally's quarters. Dr. Carwell was waiting for
them as they came up to the entrance of the wing.

"Who's that?" Carwell said, moving toward them
in the gloom. "Oh, Mr. Ho. Were you going to look
in on your brother?"

"Yes," said Ett. Somehow, he had expected
Carwell to be a poor liar. But the big man surprised him. Carwell's words sounded more natural
than Ett's own planned responses.

"Cel, this is Dr. Morgan Carwell, my personal
physician—and my brother's," said Ett. "Dr. Carwell, Miss Cele Partner."

Cele and Carwell murmured acknowledgements
of the introduction.

"Wallace is asleep. He's had quite a day," Carwell said. "If you don't mind, Mr. Ho, I'd prefer he wasn't disturbed, now that he's sleeping. These first few weeks are often crucial, particularly in a case like this where he's regaining the mental acuity he lost earlier. We want to give him every chance to rebound as far as he can."

"Perhaps," said Ett, "Miss Partner could just look through the observation window from the therapy room?"

"Of course," said Carwell. "Let me lead the way."

He took them in through the wing, to the therapy room, and across its padded floor to the observation window that gave a view of Wally's bedroom.

"I could turn on the lights without disturbing him," Carwell said to Cele. "One-way glass. But with the glare of light on this side you wouldn't be able to see him so well in the dark. If I leave the lights off here, the night light in there is just enough . . ."

"I see," said Cele, looking through the glass. Her voice was thoughtful. "You're right, Ett; he does look a lot like you."

"That's what people say," said Ett.

Wally lay on his side, in the position they had taught him, rather than flat on his back as he had on first being revived. The night light showed his unlined face clearly against the pillow, the mustache a black smudge on his upper lip.

"Yes," murmured Cele, gazing at him. "A remarkable resemblance . . ."

She turned abruptly away from the window.

"Well, Ett," she said, suddenly energetic, "what else haven't you shown me on this island of yours?"

"You've seen it all outdoors," Ett said. "How about indoors?"

"Of course. You've got a terrace somewhere, out under the stars, haven't you, where we can sit and have a drink? Come along and have a drink with us, Dr. Carwell, won't you?"

She put a hand on Carwell's thick arm.

"I'd enjoy it," he told her.

"Good—Morgan," she said. "And you can tell me all about Ett's brother. It fascinates me. Someone brought back from a terminal situation in better shape than he went into it."

They went to the terrace. Ett had thought that one drink would probably be the end of it, but Cele turned out to be as fascinated with Wally's revival as she had said. She kept Carwell in conversation about Wally until Ett's head began to spin achingly from fatigue plus his own new vulnerability to liquor and late hours. Finally he excused himself and went to bed, leaving them still talking.

He dreamed, but of Maea. He woke and lay in the darkness, remembering the sight of her laughing with Al on the boat, before he finally rolled over on his other side and got to sleep without dreams.

When he arose the next morning, Cele was gone. That evening, after dinner, Rico called Ett down to the room where he had been reconstructing the information obtained by the crystals from the 0–0 files.

"I've got it," Rico said. "Everything you asked me to find out." There were real dark smudges under his eyes, the shadows of fatigue and strain. Ett looked at him closely.

"How long is it since you've been to bed?" Ett said.

Rico groped for an answer, and Ett cut him off.

"I take it you were up all last night. In here?"

"Not all the time," Rico said. "I was monitoring the conversation on the terrace after you went to bed, just in case Dr. Carwell let something slip. But he did fine."

"I see," Ett said. "Yes, that was good thinking. I was too tired to think straight just then."

"You still look washed out," Rico said. "You could use a couple of days just resting quietly."

"I plan on it," Ett said. "I've got to be in good shape before this last part starts. But let me see what you've got so far."

"First," said Rico, "Cele Partner." He punched buttons below a viewscreen, and a paragraph of close print leaped to their eyes on its gray surface.

"There's her dossier," Rico said.

Ett looked. It was not a short dossier, either. Cele, he learned, had been born with the name Maria Van Pelt, in Brussels, Belgium. She had evidently deduced for herself the existence and power of what Rico called the bureaucracy, and set out to join it for her own benefit. She had taken a clerical job with one of the EC subsidiaries in Rangoon and proved her worth to the Accounting Section by uncovering a number of instances there of regulations being broken. She had attracted the attention of St. Onge, and since that time had been on special duty, responsible only to him.

"Good enough," said Ett. "With any luck, she'll have taken the bait; she'll be telling St. Onge right now how convenient it'd be to have Wally in my place. What've they got on Lee Malone?"

Rico punched buttons again. The dossier this time was even longer. As they blew it up to make it readable they filled the whole screen several times with successive sections of it.

"Now that's hitting paydirt," said Ett.

"I thought you'd say so," Rico answered. "Note that Master Malone is recorded as having been treated not with RIV-II, but with something called RIV-IV. Also, there's no mention of the laboratory in his basement. If the EC knew about it, mention of it would certainly be here."

"Those are two things I was reasonably sure about anyway," said Ett. "What pleases me more is that they've taken him at the assessment he wanted to create—they evidently believe he's nothing but a talker, with no real revolutionist fire in him."

"Can we be sure that isn't actually all he is?" Rico looked sidelong at Ett.

"I'm sure," said Ett. "A man who was a talker rather than an actor wouldn't have worked that long, that hard, and kept the secret of his laboratory that well—if he were only a talker, he'd have had to tell somebody, show somebody. No, Malone is safe for the moment—and he ought to be able to stay safe at least while he makes enough of the improved RIV for our use. You did find information here about the improved version of RIV?"

"Yes. Here."

Rico punched buttons again. The image that formed on a screen off to one side looked to Ett like nothing so much as a page from an advanced chemistry text.

"Can Malone follow that?"

"If he can't," Rico answered, "I can. The chemistry at this point is simple enough. Actually what I'm showing you is the end result, essential information on a long process of research and development of the drug we know as RIV. This variation is called RIV-VII."

"There's always the chance, though," said Ett, "that it isn't the actual, final variant. They might have found that and then thrown away the information as too dangerous."

"No chance of that," said Rico. "If I know anything at all, I know the bureaucratic mind. It never throws anything away. It's exactly in character with whatever eighteen Section Chiefs sit on the EC at any one time, to make sure that RIV was refined to the ultimate point—and then to bury the results here, where they'd never be used. Give me Malone's equipment and properly qualified chemists, and I'll produce the actual drug for you."

"All right, I'll take your word for it," said Ett. "Now let's look at some more dossiers. Yours, to begin with."

Without a word, Rico punched buttons. The dossier that appeared on the screen was lengthy and remarkable in the skills it attributed to its subject; and there was no hint that he was considered anything but utterly loyal to the EC.

"All right," said Ett. "Wally."

Wally's dossier was quite short, containing only a notation directing the reader to the Central Computer's biographical files, and these words: *Analysis of social contacts and expressed opinions indicated possible active member of MOGOW.* This was followed by a short mention of his recent history, including the revivification, and a cross-reference to Ett himself.

"Maea," said Ett.

Maea's bio was similarly brief, except for an appendage concerning her apparent attempts to cultivate Auditors Cele Partner and Patrick St. Onge, for unknown purposes; the note ended with the phrase: *possible MOGOW sympathizer?*

"Carwell." But Carwell was not mentioned in the zero-zero files. Ett frowned.

"Try me," he said.

His own entry was only slightly longer than those for Wally and Maea, becoming detailed only upon his recent transformation into an R-Master. There was a mention of his unusual connections with suspected MOGOWs such as Maea and Wally, as well as with R-Master Lee Malone. There was a note that, over Medical objection, Patrick St. Onge had been assigned to surveillance of him.

"Why 'over Medical objection'?" Ett asked Rico. "And why the capital M?"

"The different Section Chiefs of the Council are always feuding," Rico said. "In particular, Wilson of Accounting and Sorenson of Medical have always been at each other's throats, perhaps because they've come to be heads of the two Sections of the EC with the most personnel and the biggest budgets. Probably there was some political nit to be picked, for Sorenson to object to you being placed under surveillance; chances are it had nothing much to do with you personally."

"No?" said Ett. "I'd guess it had a great deal to do with me personally." Rico looked at him questioningly, but Ett moved on. "Let's see the entry on Dr. Garranto y Vega."

"Garranto?" Rico looked surprised. "Why would you expect him to be in here? He may be the most apolitical person I've met."

"Try," said Ett.

Rico punched buttons, and an entry was found. It was brief. It noted Dr. Garranto y Vega as an individualist who had the bad habit of ignoring Medical Section regulations; he had apparently been secretly reprimanded for some breach of the regulations about four years earlier, but the details of the case remained a Medical Section secret.

"I don't understand," said Rico, looking from the entry to Ett.

"I see a connection," Ett said. "Tell me, what besides the size of the membership in their sections would bring Medical and Accounting into conflict in the Council Chamber?"

"Well, Accounting contains the Auditor Corps, the police arm of the EC," Rico said thoughtfully. "It's known Medical doesn't like its physicians hassled by Field Examiners—it seems to think professional people should be above that. Of course, this is all very polite, and kept to arguments in the Council itself. No one in top position in the EC is going to rock the boat."

"Perhaps," said Ett. "I'd been suspecting that Medical and Accounting weren't together on everything, and I rather suspected what we found out about Dr. Garranto."

"Then maybe you'd tell me what it has to do with what we're trying to do," said Rico. "We're just trying to get the RIV-VII drug loose and out to people, aren't we?"

"Not exactly," said Ett. "We're trying to get

RIV-VII loose and out to people—but under conditions where it'll do some good."

"I've been taking that particular qualification of yours for granted," said Rico.

"You shouldn't," retorted Ett. "What if we got the drug into production and some new R-Masters made, only to have it and them suddenly swept up by the EC and quietly eliminated? What you tell me about Medical and Accounting backs up the way the whole picture's been fitting together. If the feud between even two EC Sections is serious enough, we can't trust these zero-zero files completely."

"But these files are the one thing none of the Section Chiefs would monkey with," began Rico.

"It wouldn't take monkeying with the files themselves," said Ett. "Suppose these files are only . . . incomplete? We don't know there aren't *other* secret files elsewhere in the world— isn't redundancy a bureaucratic habit?" He stopped.

"But never mind that now. You'd better get the RIV-VII information to Malone as quickly as possible. But don't transmit it." Ett stopped to think a moment.

"Didn't I see Al around here last night?" he said.

"You could have," Rico said. "I sent the helicopter for him yesterday, figuring we might need him now. The security men and Hoskides are still on the yacht, without working communications, and will have to bring the ship back by themselves. That'll take a while."

"Good," Ett said. "Take him with you in the flyer. You get some sleep on the way to Malone's. When you reach him, tell him to pack up his necessary lab equipment and clear out—he'd better use his more militant MOGOW connections for hiding places and keep on the move, if he can do it while making the new RIV. You understand?"

Rico looked at him for a moment as if about to speak, and then apparently changed his mind. He nodded.

"Leave Al with Malone," Ett continued. "I particularly don't want the EC getting their hands on him. Meanwhile, I take it Wally's been brought along by the response therapists to the point where he can put on a fair imitation of me, as long as he doesn't have to talk to anyone?"

"Not yet, but he'll be there soon," said Rico.

"When I give you the word, it'll be up to you to set Wally to face the Section Chiefs, without anyone else knowing about it. You're sure you can handle all that without trouble?"

"Mr. Ho," Rico said, "I'm not going to let that remark irritate me. I know you're suffering your usual discomforts, and you're under pressure as well."

Ett sagged a little.

"All right," he said. He wiped his hand across his forehead and it came away wet. "I'm sorry. Forgive me. I trust you, Rico, of course. We have to trust each other. Tell me again, though—you're sure nothing can ordinarily be smuggled into a meeting of the EC Section Chiefs?"

"Believe me, it can't," said Rico. "Everyone coming in is searched to the skin by guards, as well as by detectors."

"All right. Then I'll get going," said Ett. "I—Wally that is—had better leave the island tomorrow, af

ter all. Time's short. Have that make-up man come
to my room and fit me with my fake mustache,
early, would you? I suppose you've already spoken
to Al about the boat?"

"Yes," said Rico.

"Good," said Ett, opening the door from the
room to the outside and the warm island early
evening. "In twelve hours *Pixie* and I are going to
be in open water."

CHAPTER SEVENTEEN

Ett, now wearing the persona of Wally, sailed the *Pixie* to Fort-de-France, and left her there, moored in a public marina on the Madame River. He had Wally's citizen card, to the credit account of which he, as Ett, had deposited a healthy amount of dividend units, to reinforce the arrears of Wally's own allowance, which had been automatically re-activated on his revival. Thereafter, he took a private room on an intercontinental to London and began to wander, tending eastward, around the globe, drinking, gambling, scattering units about— and making it a point to get into arguments and fights wherever he went.

On the fifth day he was in the Istanbul area, in a pleasure hotel in Galata, sitting on a grav lounge by the huge interior swimming pool of the hotel, when he heard his—or rather Wally's—name called.

"Wallace Ho?"

Ett was half-asleep. The strain of appearing to lead the sort of dissipated life that a physically healthy Wally was supposed to be leading had brought him close to a state of exhaustion, for all that he spent most of his time, when out of the public eye, sleeping. But the voice that spoke to him was that of Cele Partner, the woman he had first met with St Onge, and the recognition galvanized him, bringing a surge of adrenaline that woke him thoroughly. He kept his head down and his eyes half-closed, however, so his reaction would not show. She spoke again.

"Aren't you Wallace Ho?"

He looked up and to his right, and saw her sitting at a table under a pool umbrella—only ornamental here inside—just a few feet away. She was not dressed for swimming, however, but for the street, in casual skirt and half-blouse. Hair bound in a red kerchief, she nonetheless managed to look as impossibly beautiful as a dream out of the Arabian nights.

"Who're you?" Ett said.

"I know your brother—slightly," Cele said. "I passed by his island and stayed to talk to a Dr. Morgan Carwell. I saw you. You were sleeping at the time. But Dr. Carwell told me all about you."

"Very damned interesting," said Ett. "But you still haven't told me your name. That was my question—who're you?"

"Cele Partner," she said. "Morgan Carwell never mentioned me?"

"He never mentioned anything," said Ett.

She laughed a warm, low-pitched laugh.

"Maybe he was a little jealous," Cele said. "I

told him you fascinated me. Someone who'd been brought back not just from the dead but from a bad reaction to RIV. Do you know that you're unique?"

"Being unique doesn't do me any good," said Ett. "It's my brother who gets all the advantages—just for being lucky. But then, I never was lucky."

"Aren't you?" said Cele. "I'd have thought you would be. Now, your brother Ett didn't impress me at all."

"Oh?" said Ett. "That's a change. Women used to fall all over him. None of them ever fell all over me."

"Maybe they didn't have the sense to appreciate you," said Cele.

He sat up in his chair. "You're serious, aren't you?" he said. "You're actually telling me you get some kind of lift out of me. You've got strange tastes."

"Why don't you join me?" she said.

He got up from his lounge and sat down at her table.

"Actually," she said, "I'd heard you'd left the island. I've been looking for you. I'm glad I finally found you."

They were together for the next five days, an experience that threatened to shake Ett loose from most of his certainties. This Cele Partner was entirely different from the one he had met as Etter Ho. The former Cele had been aloof and seemingly preferring to stay on a pedestal, rather than stepping down to common earth with any man. This new Cele was just the opposite. The less Ett, in his guise as Wally, tried to please her, the more attentive she became to him. There was a fire in her now that he could not have imagined before. In spite of himself—though he was careful to hide the reaction—his own feelings toward her were kindled by it. He was absolutely certain that he did not love her. But acting as she did, how could he fail to want her as he constantly did?

But what was real about her and what was not? Was the Cele he had first known the true Cele Partner? Or was this present woman the true version? Was what he now saw an act put on at the orders of Patrick St. Onge, or someone else? Or had the earlier Cele been acting a part?

Meanwhile, he was moving them both eastward to his destination, which was the same gambling area around Hong Kong that he had visited before as Ett. Once more he gambled, and this time he made sure to lose steadily. Two days after they got there, his credit was exhausted, and he turned to Cele for units.

For the first time, she refused him something, though the refusal was given sweetly enough. She sat in his lap and ran her fingers through his hair, begging him to understand that she lived almost on a day-to-day basis as far as her GWP allowance was concerned. It was a slightly better allowance that the basic level for her job, because she had once written a play that was still being performed, but it was barely enough to keep her going.

He shoved her away, onto the floor.

"You're no good to me," he said and stalked out.

Once beyond the door of the hotel suite, he went down to the main bar and drank for a while, using what little credit remained to him. After a bit, he went to a phone booth. Luckily, communications, like local transportation, were free, a fact he had taken advantage of in the old days when operating the *Pixie* took most of his basic allowance.

After some little delay, the face of Rico looked at him out of the phone screen. Across a satellite communications circuit that was sure to be tapped and recorded by the EC— unlike bugging of homes, that was legal—they exchanged glances.

"I don't want to talk to you!" Ett snapped. "Get me that brother of mine. He'd better talk to me, or he'll be sorry he didn't."

"Mr. Ho," said Rico, "Master Ho has asked me to tell you that not only won't he talk to you now, but he doesn't want to talk to you at any time in the future; and he also says that it'll do you no good to keep calling, because that decision is final."

"All right," said Ett thickly. "You give him a message for me then. He can shut me out all right, if he likes; but he's not going to go on living like a king while I have to scrape along on a basic allowance. He can sit on his island and pretend I don't exist, if he wants, but he's going to have to pay for the privilege. I can be trouble for him. Wait and see if I can't."

"What are you going to do, Wallace?" Rico asked.

"Never mind what I'm going to do. Maybe I've got a friend. Maybe I'm going to have more friends. Maybe things'll start working for me; then he'll wish he hadn't acted so damn high and mighty."

Rico sighed.

"Do you want me to tell Master Ho that?" he said. "I don't think it will improve the way he feels toward you at the moment."

"I don't care how he feels," Ett said. "He and his feelings can go to hell. All I want is some funds to make life livable. He's got all the credit in the world."

"But he can't use it to give to other people, even to his brother. That's one thing the Auditor Corps has already told him they won't allow any more."

"Don't tell me that. He could sneak all the units I want and they'd never know it, let alone complain about it."

"How much do you want?"

"How much can I get?"

"I . . . it's not for me to say, of course," said Rico. Once more in the screen, his glance held Ett's, meaningfully. "It would depend on how soon you wanted it. The best estimate I could give you would be that in a week you could have, say, a couple of thousand units."

"A week?" said Ett. "How about three days from now? How about tomorrow?"

"I'm afraid," said Rico, slowly, "that if it had to be tomorrow or even three days from now, it would have to be nothing. It'll require at least a week to get you anything. But then you could have two thousand. If you could wait, say, three days longer than that, it might be possible to make it four thousand.

Ett inclined his head, almost imperceptibly.

"Go to hell!" he said, and punched off.

He got up and left the phone booth. He did not have to pretend to be half drunk, because the drinks he had had at the bar were affecting him heavily. But in spite of this, his R-Master mind was able to consider the information he had just gotten. The request for funds had been set up ahead of time with Rico as a code to allow Ett to discover what Lee Malone would be able to do in the way of producing doses of RIV-VII. The answer from Rico that it would take another week to produce the first two thousand doses was not encouraging. Even two thousand new R-Masters was a tiny assault force with which to threaten the bureaucratic organization tightly controlling every technological service and every source of supply for a world whose population was nearly six billion people—all thoroughly controlled, whether they knew it or not.

But judging from Cele's refusal to feed him more units to gamble with, things were moving to a climax in a game he was playing with her, St. Onge, and those behind him.

Well, if they had to make do with two thousand doses, they would have to make do. He went unsteadily back up to the hotel suite he shared with Cele and found her gone. He collapsed on the bed in the bedroom and let his drunken stupor pull him down into heavy sleep.

He was awakened by hotel employees who had roused him in order to evict him. Cele was still absent. He allowed himself to be put out into the street, although he put up a show of protest. It was a new day; half a block down the street was a bank where he could draw one more day's worth of his basic allowance. It would not be enough to regain the hotel suite he had just left, but it would be enough to feed and house him in a more reasonably-priced hotel.

However, when he got to the bank, he discovered that an almost unheard-of thing—a debit—had been charged against his account. The bank had somehow discovered charges of his which, through some sort of error, had not been placed against his account earlier—and now these charges had to be paid. In fact, they would be drawn from his basic allowance until they had been paid, which would take the next thirty-nine days. He would get no more during that period.

It was a step Ett had expected. There was one stage lower than that of someone on Minimum Basic Allowance. That was to become an occupant of the Earth Council Free Shelters— generally, last refuges for people who because of mental or physical deficiencies could not take on even the small responsibility of drawing a daily allowance and using it correctly to maintain themselves. Ett looked up the nearest Free Shelter in the local directory and went to it.

He was given a small cubicle of a room and a filling, if unremarkable, breakfast, in a general dining room where he was surrounded by the incapable, the aged and the infirm of both sexes. This meal over, he made his way to the Sunset Mountain, the same sprawling hotel and casino he had visited shortly after becoming an R-Master. He took his time, wandering in apparent aimlessness, until he found himself at the hotel.

Inside, Ett searched out the desk of the Director of Services.

"People say," he said, "there's a fencing school here at the Mountain."

"Yes, sir," said the woman behind the desk. "Wing Forty-four of the hotel, and follow the signs."

Ett made his way to Wing Forty-four of the hotel and found, as he had been advised, plaques on the wall pointing the way to Fencing. These brought him eventually to what looked like the outer lobby of an athletic club.

"Sir?" said the male attendant behind the desk, smiling politely.

"I heard," Ett said, "that a man in need of money could earn some here, if he could fence, and volunteered for bouts with unbuttoned weapons."

The politeness dropped from the man like a discarded mask.

"I'm afraid not," he said coldly. "You've been listening to one of the stories that circulate around the gaming tables."

Ett started to turn away.

"However—" said the clerk.

Ett turned back.

"However," the other repeated, looking sour, "we do have gentlemen sometimes willing to sponsor amateurs in bouts with unbuttoned weapons. I could put you on a list. You do fence?"

"In secondary school I was on the school team," said Ett.

"All right." The clerk reached under the counter separating them and came up with a sheet of paper and a plastic tab on which was printed a number. "You're now number eight-seven-three in priority. Sign this release; then go in to the aid station. Tell them to give you a physical. After that, come back here and wait. Your number tab will give you credit for food and drink while you're waiting."

Ett followed the instructions. It was a good three hours after he had been given a cursory going-over by the medical technician in the aid station before he heard his number called over the public-address system.

"Number eight-seven-three," said the bored female voice which had been reading various announcements steadily for the last hour, "report to Gym Twelve-B. Number eight-seven-three to Gym Twelve-B immediately."

Ett consulted a map of the hotel wing he was in and found his route to Twelve-B. When he stepped through the door of its entrance he found himself on a gym floor in a room with a balcony—very much like the one in which he had witnessed the sword fight once before, except that in this case the balcony seats were empty. In fact, there was no one visible in the room at all, except a man holding a pair of weapons, very like fencing sabers, but with sharpened points.

"Are you—" Ett was beginning, when the man cut him short.

"Of course not. Here, take one of these. Your sponsor will be in directly."

"Are you the one I'm supposed to fight?" Ett insisted, taking one of the blades. "Where's the crowd?"

"No, I work here. And there isn't any crowd, just you and your sponsor."

"But if he's sponsoring me to fight someone—"

"Don't be more of a damn fool than you have to be," said the other impatiently. "He's sponsoring you to fight him, of course. He specified no crowd, and as long as he's willing to pay for privacy it makes no difference to us. As far as your own terms with him go, you work those out with him yourself; we don't even want to know about it."

He pushed the other weapon into Ett's hands.

"Here, give him this when he shows up. I can't wait here all day."

He went out.

For a long moment, Ett stood alone in the room,

holding both blades. Then there was a sound—the sound of a door opening off to his right. He turned, and saw Patrick St. Onge, wearing the type of tight-fitting black suit Ett had seen before on his previous visit to this part of the Sunset Mountain. St. Onge came across the gym floor toward him. At the same moment there was the noise of another opening door, this time above him and behind. Looking up into the balcony, he saw Cele, dressed in something gauzy and springlike and looking delightfully old-fashioned; she came down to the edge of the balcony and leaned over.

"Wally," she called. "Here's a gentleman who wants to meet you. His name's Patrick St. Onge."

Ett looked back at St. Onge. The tall man came up to Ett, took one of the blades from him, and stepped back to salute with it.

"Guard," he said, and he himself fell into guard position.

"Wait a minute," said Ett. He looked up at the balcony. "Cele!"

"I'm afraid I can't do anything more for you right now, Wally," called Cele sweetly.

"Guard," said St. Onge again.

Slowly, Ett moved his blade up into a guard. He felt unbelievably clumsy while, facing him, St. Onge looked as if he had been born in the guard position. The other man's face was expressionless. Only when Ett looked at the auditor's dark eyes closely was he able to make out something a little eager, a little hungry, in the squinted lines about them.

Ett knew he had put himself into a situation where St. Onge could legally kill him. He had calculated that St. Onge would not do so. Now he hoped he was right about that.

"Come, come, let's not waste time," said St.
Onge.

He dropped his saber point carelessly to the
wooden floor and seemed to relax. Ett lunged; and
there was a flash of light reflected from metal,
a ringing, clashing sound as the blades came
together—then Ett's weapon was wrenched out of
his grasp. He didn't see where it went, his eyes
were unable to move from the blade of St. Onge
which circled slowly before his eyes. He stood
frozen, and watched the point approach, until the
sharpness was pricking the skin at the base of his
throat.

In the moment of silence that followed Ett felt
the coldness of new sweat breaking through his
skin; he was afraid—but even as he catalogued the
sensations, a part of him was noting coolly that
such fear was exactly the right reaction to show,
just now.

St. Onge laughed, but without moving his blade.
The point stayed poised and ready; he could feel
it.

"Do you realize," St. Onge said quietly, "you
didn't even set a price on this carcass of yours
before you started? Tell me now. What's your body
worth—and where should I send the money? To
your brother?"

"Damn you!" swore Ett. "You can't kill me—
just like that!"

"Can't I?" St. Onge laughed, his point still pricking Ett's throat. "Why not? You signed a release.
An aberrant act, but not an unexpected one. You
apparently came out of that revivification from a
cryogenic state with an improved intellect but with
an emotional instability, Wallace Ho. I'm an

auditor, from EC Accounting, and I've had some experience with unstable personalities. Give me one reason not to kill you."

"All right, I'll give you one!" flared Ett. "You can use me. The EC can use me, if you want to get rid of that brother of mine!"

"Oh?" St. Onge's eyes flickered suddenly, up to the balcony where Cele was and then back down again to Ett. "What makes you think the EC would like to get rid of any R-Master, least of all our newest one?"

"Do I need to tell you?" retorted Ett. "I know he'll have been trying to make trouble for you. That's the way he is." Ett laughed with what he hoped was the right note of bitterness. "That's life for you. I'm ready to cooperate any way you want. He would never cooperate. And which one of us are you trying to kill off right now? Me! When you'd be ten times better off with me in his place and him dead!"

The point of the unbuttoned saber fell away from its touch against Ett's neck.

"Well, well," said St. Onge, softly. "So you think you'd make a better R-Master than your brother?"

"I know I would."

There was the sound of feet on steps. Cele descended by a stair at the side of the balcony and came up to the two of them.

"Well," said St. Onge, tossing his weapon aside, "maybe you'll have the chance to prove that, Wally. Come along."

There was an unmarked autocar waiting for them outside the Sunset Mountain. It took them back to the same hotel and suite that Ett had been in the day before, the one he had been evicted from.

Once there, Cele and St. Onge waited while Ett shaved the mustache he had grown to replace the fake he'd begun wearing when this masquerade started. Ett also cleaned up and put on fresh clothes.

"All right," said St. Onge, when Ett came back into the room. "I'm convinced. You look enough like your brother to pass a casual examination. Now sit down and listen to me."

Ett sat.

"Your brother Etter," said St. Onge, "avoided normal society most of his life. As a result, he managed to grow up without acquiring the almost instinctive understanding of how the world works, that all the rest of us have. But I think you understand."

"Try me," said Ett.

"I think," said St. Onge, "you, like everyone else, learned a long time ago that there's one price everybody has to pay to have our world the good place that it presently is—without wars, without starvation, without plagues, with a good life possible to everyone. In return for all this, there's just one requirement: we all have to live by the regulations. Unless the overwhelming majority lives by the regulations, the system won't work. That's why we crack down on criminals—and that's why you're going to get the chance to take your brother's place."

"You mean," said Ett, "if I do step into his shoes I've got to stick by the regulations? Of course I will."

"Don't say it so lightly," said St. Onge. "Because you're going to have to start out by breaking a regulation, at your own risk. You're going to have to be the one to claim to be Etter Ho. All we'll do is help you take your case to the Earth Council. Neither Cele nor myself nor anyone else on the Council is going to so much as bend a regulation in its own right for you."

"Well, what good is that?" said Ett. "He can prove who he is by fingerprints, eyeprints, and a dozen other things."

"To be sure," said St. Onge. "But we'll make a point of discovering that one of the Ho brothers, aided by someone we haven't yet identified, got into some ultra-secret government files. We guess that their purpose was to get the codes that would enable them to switch the master identification files of Wallace and Etter, in the Central Computer. Since we think the files may have been switched, and since you claim to be Etter, the man now masquerading as Etter must be Wally, the brother Etter managed to have revived from cryogenic suspension. Unfortunately Etter—you, that is— didn't realize that such subjects of cryogenic suspension can suffer brain damage in the process of suspension, with the result that they emerge with criminal inclinations. Apparently this may have happened to your brother Wally, who then got into the files I was talking about and switched them in an effort to gain for himself the perquisites of an R-Master. Understand, none of us know this to be true, and you swear that you are Etter— don't you?"

"Of course," said Ett. "But what about lie detector tests, or a dozen other ways of checking—"

"None of those are completely reliable. Under proper drugs, the truth can be gotten at, of course," said St. Onge, getting to his feet. "But the man now masquerading as Etter has made a point of refusing to take drugs; the record will show him doing that still. The regulations protect him in that sort of refusal, of course. There's no way we could force him to do any such thing. On the other hand, you'd be perfectly willing to be questioned under the proper drugs, wouldn't you?"

"Of course," said Ett, almost without hesitation.

"Don't worry." St. Onge smiled. "I have great faith that you'll confirm your identity as Etter under any drugs we give you. Just as I have confidence that, faced with this evidence, the EC Section Chiefs will confirm you are Etter Ho, R-Master. Of course, once you're reinstated in your proper identity, you'll naturally have no objection to putting yourself under the direction of Dr. Hoskides, Etter Ho's assigned physician, who will be at hand at all times from then on to alleviate your discomforts with other drugs."

"I see," said Ett. The words stuck in his throat. "I'll be under medication part of the time, then, once I'm confirmed as Ett."

"All of the time," replied St. Onge, with a gentle smile. "It's part of being an R-Master."

Ett nodded his head grimly.

"All right," he said. "It's a deal. I just want one thing."

"You're not in a position to make conditions," St. Onge said.

"Aren't I?" Ett answered. "You wouldn't be going to this much trouble unless you wanted me pretty badly. I say, I want one thing."

"All right, let's hear it then," said St. Onge. "But it's going to have to be something within the regulations."

"It is," said Ett. "But it's also protection for me.

When the Section Chiefs of the Earth Council—how many are there?"

"The Section Chiefs?" St. Onge said. "Eighteen."

"When they agree that I'm R-Master Etter Ho, I want to be there. I want to be there, physically, in the room with them, so that I can hear them say I'm R-Master Etter Ho. And I want the whole meeting a matter of public record. If something goes wrong later on, at least I'll know it wasn't because one of them thought it was safe to back out of the matter."

"What you're asking just can't be done," said Cele, speaking for the first time. "They hold their meetings by phone."

"Always?" demanded Ett. "I heard—not always."

Cele said nothing.

"Almost always," said St. Onge. "In special cases they all meet together, physically, in one room. But there are still enough fanatics in the world to make a meeting like that dangerous. I don't think I can promise you that."

"I know you can't," said Ett. "But you can't say no, either—not without asking someone, whoever your superior is. And you'd better ask him, because without this I won't promise you anything, either."

He laughed. "You're forgetting that I'm already at the bottom. How much have I got to lose by not going along with you? I've got to have some reason to trust you—you and all of them—or it's no good. It's me who's breaking the regulations in all of this, and you've got to pay me for that."

St. Onge stood for a moment.

"All right," he said, then. "I'll ask. And if they

agree, you'll meet them all, in the flesh, under one roof. After all, this is an extraordinary situation."

He headed toward the door of the room. Cele followed him.

"Wait a minute!" Ett called after them. "You can't just go off and leave me here, dangling. How long before I have this hearing? A month, a couple of weeks—?"

St. Onge stopped and looked back. He smiled oddly.

"Now that I really can't tell you," he said. "If it can be done at all, it may take a while to get schedules worked out." He paused.

"But if it's done," he said, smiling more widely, "then probably it'll be right away. Let's guess tomorrow—twelve hours from now, Hong Kong time."

CHAPTER EIGHTEEN

Ett sat where he was, counting the seconds and trying to restrain his impulse to move, until St. Onge and Cele had been gone long enough to get them to the entrance of the hotel and outside. Then he got up and went to the phone in his room, where he made a show of enquiring of local information before punching out the number of a nearby bookstore.

After a second, the face of a young Oriental woman appeared on the screen.

"I'm at the Hotel Oceania," Ett said. "The name is Wallace Ho. Do you have some kind of information on R-Masters you could send over to me right now?"

"Right now?" The smooth, almost childish face stared at him out of the screen. This was an emergency contact. He had no idea even what this woman's name was. Rico, with the aid of the

MOGOWs, had set up at least one such blind contact for him in each city he was to stop in over-
night on his way to Hong Kong.

"Right now," said Ett. "Twelve hours from now
I won't be here any longer. I won't have any need
for it."

"Twelve hours?"

"That's right."

"Let me see what I can find for you here in the
store, then, please, sir."

"Thanks." Ett punched off. Just in case there
should, in defiance of regulations, be some kind of
human or mechanical eye observing him, he went
to the bar of the room, made himself a drink, and
carried it back to his chair by the window. But he
only pretended to sip at it.

It was nearly four hours before the phone rang.

"Our last copy of the best available reference on
R-Masters was sold to a lady in your hotel," said
the face from the bookstore. "But I've just talked
to her and she is willing to lend it to you, though.
At this moment she should be down in the lobby,
checking out. If you go down she will lend you her
copy."

"Thanks," said Ett.

He left the room and took the nearest elevator
shaft down to the central main lobby of the hotel.
There were perhaps half a hundred people milling
about, and he suddenly realized he had been given
no description of the "lady" he was supposed to
meet. But common sense came to his rescue, and
he found a seat among a group of comfortable
grav floats in a gardenlike, secluded corner of the
lobby, and sat down to wait.

A few minutes later, a somewhat stiff-moving but slim-bodied elderly Occidental woman walked into the same area and took a seat opposite him. He looked into the woman's face and under the graying hair of the wig she was wearing, and the lines and make-up, he recognized Maea. He hadn't really thought of her as being that thin, he realized.

"Mr. Ho?" she said, in a filtered voice.

"Yes."

"My bookstore told me you very much wished to read a copy of a book I have; evidently I bought the last one they had in stock." She passed a small, brown film card case to him, leaning forward. "Here you are."

"Thanks," he said.

She sat back on her float, which had drifted closer to Ett. She did not seem to be lowering her voice, but now it seemed to Ett not to have the carrying quality it had had a moment before.

"What is it?" she said.

"Things have gone well," he said. "Too well. St. Onge took the bait, just as I told Rico he would. They're going to give me the chance to switch from Wally Ho to Etter Ho, but there's a problem. I'm to be taken to meet the Earth Council's Section Chiefs, probably early tomorrow. And Rico told me it would take two weeks to make even the first two thousand doses of RIV-VII. That means we may just have gone bust, and the rest of you'd probably better split up and try to hide out."

"We couldn't hide long," she said, a little bitterly. "You know that."

"What are you doing in this, anyway? Rico, Carwell, the make-up man and I were supposed to be the only ones in on this part of it."

"The make-up man was MOGOW," she said. "Of course he came to us." She paused, and looked at him. He thought wonderingly that she was about to cry, but she did not.

"Ett," she said—and reached out to put her hand on his, where it lay on the arm of his float—"we haven't really been very honest with you, through all this. You see, there's an organization within an organization, a special secret group in the MOGOWs—and I'm one of that group."

Ett nodded for her to continue.

"We believe that we have to get results, and so sometimes we end up doing things we don't especially care for," she said. "We use the regular MOGOW organization as a kind of cover, and people think that because that group is so ineffective, none of us are any danger." She stopped and lowered her eyes.

He smiled. "Am I supposed to be surprised?" he said. As she looked up, swiftly, he went on.

"There had to be something like that, considering the competence of those few MOGOWs who came to help us on the island, and how quickly they got to us. It was obvious the MOGOW organization had to be a lot stronger and more able than it appeared generally, some time ago."

Her eyes met and held his, levelly.

"I'm glad to hear you know that," she said, "because you'll need to believe what I'm going to say."

She stopped, and took a deep breath.

"Our inner group decided a long time ago that if RIV could be improved and used on our people, we could take some giant strides forward," she

said. "We've had a research program going for
some time. One of our main workers was a physician at the same RIV Clinic where you—and
Wally— had your injections."

She paused for a moment, now. Her voice
tightened.

"Wally was one of the regular members," she
went on, "and I introduced him to the inner group.
We needed a volunteer, and he was willing. We
needed someone to be our . . . our guinea pig, for
that new variation of RIV. So Wally went to the
Clinic, and our researcher there gave him what we
thought was our improved version of the drug. But
it wasn't— wasn't improved. It ruined him instead
of making him an R-Master, the way we'd hoped."

Ett knew he was staring at her. Once more he
heard the roaring in his head, and felt as if he
were watching her from inside a long tunnel. He
felt a trembling as if something inside his chest
were about to cave in, and he tried to get some
sort of grip on it, as if to control it. When he tried
to speak he found a lump in his throat, in the way,
but he conquered it.

"Why didn't you tell me this before?" he asked.

"I'm sorry." Her voice was bleak. "We talked
about it, and decided we simply couldn't trust
you. Up to then you'd never shown any concern for
another human being in your whole adult life. To
us, you were nothing more than one more of the
many who just idled their whole lives away. I'll
admit we were surprised when you came to take
responsibility for Wally, and tried so hard to get
him revived—and even more when you made arrangements to take RIV yourself. But we still

couldn't believe that you could really change over-
night into someone who wanted to help cure this
sick world. I believed that about you, too, even
though I liked you," her voice was almost harsh—
"until just a short time ago. I managed one night
to get Al to open up about you, on your boat, and
he told me a lot that suddenly made sense."

"Oh," said Ett. The syllable was drawn from
him, almost as a sigh.

She went on.

"Al gave me—gave us—a lot better picture of
you than we'd been able to get before. You've been
an imposter all your life, we know that now. Like
Wally, you really cared; but, not like him, you
took it out by pretending you didn't care at all.
When Al told me that, it rang true to me—it fit
what I'd seen in you."

She paused, leaning forward in her chair a
fraction. "Are you all right?"

"All right," he said. "Yes." He could feel perspi-
ration beading on his skin now, cold and sticky.

"Go on," he said. "Go on."

"I went to Rico then, and told him the truth
about myself and the MOGOW organization." As
she talked, she was watching him steadily now.
"But by that time you'd already gone off as
Wally—" She broke off suddenly. "Ett? Are you
really all right?"

"All right," he answered mechanically, but in
spite of himself, now, the fury was with him, rising in him, and he rode it like a wave. It had been
these people all along who had caused what had
been done to Wally, after Wally had trusted them
with his life.

"How could any cause be worth that?" he said. He could feel his eyes narrowing as he watched Maea now, could feel his pulse quickening and his skin heating, as if to burn off the sweat. He sat up, and then quickly rose, standing above her and looking down, as if from a pulpit or the top of a tree. She looked small, he thought, like an old lady shrunk back to childsize by age; and he felt that he could simply reach out and crush her in one hand.

"You knew what you'd done to him," Ett said, "You'll tell me now you regret it. But then when I became an R-Master, suddenly there you all were again, like vultures, figuring to use some poor, trusting slob in your dirty little schemes while the rest of you sat back, safe!"

He was caught up in his anger now, borne on its crest like a sloop caught in the big swell. He saw and heard her trying to break in on his speech, but he overrode her with the force of his low-voiced vehemence.

"Well, you're not going to use me the way you did my brother!" he whispered savagely. "If I'm going to be cut down by the EC in a few hours, that is the way it's going to be, and it doesn't matter. Because I'll be trying to take them with me—and you MOGOWs, too!" He laughed. "We're in the Twilight of the Gods," he continued, "and now comes Gotterdammerung!"

She was staring at him, eyes wide; he looked into her eyes and laughed again.

"Can't believe it, can you?" he asked. "You can't get it into your head that poor old Ett could have so much hate inside him ..." he heard his own voice, and paused, a new thought beginning to stir somewhere in his mind. Suddenly his R-Master acuity of mind was at work again. But he went on in the same tone and words. "None of you knew what it's been like, to have to hide, all these years. And I'm now so tired of it all, I just want to end it!"

She continued to sit, looking up at him. She had stopped trying to answer him, but he was now able to see the shine of tears in her blue eyes. His head had begun to hurt him again, and his own eyes felt as if he had sharp sand under their lids. Deep inside he felt a faint note of discord, as if a movement was in the offing that would eventually bring him the familiar, churning nausea he'd learned to hate. Acid built up low in his throat, and twisted his lips as he spoke again.

"Have you got a handkerchief?" he said, coldly. "Wipe your eyes. We may as well play out this little game to the end."

She nodded, and looked down, rummaging in her old-woman's bag for a piece of linen. He sat back, waiting.

"All right," he said, when she was done, "this really doesn't change the situation from what it was when I called my contact. In less than twelve hours I might meet the Section Chiefs, and, as I just told you, according to what Rico told me there's no RIV-VII at all."

She looked at him. "You mean you'd still want to try to use it, if you had it?" she said. "I thought you meant—"

"I know what you thought," he said, "but I've got to use what I have on hand. So I want you to go back to Rico, right away, and tell him what I said about the meeting. He might not have any two thousand doses, but he should already have had time to do a test run. Ask him. See if he can think of a way to use those. Do you understand?"

"Of course I understand," she said, an edge of bitterness in her voice.

He held up a hand to override her words, and continued.

"Tell him to get out of there as soon as he gets something set up—they'll be coming for Wally very soon now. And you and Carwell had better leave too. It'll be up to me and Wally now."

He grinned, suddenly, a little wryly.

"Wally and I had a great-grandfather who was a missionary," he said. "Great-grandfather Bruder. He had a line that would fit this situation well, I think: *'Not in my time, O Lord, but in thine.'* "

He stood up.

"Well, let's try it, then," he said. "Get back to Rico and tell him. And you'd better get away from me now, before you attract the wrong kind of attention to yourself." He laughed quietly. "But go. You'll need to hurry."

She stood up with him. He nodded.

"Thank you very much for lending me the book," he said, in a normal tone of voice. "I'll send it back to you just as soon as I'm through."

"Take your time," she answered, and turned away. He watched her vanish into the crowded lobby. Then he turned, himself, and went back up to his suite, to lie down on his bed while he ran the book through a viewer just in case the room was bugged and he was under observation. As he watched the pages projected on the small screen-surface of the book, sleep came to him, easily and comfortingly, much as it had in the days before he'd been injected with RIV. He welcomed it even as he dropped off, the book still with its viewer screen lit before him and the windows open to the early evening's light. He slept until he was roused.

CHAPTER NINETEEN

Two armed Field Examiners from the Auditor Corps
came for him at three in the morning, Hong Kong
time, without using the annunciator. They took
him to an intercontinental and lifted him over the
bulge of the world into late afternoon, landing him
in the center of the complex of EC administrative
buildings in Halifax, Nova Scotia. The sky there
was clouded and wind-swept, cold and gray like
the buildings.

Ett was led to a basement level far below the
surface of a hill that still retained ancient fortifica-
tions half-buried in the earth, now frozen and sere.
There he was stripped, showered, irradiated, and
generally searched. He was redressed in a loose
suit of gray coveralls and taken onward by two
different Field Examiners.

By slideways and tunnels over some distance
they conducted him at last to an unremarkable-

looking conference room which held a horseshoe
table capable of seating perhaps twenty-five people.
He was given a chair off by itself in an open space
some distance from the open end of the horseshoe,
and left to wait with one Field Examiner standing
behind him and the other watching him from a
post at the wall to his right.

Some minutes went by with nothing happening.
Then people began to trickle into the room. There
were about an equal number of males and females,
and most were of middle-age, if not beyond that.
They took chairs at places they seemed to know
around the horseshoe, and their companions took
seats behind them, revealing themselves to be aides
or deputies. Wilson, Patrick St. Onge's boss and
the Accounting Section Chief, was the only one Ett
recognized immediately. Some of the others he
identified more slowly as EC Section Chiefs whose
images he had seen in the news releases. Patrick
St. Onge came in, glanced at Ett, and then had a
brief, quiet conversation with Wilson. He went out
again, not bothering this time to make any pretense of apology for the fact that a citizen had
been brought in under guard by armed Field Examiners, without concern for the legal niceties.

Around the table, those who had already seated
themselves were chatting with their neighbors.
There was a relaxed air as if this was very much a
part of the ordinary day's routine in some ordinary office setting. But the room was filling up
rapidly. St. Onge came back in, followed by Cele,
but they did not take seats, instead standing along
the wall near the door, which was behind Ett and
faced the open end of the horseshoe. Nearly all the
other seats had filled by now, except for the one in

the very center of the upper curve of the table. This remained empty until a tall, bony woman in her late forties came in the door and moved around the table towards it. As she did so, Wilson rose from his place and moved up the other leg of the table, arriving at the empty seat at the same time she did.

They exchanged a few words, and then Wilson retired to his seat. The bony woman sat down in the empty seat in the center and reached for a gavel lying within reach. She rapped it twice on the wooden sounding block that was with it, on the table-top.

Conversation died away around the room.

"All right," said the woman. "Saya Sorenson presiding at this policy meeting, it being Medical Section's turn in the rota of the Chair— this for the record. Everyone present? Yes, I see you all are. Are the recorders on? Very good. Go ahead, Patrick."

"With the permission of the Section Chiefs," Patrick St. Onge said, advancing into the open end of the horseshoe, "I've asked that today's policy meeting be an in-person one because we've been concerned lately with a possible abuse of the RIV Program, and in particular the making of R-Masters—"

"Excuse me, Patrick," broke in Wilson. "Perhaps we could have identification first?" He glanced at Ett. "This, as I remember, is our latest Master, Etter Ho?"

"That," said St. Onge, "is one of the things I intended to ask the Section Chiefs to decide. He's either Etter Ho or a conspirator against the regulations—or possibly both. But there are some other possible conspirators against the regulations involved in this situation. If I might bring them in now?"

"Go ahead," said Saya Sorenson.

There was a sound behind Ett, and he turned in his chair to see the door opening and several Field Examiners ushering in the coveralled figures of Maea and Carwell. After a second, another figure was ushered in, to stand by the wall. Ett's heart jumped in his chest. The latest person was Wally, also in coveralls. He walked as Ett had walked, and when they stopped him, he folded his arms and looked down thoughtfully, as if abstracted from what was going on around him. There was no sign that the Field Examiners had yet realized that he was nothing more than a trained body, although undoubtedly they must believe him quite unusual.

There was a little murmur around the table as the Section Chiefs looked from Wally to Ett and back again.

"A remarkable resemblance," Saya Sorenson said. "For the record, Patrick, are they twins?"

"No, doctor," said Patrick. "Only brothers."

"Continue, then."

"Thank you," St. Onge said, bowing slightly in the Chair's direction. Then he turned at an angle, so that he could view Ett and the standing figures of Maea and Carwell without turning his back on the Council.

"The Auditor Corps," he said, "must admit to being uncertain as to just what may have occurred recently in regard to these people. We suspect we know, but our evidence is only circumstantial. For that reason we have brought the matter to the

Council's attention—because a quick resolution of the affair is quite important."

"I must say I never thought to hear such words from the Corps," said a small, gray-haired woman on the right of the horseshoe. St. Onge remained silent but Sorenson picked up her gavel and rapped it once, crisply. Silence followed, and she nodded at St. Onge. He continued his presentation, identifying Maea and Dr. Carwell, and then pausing a moment.

"Both of these people," he continued, "are suspected—strongly suspected—to be MOGOW operatives. And both have been attached to the household of the newest R-Master, Etter Ho, under rather unusual circumstances—"

"Very interesting," said a young, slightly heavy woman with lank hair and a heavy jaw. "But what should we be concerned about with the MOGOWs, who have always been ineffective and unimportant?"

The gavel rapped again.

"If Social Control will kindly reserve her comments until later?" Sorenson said.

"I had a point to make that was pertinent," protested the younger woman.

"I support Nicolina Drega," said Wilson from the left. "Let her speak."

"Oh, come on," chimed in the voice of a portly, balding man. "If we do that we'll be here forever. Why can't we get the report out of the way and get out of here?"

"I don't want to be here all night, either," Sorenson said. "But I'm going to take Mors Lakin's words as a call for a vote. All in favor of Social

Control Section Chief Nicolina Drega speaking at this point, raise your hand."

Hands went up.

"Passed. The floor is yours, Nicolina."

"I was going to say," the woman said, "that the MOGOWs have been of no consequence until now. I fail to see why this Council had to be called in. Is there something we haven't been told?"

"We have evidence," St. Onge answered, "that the security of the zero-zero files may have been breached. Again frankly, we don't know that for sure, beyond having evidence that something unusual occurred there. Nor do we know what the particular target of the attempt may have been. But we have a theory which fits in with the case of R-Master Etter Ho. Perhaps it would be best if I simply laid out that theory for you? As I said, it's something the Auditor Corps can't prove yet, but . . ." He stopped.

Sorenson looked about, and then nodded. "Proceed."

"It is our belief," St. Onge said, "that this group of MOGOWs took control of the household of R-Master Etter Ho, for their own purposes. We think they determined to replace R-Master Ho with his brother Wallace—the resemblance you can see for yourself—who is known to be a MOGOW himself. To that end, we believe they have attempted to exchange the identity records of the two brothers in the zero-zero files, so that when the question came up elsewhere, reference to those files would give the incorrect answer. We also think they have done away with Etter Ho's secretary, a valuable senior government employee named Rico Erm, who has disappeared."

There was a stir in the chamber at this, and Sorenson spoke up. "And did they succeed?"

"We don't know," St. Onge said. "At the moment an identity check supports the man against the wall as Wallace, not Etter, Ho; and the man in the chair claims to be Etter Ho. We believe this is in fact the case, but only because the conspirators failed to achieve the exchange of identity codes that they planned."

"If the zero-zero files prove him to be the rightful R-Master Ho," said a fat man on the far side of Saya Sorenson, "what's all the fuss about? Speaking for Special Services, I propose we confirm the seated man as Master Ho, deal with the others as criminals according to whatever regulations apply, and move along." He looked around the table.

"If that is the opinion of the Section Chiefs," said St. Onge. "In the name of the regulations, however, I wished to point out that the security of the zero-zero files may have been breached, a breach stemming from a possible breaking of regulations."

"Oh, come now, Patrick, we don't need all that," said the fat man. "Naturally none of us is going to bend, let alone break, regulations."

"In that I agree with Special Services," said Nicolina Drega. "We've got more important things to do, with a world to run, than to sit in judgment on petty criminal cases."

"But," said Wilson, "is this merely a petty criminal case? It deals with a possible zero-zero file breach plus an attempt to impersonate an R-Master. The Section Chiefs of this Council may remember that Accounting—over strong objections by Medical—first insisted on setting Patrick St. Onge, here, to keep an eye on this Etter Ho, once

he was made an R-Master. Fortunately, a majority
of the Council backed us in the decision to do just
that, or this present situation might never have
been uncovered.''

"And I was saying that I doubted that—doubted
it profoundly," Saya Sorenson said dryly. "Accounting, you are ruled out of order. It happens that in
this case the Auditor Corps has let the wool be
pulled over its eyes to a shocking extent; if it were
not for the alertness of an investigative branch of
our own Medical Section—"

"Investigative branch? What investigative branch?"
Wilson pounded the table with his fist. "Since
when has Medical been concerned with EC security?
This is a matter that has been thrashed out in this
Council before. The Auditor Corps and the Auditor
Corps alone is authorized to guard the regulations
that preserve our utopian Earth—"

"And it's precisely because they've been doing
such a bad job of it that Medical has had to take
steps on its own—for which the Council will be
thankful, once it learns the facts," retorted Sorenson. "The Auditor Corps observed the operation of
a MOGOW militant unit right under its nose without suspecting what was happening. Only the superior loyalty of our regular Medical personnel
allowed our Section to be alerted."

She turned to look at the back wall against which
Wally, Maea, and Dr. Carwell were standing.

"Dr. Carwell," she said, "will you tell the Council what you know and what you did?"

Morgan Carwell rolled forward, seeming clumsy
as a bear.

"I'm a physician at an RIV Clinic," he said ear-
nestly to the faces around the large table. "I have

to admit I was a MOGOW, too, for a while. But I became convinced there was more harm than good to be accomplished in that direction. There was another physician at the Clinic who, like me, belonged to that subversive organization. For MOGOW purposes he experimented on his own to improve the RIV formula. Then he tried out the result on a young man, a MOGOW from another branch of the organization, who came to the Clinic deliberately to act as a guinea pig for him. The result was that the young man suffered an extreme negative reaction to the drug."

He turned to Wally, still standing against the wall, arms folded, gazing at the floor as if lost in thought.

"It was that young man there," he said. There was a murmur from the room.

"What—" began Drega.

The gavel banged down.

"Order. Let him finish. Go on, doctor," said Sorenson.

"So I reported the whole matter to my Medical superiors and promised to do whatever I could to stop such deadly experimentation in the future. Later on, when Etter Ho asked me to be his personal physician, I checked with my Medical superiors and they asked me to accept the post and keep them informed of what went on with this new R-Master, since there was some suspicion he had been connected, or would be, like his brother, with the MOGOWs."

Carwell stopped and wiped his forehead, which was gleaming with sweat.

"I did," he said. "I found out much more than the auditors did. The man sitting is actually Etter

Ho. The one standing is Wallace Ho, a revived cryogenic, who actually has no mind or personality. He's been response-trained to play Etter's role, while Etter, with the MOGOWs, tried to discover some fanciful hidden research concerning a developed and improved form of RIV. They believed they'd found it; I understand they were going to try to duplicate this supposed improved form of the drug with the facilities of a laboratory set up underneath the home of Lee Malone, another R-Master—"

"What? When?" snapped Wilson. "Patrick, order Field Examiners to Lee Malone's immediately—"

"It's not necessary," interrupted Sorenson. "Our own people have already raided the place. We got much of the lab equipment, but Lee Malone has gone missing, along with your Rico Erm."

"Erm?" Wilson stared.

"Exactly," said Sorenson icily. "One of the most trusted secretaries, according to Auditor vetting, I think? He's disappeared all right. But he was working with Ho and the MOGOWs all the time. I should, by the way, reassure the Council. There is no need for worry about any of this. We of Medical have allowed it to run on this long only in order to demonstrate how badly Accounting and its parasecurity arm, the Auditor Corps, have been serving us all. The time has long been overdue for each Section to maintain its own security force. Never mind that now, however. The point is that Medical—not Accounting—had this little MOGOW conspiracy under control from the very beginning. Let me tell you—"

"This is outrageous!" Wilson lifted his voice. "Medical is violating all the rules of order of this—"

"Quiet," said the fat man. "I want to hear this." There was a chorus of agreement from the other figures around the table. "Go on, Saya."

"Gladly. As I was saying, we've had the conspiracy under control from the inside all the time the Auditors were watching it and worrying about it from the outside. The injection of Wallace Ho with an experimental version of RIV raised the possibility that more efforts like this might well be made by irresponsible private groups in the future. If so, how should they be controlled? We at Medical evolved a plan for control and proceeded to test it, in this case. Wallace Ho had inadvertently been made a near-idiot—or would have been, if he had not committed suicide before the process had taken its full effect. To smoke out the conspirators who had been involved in producing the drug used on him, we offered them a bait. When Wallace's brother Etter decided to take the RIV treatment, we saw that he was not given RIV-II—"

"Not the RIV-VII!" cried Nicolina Drega. "You didn't break the Council committment against using the final form of the drug!"

"No, no, of course not," said Sorenson. "We merely used a slightly more advanced form, the RIV-IV. It was sufficient to ensure Etter Ho an R-Master development, but still left him in need of palliative medication."

"Which he refused to take!" snapped Wilson.

"Well, yes, that's true," said Sorenson, glancing at Ett in his chair. "He did refuse all medication. But that was a minor matter. As we suspected, the MOGOWs and even some others like your Rico Erm, who were at heart subversives, took the bait and gathered around him in hopes of making some profound alteration in our system. As a result, we uncovered a number of most dangerous people; not only that, we will continue to uncover more as Lee Malone and Rico Erm, in their flight, lead us to others as they turn to them for shelter and help."

Sorenson turned and looked directly at Ett, once more. "Etter Ho," she said, "was an inexperienced, ignorant young man, even though he became an R-Master. He was out of his league all along, and never knew it. But now it's all over."

Ett sat unmoving in his chair during Sorenson's indictment, his eyes focused on the shield that was embossed on the panelled wall behind her. She continued to look at him after she stopped talking, until the rising hubbub in the room attracted her attention. Wilson was arguing heatedly with several other Section Chiefs, pausing only to exchange quieter words with Patrick St. Onge, who had moved over to stand behind him.

Finally Ett turned his head, to see Wally standing unchanged in his place and Maea, still near him, still standing by the wall. Her eyes were on Ett, and her face seemed to be pleading or apologizing; but she uttered no word. Carwell had moved well away from her, and was now against the wall at the other end of the chamber, unattended and looking tired and downcast. He didn't look up as Ett glanced his way.

Ett turned back in his chair, but his eyes were now directed at the floor. The marbled pattern of its carpet swam before his eyes, blurring out of and back into focus. Within him the old feelings were back again. He could feel his eyes squinting as the skin around them tightened, and his pulse

began to race, his breathing to quicken. He sat up
straighter in his chair as Sorenson rapped for or
der once more.

It took some time, but eventually the room
quieted, and all attention turned back to the Chair

"It seems," she said, "that our first concern mus
be to find out how badly the zero-zero files have
indeed been compromised. I suggest—yes, Dr
Carwell?" The big brown man had moved forward
waving a hand to attract her attention and shak
ing off the arm of a Field Examiner who looked
rather unsure of himself. Carwell was sweating
profusely, and his voice was hoarse.

"Did I hear correctly?" he said. "There was an
improved version of RIV that you all decided to
hide?"

"Doctor, you're out of order now. Please leave
the—" She was interrupted as Carwell turned to
Ett.

"You were right after all," he said. His voice
was deep and raspy, and the coverall he wore
showed wet stains at armpits and wrists, as well
as down the back. "I didn't have the guts to admit
it."

The next instant he was in the grasp of two Field
Examiners and was being hauled out of the room
He made no protest of any sort.

Ett watched him until he was out of sight, and
then turned his eyes to Maea, still standing by the
wall and still watching him. Their looks crossed
met. He smiled slightly at her for a moment, and
then turned back to face the Council.

"That's insane!" Wilson was raging. "What
Carwell reported means that Erm and Malone are
on the loose with the RIV-VII information. Whil

we sit here, they're probably turning out doses of the drug by the hundreds, if not thousands!''

"Which need not worry us," said Sorenson. "An R-Master, whether produced with RIV-II or RIV-VII, is still nothing more than a highly effective problem-solving human entity. He or she is effective only in proportion to the power he or she already possesses. It goes without saying that the MOGOWs are, almost without exception, outside the working system of the Earth Council; it's with the EC—with us—that the real power lies. The R-Masters produced by Malone and Erm may be somewhat troublesome to us for a short while, but there's little major change they can accomplish before they betray themselves into our hands. Bear in mind that the EC is a system of world management employing millions of people. What can a few thousand, working from the outside, do against anything so massive?''

"By God!" said Wilson. "You take it calmly enough!''

Sorenson shrugged.

"I leave it to the other Section Chiefs of this Council to decide—by vote—if I'm not right," she said. "Shall we vote on it?''

"By all means," said the fat man, glancing at his chronometer. "I have a dinner engagement . . .''

There was a murmur of approval around the table.

"You're a bunch of idiots!" exploded Wilson. "Idiots, playing with matches in a fireworks factory!''

"Be quiet and vote," Sorenson told him. "No one here is about to be worried by your dire predictions.''

"How about mine?" said Ett.

His voice brought heads from around the Council table to look at him.

"Keep him quiet, you Field Examiners," commanded Saya Sorenson, brusquely.

"Stop and think," said Ett. "Not everyone wants to be an R-Master—"

The rest of his words were lost as one of the Field Examiners reached from behind him and encircled his neck with a hard forearm, choking Ett off.

"Let him talk," said Wilson malevolently.

"Yes," said Drega. "That was rather an interesting start he made there. Let him talk."

"Let go!" snapped Wilson directly to the Field Examiner. "That's an order—from me!"

The Field Examiner let go. Ett massaged his throat for a moment and got his voice back into working order.

"I was going to point out something," he said. "Not everyone wants to be an R-Master, even if the chance is given to them. Some people don't want to spend their lives being high-powered puzzle-solvers. Others have personal reasons—" he looked around the table— "like all of you here have."

"Shut him up!" snapped Sorenson.

"I figured out quite a while ago why none of you took advantage of the RIV-VII," Ett continued. No one moved in the room now. "It was part of the business of not rocking the boat, of not risking anyone getting an edge over everyone else. I'll bet you all take monthly or even daily examinations to prove to each other there's no RIV serum in you. Aren't I right?"

None of them answered.

"Of course I'm right," said Ett swiftly. "And that's why you've continued to treat people with the RIV-II at the Clinics, instead of using the problem-free RIV-VII—you want those who *do* become R-Masters, who might be able to make problems for you, to stay under your control."

He moved in his chair as he spoke, looking about the circle to see each of them in turn. "That's the one thing you overlooked in letting Malone and Rico Erm get away with the means to make the RIV-VII. The one group of people who'd really threaten the EC system if they were R-Masters are you people here."

"There's no danger of that," said Sorenson acidly. "Do you think we're going to invite Malone in to treat us all?"

"Not Malone," said Ett. "Someone else . . . *Wally! Now!*"

At the end of the line of people against the wall of the room, Wally moved, in the last of his trained movements. His face had no expression, but his hands went to his neck and grabbed, pulling away as if in a ripping movement. The skin there opened, ripped away as if it were cloth, fitted with a pocket. Inside was a small, flat plastic capsule. Before any of the Field Examiners could reach him, Wally took it in his fingers and tossed it onto the floor in the center of the horseshoe table; and as it hit two laser beams crossed in front of him, then found his chest.

The capsule exploded.

Suddenly, the room was obscured by an eye-stinging mist. Sitting in his place in front of the table, Ett felt as if the whole place moved about him. He started to hold on, but his fingers slipped from the sides of his chair, numb and useless. His mind was spinning, and he felt himself beginning to fall from his seat. Then the mist began to thin and his strength to return. He caught himself, still upright in the chair. But now the clearing lights of the room hurt his eyes. The sound of voices roared and thundered in his ears, so exaggeratedly loud that he could not make sense of what was being said.

Now it was clear enough to see that Wally had fallen. He lay face down and still. Near him Maea was sitting with her back to the wall. She looked different. Her face had changed. No, thought Ett, not her face, just her expression—the way she was looking at things. Had he looked like that, he wondered, in that first moment at the clinic when the advanced form of RIV had taken effect? Or was RIV-VII more potent that way?

But he had no time to puzzle over such things. Around the room they were all changing— Maea, St. Onge, Wilson, Sorenson, Drega, all of them— even the Field Examiners. Ett's strength was still diminished, but he forced himself up onto his feet. He stood, walking into the opening of the horse-shoe shaped table, to look down at Wilson, still in his chair but totally helpless. Ett could feel himself, still weak, but there was strength enough in him to kill anyone here if he needed to. He was the only one so far able to rise.

But then he turned back from the table, walked slowly towards Maea, instead. Whatever the effect of a double exposure to the RIV drugs might be was yet to be learned. But at the moment he was strong enough—and sensible enough—to reach the young woman and kneel beside her.

He stroked Maea's hair and she looked up at him, eyes wide and hands caressing the carpet she leaned above. He let himself down slowly, to sit beside her on the floor, and leaned his head back against the wall. His eyes wandered from light to light, and across the spaces between the fixtures in the ceiling. About the room there were noises of abstracted, almost rhythmic movement. But it seemed remarkably peaceful. He closed his eyes, realizing that they had begun to unfocus once more.

"Not in my time, O Lord, but in thine," said the voice of great-grandfather Bruder, somewhere nearby, and the phrase had a sound like trumpets. It began to reverberate about the room, echoing in his head, becoming a roar.

The light was becoming too much for him. It hurt his eyes—but no, his eyelids were already closed, so . . . There opened before him a world—no, a universe—made available by the RIV-VII, a universe in shape and distance, depth and content, such as no one had ever imagined before. He had won.

CHAPTER TWENTY

The *Pixie* swayed slightly, riding the tropical Pacific swells so lightly that it seemed it was the stars that were dancing circles in the dark sky. The ship was almost becalmed, and the ocean was unruffled, strangely smooth except for the rise and fall of the glassy surface. Dark threads that were sea snakes writhed in the moonlight down the glinting surface of the water.

Al was down in the cabin with a light on over his bunk, reading—the reflection of that light could be seen on the water to starboard. Undisturbed by it, up in the cockpit of the sloop Ett and Maea had the vessel, the sea, and the stars to themselves.

". . . and there's the Southern Cross," Ett was saying.

"How strange," Maea said. "I've seen it before, but right now it's like looking at it for the first time."

"And there's Alpha Centauri," Ett said. He was half sitting, half lying, on the cushions of the stern seat with Maea on his right side and the rim of the wheel under his left hand. He could have roped the wheel but he liked the feel of it, alive under his fingers, as the boat eased into every little breath of air.

"Where?" asked Maea.

"See, one of the pointers, there, for the Crux— the Southern Cross. See it now?"

"Yes," said Maea. "Do you think we'll ever go there?"

"Why not?" said Ett, and stared up into the night. "Now that we're starting to get the world moving again."

She shivered slightly.

"Are you cold?" he asked.

"No, no," she said. But even as she said it, she shivered once more. "Just a psychological chill, I guess."

"Someone step on your grave?" he said, smiling at her, but watching her closely.

"No," she said, looking down at the decking beyond her feet. "Yours."

He raised an eyebrow and tilted his head to the side. "You're still thinking about that day in the Council chamber," he said.

"Before that," she said. "In Hong Kong, in that hotel lobby. I'd never seen you like that before—I'd never seen anyone look like that."

She lifted her head and turned it to stare straight into his eyes.

"I'd never have believed such fury—" her voice was almost empty of emotion—"in anyone." Her words lingered on the soft, night sea air about them. After a moment he answered.

"It's genetic, I think," he said. He heard his own voice, also empty. "I told you about my great-grandfather Bruder—he was intolerance and fury incarnate in the flesh."

"But you don't have to do what he did," she said. He shook his head at her.

"No," he said. The word came out hard and unyielding. "I can promise you that."

He felt her hand slip into his; and it felt oddly comforting, reassuring.

"Wally used to talk about him, too," she said. "How could he be so important to you both?"

"I don't know if 'important' is quite the right word," Ett said. "He was more than that . . . it was as if he could only worship God by taking over God's role in our universe. Dealing with him was like dealing with an elemental force, one that was always there, eclipsing everything else."

He shivered, unthinkingly, and she rubbed her left hand down along his right arm.

"Were you afraid of him?" she asked.

"No," he replied. "Not the way you mean. I've only been afraid because I've always been too like him, all my life."

"In your anger, you mean," she said. "But you can be like him in more ways than his anger."

He forced a smile.

"Yes," he anwered. For a moment he did not know what more to say. Then he sighed.

"For Heinrich Bruder, that anger and intolerance were all he had—and it became him. So when I learned I had it in me, too, I was frightened. And what scared me most was becoming like him. So I fought it."

There was a moment of silence before he went on.

"After Wally's death, I thought I'd finally lost that fight, after all," he continued. "Even though I managed to come up with a lot of logical reasons for the things I did, I knew I was only fooling myself. It was the rage in me—his rage—all that time."

"Yes," she said, "I can see that now."

"I knew it in Hong Kong," he said. "That explosion, my second time there, showed me what I was doing, how I'd been deceiving myself. So I decided to give in—to *be* Heinrich Bruder—and go ahead with a plan that could destroy the EC, and the whole world's society."

"What changed your mind?" she said. "You'd planned to kill all the Council Members after the RIV-VII explosion, hadn't you? What stopped you, there at the last moment?"

"I don't know." He frowned. "Suddenly, there was nothing to be gained by it. Maybe it was because I'd been fighting the old man for so long that I'd finally broken free. All I know is that when everyone was reacting to the RIV, there in the Council chamber, suddenly I was just me, and the fury—well, it was there, still, but it didn't control me, any more."

"Ah," she said. "You finally struck a balance."

"I suppose," he told her. "And I think I did it by surrendering. By giving up. Once I could do that, then the tension was released and, well . . . I healed, even though I didn't understand what was happening."

"So when did you understand?"

"When they were taking Morgan Carwell away, I think," he said. "As they were dragging him out of the room I could see that even though he'd betrayed first me, and then the EC—the important thing to him was that he'd been true to himself all along."

He paused, musing. "At that moment, if I'd really been Heinrich Bruder come back to the flesh again, I knew I'd have hated Carwell for what he'd done to my plans ... but I suddenly realized I didn't. And when the RIV explosion came, I knew I was free."

He sobered.

"It's still in me, of course," he said. "That rage. It's part of me, part of why I'm who I am. But it's not walled away from my control, any longer."

"And you're not afraid of it any more?"

"No," he said. "How could I be? Now that I know it's *me*! It's not my great-grandfather, still alive somehow, after all, there in the dark at the back of my mind—it's only me. And I can handle myself."

Quieting, he went on. "Heinrich gave himself up to the monster he chose to be. He let himself be submerged by it, and everything else that he was vanished underneath it, somewhere. I tried to go the other way, and then almost bounced back onto his path. Both routes were wrong."

"You're sure now, then?" she said, watching him. "You're sure that the bureaucracy'll go smash, that a better kind of society'll be born—you're even sure we're safe?"

"Of course we're safe," he said. "I told you that."

"Tell me again. I'd like to hear you say it."

"Why, just as I told you," Ett replied. "We're just counters, chips, you and I—particularly me. If I'd died after that double dose of R-drugs, none of the powers that still be would have missed me. But since I didn't die, maybe I'm supervaluable. Who knows? They'll want to wait to find out if I can be used by one or more of them."

"Are you supervaluable?"

"I don't know!" Ett laughed. "I didn't feel any difference when I had one RIV-IV dose inside me. I still don't feel anything, with that plus the RIV-VII. Maybe I can turn the universe inside out—but what good does that ability do me, if I don't know I have it?"

"Be serious."

"But I am being serious!" he said. "Well, almost serious. All right, no, as far as I can tell, that second dose didn't do anything except make me a little more resistant to the side-effects, the aches and pains I'd been stuck with as a result of the first dose. But what does it matter? The point remains I might be too valuable to destroy. You too—and Al and Rico. So none of the R-Masters we now have as Section Chiefs are going to risk being the one to get rid of something that might be valuable and useful to them later on. Risk is what they've always avoided, and being R-Masters themselves doesn't change their attitudes. By the same token, each one's watching every other one to make sure that no one else tries to make use of me. So . . . standoff. They all leave me alone."

"And me alone?" she asked.

"And you. And Al, as I said," Ett nodded toward the lighted cabinway forward. "We're a package. So here we are, free to do what we want."

"But what makes you so sure they'll end up, in the long run, tearing each other apart, the way you seem to think they will?"

"Not tear each other apart," said Ett. "Just, over a period of time, they'll eat each other up. The RIV-VII apparently can make anyone who wants to be super-capable. But then the new super-capable individual's got to deal with all the others just as capable as he or she is. Capability leads inevitably toward responsibility—and there's only so much responsibility for others to be shared before you bump up against others' desire for freedom and self-responsibility. The Bureaucracy is going to disappear, as its members come to terms with each other."

"And those who won't come to terms will eat each other up," Maea grinned, a little wickedly, "like the gingham dog and the calico cat."

"What's that?" Ett frowned at her.

"You don't know that old poem by Eugene Field?" She quoted:

> *"The gingham dog and the calico cat*
> *Side by side on the table sat,*
> *'Twas half past twelve, and (what do you think?)*
> *Neither one nor t'other had slept a wink.*
> *The old Dutch clock and the Chinese plate*
> *Appeared to know as sure as fate*
> *There was going to be a terrible spat . . .*

". . . and so it goes for three or four more verses like that," Maea said. "Until it winds up:"

> *"Next morning where the two had sat*
> *They found no trace of dog or cat;*

And some folks think unto this day
That burglars stole that pair away!
But the truth about that cat and pup
Is this: they ate each other up.''

"Which," she concluded, "is what our EC Section Chiefs are going to do to themselves and to the EC bureaucracy—if you're right."

"I am. You'll see," said Ett. "You see, they didn't realize how wise they were, originally, in all leaving RIV-VII alone. They made things work by everyone agreeing to play by the rules. But it was easy to play by the rules when they were ordinary—even mediocre—men and women. Now they're stuck with minds that can see too many ways of playing the angles and cutting corners."

"For people like that, I think you're right," Maea nodded. "They're not only stuck now with the problem-solving minds of R-Masters— they're stuck as well with the R-Master compulsion to use that ability when they get squeezed. They might hold the line for a while and try to keep on playing by their special rules. But sooner or later one of them is going to take an unorthodox route to some end he particularly wants, and just as soon as one of the others catches him at it, the one who did the catching's going to begin breaking rules also—just to keep even. Result: the gingham dog and the calico cat syndrome."

They sailed in companionable silence for a long moment or so.

"Don't forget, too," said Ett, then. "This is going to be a crumbling of the pyramid from the top down. These people control the system. Big chunks of it. They'll end up using those chunks in rule-breaking ways, and taking the chunks along with them into battle with each other. In the end, the whole hierarchy will break up into so many small pieces you won't be able to count them. Meanwhile the RIV-VII that we'll go on making is going to be spreading and increasing the new crop of independent problem-solvers outside the bureaucracy, as well, ready to help take over when the original system crumbles."

"Oh, I believe that," said Maea pensively. "After all, technically, I'm an R-Master myself now, too. I can believe in things crumbling. But what's to say it'll be put back together any better than it is now?"

"We're a self-improving race—by inclination," Ett said. "Also, we need order and law. Besides, remember, not everybody wants to be an R-Master."

She looked at him doubtfully in the moonlight.

"What makes you so sure about that?"

He grinned at her and then turned to shout down the companionway to the cabin.

"Al!"

"What?"

"How about we get some RIV-VII and make you an R-Master too, next stop we make?"

"Go to hell!"

"Al," shouted Ett, "you don't mean that!"

"The hell I don't!" Al's voice was positive. "That's for the rest of you. The earth, the sea, and me—we like ourselves just the way we are."

"You see," said Ett, more quietly to Maea, "why I wanted to keep Al out of the Council Room that day. He was my touchstone. You and I—the bright ones, the flaky ones, the earth-shakers—we show up and disappear. Al stays on forever, generation after generation, and produces more like us when he needs us."

She did not say anything for a moment.

"You don't like the way we are, then?" she said, not looking at him.

"Of course I do," he answered. "But that's the kind of human critter I am—and the kind you are. Al's a different kind, and there's more like him than there are like you and me."

"What's the use of civilization, then?" she said. "What's the use of anything? If it isn't becoming better thinkers that we're after, what is it?"

"I don't know," he said. "How can I tell? I'm a man of my time, just like you're a woman of your—our time. But I can guess that the R-whatever drugs, and everything else like them, aimed at making us smarter, may turn out to lead us down a blind alley."

"What makes you think so?" she said. "As I say, if being smarter isn't what we're after, what is?"

"And I say," he said, "I don't know what is. But there's lots of things brains can't do for you. All the intelligence in the world won't help you build a boat like this one, until you've learned the craft of boat-building from the keel up. Being very smart doesn't automatically make you paint a better picture or compose a better piece of music. The best you can say for intelligence is that it helps you along the road toward the things you want. But the things themselves—the actual things—have to be something more than just intelligence products."

There was a moment's silence between them. Then she spoke.

"There's children," she said. "The next generation."

318 Gordon R. Dickson

He looked at her quizzically through the darkness.

"Already," he said, "you're bringing that topic into the conversation."

"It was never out," she said. "Everything else in the world and time adds up to it. But you never did really answer me when I asked you why you are so sure not everybody wants to be an R-Master; all you did was show me that some people like Al *believe* they don't want it. But what makes you, yourself, so sure you can trust them to go on believing it?"

He looked at her for a long moment; and when he spoke his voice was more quiet and serious than she had ever heard it.

"Laugh if you want," he said. "But it's just something I believe about them. I have faith."

She smiled at him then, tenderly.

"And I believe you have. Etter Heinrich Bruder Ho," she said.